CAPO

Champagne and Black Roses

Malik "Kazi" Jones

INTRO TO CHAMPAGNE AND BLACK ROSES

This part of Capo's story began in 1976. Tito Shakur, a Black Latino from Cuba, was dragged to go to the military for The United States. As an army ranger, he fought beside some good men and women and as a cook, he fed the poor. He was awarded a purple heart for his bravery in saving a village of people from being executed by Nazi's. While on base in Germany, he met a woman named Christi Blake, who was an officer assigned to be the ambassador of Germany. She was the delight of his eyes. Pretty, brown-skinned face, wide hips, and a small waist with a Brazilian Accent. By both being Latin, they instantly took a liking to one another. They went on a few dates off base that would eventually lead to a sexual relationship. Not long after, they found themselves in their commander's office. However, instead of being reprimanded for the love affair, they were given a joint mission to infiltrate the Cuban government and assassinate their ambassador and the carrier for Fidel Castro. But by no means would Tito betray his country, so the two opted to go absent without leave and continue their love affair in Havana, Cuba. The U.S. government was told by the Cuban government they had two of their spies, and unless they released all political prisoners with family in Cuba, then they would be executed. The message was a favor for the information Tito had given the president Mr. Castro.

In 1977, Tito and Christi were married under the assumed last names of Placencia. The following year, they had their firstborn and named him Juelz, which was another name for chapters in Christi's Holy Qur'an. Eighteen months later, on New Year's Day, they saw their second son born to this world and named him D'Juan after Tito's grandfather. They believed their children would bring them good fortune someday, but both agreed it wouldn't be in Cuba. The Revolution for freedom had spread worldwide, and the hopeless began to have hope. The voiceless began to speak, the deaf started to hear, and the blind began to see. Tito was raised on the belief that no one could conquer a country without corruption, so when fighting for justice and equality, he prepared to be met with resistance. Although that was his belief and the lessons he shared with his sons, his younger brothers, Kaboobi and Santana, must have forgotten this core principle. Unbeknownst to him, they were back in the U.S. involved in more corruption and scandal than a revolutionary should be. In fact, they were even sold on the American dream.

While D'Juan was facing a hunger and health crisis, his uncles were in America living like kings. There was Kaboobi Shakur, who made a name for himself by introducing the West Coast to grade A heroin a.k.a China White. After settling in the San Francisco Bay Area in 1977, he hooked up with other Latin families and founded what was known as The Familia. Within three years, China White was in such high demand that he organized an import business. Important figures in the early developments were Topaz Deguzman and his nephews, Carlos and Poncho aka Pappi. Topaz already had territory in the Silver Street Projects with an army commanded by a well-respected capo named Remo. Formerly known as an enforcer, he was without question the guy you'd need to safeguard a multi-million dollar empire.

Pappi and Carlos was the oldest of his sister's four boys, smooth operators with the gift of gab and already accustomed to transporting Columbian gold weed to Chicago and Cuban cigars from Florida. Their mother, Monese, worked for Amtrak and, quite frankly, was the key to their success. Her carry-on bags were seldom checked, and after doing a few favors, she was rewarded with a nice home on the south side of Chicago. That marked a new beginning, and Kaboobi thought expansion. He wasn't satisfied with controlling the heroin market. He wanted to control the real estate market as well.

His younger brother, Santana, controlled the Columbian gold market and had a lot of success. While Kaboobi was thinking of expansion, Santana just wanted the streets. To strengthen his position, he chose some projects on the south side of Richmond, California. When he witnessed the power and opportunities that came from selling heroin, he transformed the Easter Hill Housing Complex into what became known as Sugar Hill. By 1981, he was being called The Sandman and respect ran deep.

His captain, Lamont Bishop, was a stone-cold gangster and a gentleman. In his early teens, he and his younger brothers, Junior and Silk, worked out of Little Ricky's pool hall selling powder cocaine at fifty dollars a gram. Then it evolved into a gambling shack, where the pool tables would become crap tables. The maximum capacity of sixty was exceeded by a hundred percent daily. Forcing the owner into either selling out or joining into a partnership of buying the old theater building on 2nd and Cutting Boulevard. As a friend of The Familia, he agreed to the terms. They'd finance, and he'd handle business affairs. It couldn't have been a better gift to Richmond than Candlelight aka rhythm and blues headquarters. The Multiplex was divided into three sections and served as a venue for holiday celebrations and live performances with a maximum capacity of thirty-eight hundred guests. The main entrance led to the lounge, bar, and grill area. The right wing was for adult entertainment along with private rooms for VIP's. Top shelf champagne and Cuban cigars were catered to each of the twenty rooms at the top of the hour. The left wing was a casino for high rollers with a security room and office occupied by Squalito Blake and his nappy roots team of assassins. Sitting in a neutral area, The Candlelight attracted players, macks, and high rollers within a two-hundred-mile radius, leaving Little Ricky's as a designated rendezvous for Richmond's finest capos and boss madams.

Together, Kaboobi, Topaz, and Santana organized a powerful regime respectfully known as the Family of King's, F.K in short. From a traditional stand point, they didn't trust banks or I.O.U's for that matter. Cash on the ebony coffee table made the business good.

Tito and his family arrived back on American soil in 1982. Juelz had just turned four in May, and D'Juan was two years old. They were immediately embraced by The Familia and offered a piece of the business sector. Christi worked as a real estate agent, and Tito as a cook and manager at The Candlelight. Juelz and D'Juan was often left to hang around the younger members of The Familia. Sonny 'Money Man' Montana was an emerging ghetto star. He was D'Juan's role model. His uncle Kaboobi raised him since the age of five after his parents were executed by Columbian drug lords. The Silver Street Projects was his playground and place of business as a teenage hustler. He was one of those kids that wanted it all before his time. Legend had it, he rode a bike before a tricycle, bought a BMW at age fourteen, and counted a million dollars cash for his fifteenth birthday. Kaboobi called him their golden boy, smooth as cashmere but tough as leather. So, one could expect he would also make an easy target for a dealer wanting to make a name for himself.

By 1986, the F.K organization expanded into the cities of Rodeo, Vallejo, Oakland, and six different states, Washington, Nevada, Nebraska, Illinois, New York, and Florida. Hearing of the movement was like a fairy tale, but witnessing it was shell shocking. On one hand, they gained power and support from the people by paying mortgages, property taxes, and putting food in their refrigerators. Then, on the other hand, there was innocent blood and gasoline from cocktail bombs, which terrified the working-class citizens.

In the midst of chaos, Tito kept The Candlelight Diner at maximum capacity. It soon became the place to be seen and for musicians to be heard. Squalito, aka Poppa Squally, managed the events, bringing in different performers every week. From B.B. King with the blues, to the Debarge Brothers and Ohio Players with the rhythm, and The Whispers with the soul, not to forget Ella Fitzgerald with the jazz and Johnny Guitar Watson with the funk. Many of these musicians attributed their success to Squally and this fine establishment.

It was 1988 when crack cocaine became the new monster Over six hundred teenagers and fathers were killed during this genocide called the drug war. What followed over the next year was even more devastating. Mom-and-pops stores, gas stations, a laundromat, along with other small businesses, were facing foreclosure. Even homes and over four hundred acres of land, which had been in some families since the Renaissance Era, was in jeopardy. Just as the urban communities were established through trade and good relationships, they were destroyed with a hit of crack cocaine. With every transaction came problems, so as the dealer got rich, the user brought their problems home. As a result, families separated from the head. With single-parent homes becoming a norm and an enigma for instability.

During the Regan and Bush administrations, the drug trade was the driving force of the economy. Maybe by mere coincidence, but even Stevie Wonder saw the destruction on the road ahead. He tried reaching the people with powerful messages in his music, but evidently, it wasn't heard in Rich City.

Guys like Sonny, Lyfe, and Remo were tempted by their selfish desires and the belief they could rule the world. With the power to take a life and buy a twelve-unit complex with the snap of a finger, they became a dangerous group to hang around, to the point they couldn't even hang around each other. Consequently, there was a growing threat and several attempts made on Sonny's life, so he set up on the south side in the Globe Town Projects. Being only six blocks from Santana, he felt a little more secure. Forming his own crew with the support of Lyfe, they called themselves The Globe Boys. With Remo now in control of the Rodeo Projects, they dominated the opposition, feeling invincible. That was until December 24, 1989, a night that would impact D'Juan's destiny more than he could imagine.

Sonny was leaving The Candlelight casino with a hundred and fifty grand more than he came with. His role was like magic, and at one point, the other gamblers just watched. For a little less than a hundred grand, he'd brought an '89 Jaguar and the king of the road, a '67 GT500 Mustang Shelby. His crew, Dorian, Rocky, and Slim, escorted him outside of his Mercedes 560 SEL. Suddenly, they were confronted by three men with Tommy guns. A gun battle broke out, leaving four people dead, one of which was Sonny. Kaboobi, Remo, Lyfe, and Dorian amongst the rest of 'the familia' grieved for weeks over his loss. In the wake of this incident, The Candlelight was closed indefinitely pending homicide investigations.

When D'Juan asked his Uncle what was going to happen next, Santana said, "It's the game, babii. The playaz gon' continue to play, and the hustlers gon' continue to hustle." Whatever that meant, he had yet to understand. But what could be seen with his own eyes was his family separating. While Carlos, Pappi, Spider, and Dorian found it to be more lucrative in Chicago, Illinois. Kaboobi went into hiding in his mansion in the Richmond Hills, and his ma complained about everything from where they were going to live and it not being enough food. However, Tito made a promise to his late father that he would never be like his oppressors and sell out for corruption. Once he finally realized what his brothers were involved in, he decided he wouldn't accept another dinar from them. Eventually, Christi's account was frozen pending investigation into her brother Romelo Black Sr. and his connection with Santana's criminal empire. As the most flamboyant gets all the attention, fame and power creates jealousy and envy in the hearts of men. Not to mention, those Federal agencies who make a living by busting and seizing Drug dealer's property.

Richmond was known as Rich City and the murder capital of killa Cali. President H. W. Bush declared a state of emergency and ordered the National Guard to patrol the streets. Whoever thought the death of one man could trigger so much bloodshed? Romelo, Lyfe, and Remo orchestrated train robberies for military weapons. With heat coming from the ATF and homicide detectives, their job still wasn't finished.

Shortly after D'Juan's tenth birthday. Tito had taken him and Juelz back where it all started, Harlem, N.Y. His mother, Mrs. Nina Perez-Shakur, was Puerto Rican and well known in the uptown district. As a refugee from Cuba, she still stood for the revolution of peace and equality. Her late husband, Mr. Dejon Shakur, wasn't only a revolutionary but also a respected businessman in Manhattan. So, when Tito decided to start his own business, he had no problems finding legitimate investors. He enrolled Juelz and D'Juan into Malik Shabazz Charter School in hopes that they would get a meaningful education. However, D'Juan felt the pain of his parents' separation, and in his mind, it was due to being poor.

In Champagne and Black Roses, he tries to reconcile his family the only way he learned how; *Gambling large and hustling hard!*

Chapter 1

D'Juan looks up at the sky, and into the starlight. The smell of Cigarillo and urine reek from the alley below. Suddenly he hears two men having a discussion about pick-ups and drops. Followed by a beer bottle breaking against a brick wall "hey poppa what's up. You rolling in some mad doe huh?" One of the two guys ask a presumed to be hustler. The mid-aged man stands firm and without hesitation respond "Yo, my man's. What I'm doing is my business. So if you ain't buying, keep it moving up the block."

The elder man looks toward his younger soldier who steps back into the shadows, then back to this hustler "Let me enlightening you on som'thin my man's. You don't call shots around here, I do. Every block, bodega, and alley in Spanish Harlem belongs to the Kings-men and I don't know you. So that means, you're trespassing and do you know what happens to people like you?" The man asks; cool, calm, and collected.

"Yo, I don't know about all that. My man's put me on and said it's good to move this work, and that's what I'm gone do, B. So if you ain't God, you can get the fuck outta here wit the empty threats, straight up" the hustler says boldly.

"BANG", One shot rang out, echoing through the Alley. The hustler was startled as he clutched his stomach. "I decides who lives and dies you maggot. ***And you***," another shot was fired into the hustlers face, simultaneously with the word ***"die."*** As blood oozed onto the concrete, the two guys casually steps over the dead body and walks through the Alley.

Apparently D'Juan drew attention to himself after the first shot. The shooter glanced up at the rooftop but act as if he never minded the kid. All night he was worried and didn't know rather to tell Julian or not. Then, the morning comes and D'Juan is awaken by a knock on the door. "Who is this he thinks upon opening it."

"Hey Mijo. Your Nana home?" The man asks.

"No senor."

The man then stoops down, removing the sunglasses from his face. "Aye, ah. I know you were on the rooftop last night. I hate you had to see that, stuff like that is not good for kids to see." As D'Juan begins to denied he seen anything, the man insists "don't worry about it. It'll be between me and you. I'm indebted to you. Whatever you need, or your family. Come see me yeah." He then reaches out his hand with a wad of hundred dollar bills "I'm Arnesto. And you, from now on is Cuba, o.k."

"See, senor." D'Juan nods his head and shuts the door.

Harlem World U.S.A, While it's a historic and beautiful place, Harlem's dark underworld was similar to that in Rich City. They had Crews reigning supreme like the F.K organization dominated the opposition with money and power. Yeah, Harlem's brightest stars drove luxury cars, wore expensive fur jackets with gold ropes, and four-finger rings representing who they were, and their level of success.

D'Juan and Juelz loved their second home, and in return Spanish Harlem embraced the Shakur boys as their own. Their bloodline is considered royalty, so anything they needed they could get. The problem is their father Tito, refrain from asking for anything. Even if they were a day from being thrown in the streets. He reasons, a man works with his hands, not stand with his hands out.

Over the past summer they grew accustomed to the culture and B-boy style, especially Juelz. He could freestyle break dance and connect lyrical bars with the best of them. D'Juan was a Timberland and skull cap, leather coat wearing kid from jump. Like history was to be written, he learned how to hustle, where he witnessed his first murder; on 106th and 7th Avenue.

Tonya was the prettiest girl on the block. Puerto Rican with long, black curly hair, petite frame and smart. She was quite popular in the neighborhood. Played stick ball with the older boys, but didn't take no mess from no one. The moment she cursed someone out in Spanish, either her fists or other objects would be thrown, no doubt about it. Every afternoon, coming home from school, D'Juan looked forward to seeing her smile from the stoop with her friends. That attention made him feel like a celebrity, and the fly girls was his fan club.

Juelz hooked up with a Jamaican princess in the neighborhood named Jamelia. A honor student and athlete with sex appeal out of this world. And being a popular athlete himself, he was getting all the sexual favors a young man could dream of.

Their father Tito, overhears their late night stories about sex, money, and power but keeps to himself. He contemplate on a daily basis, how do he reach his son's but the influence of Ill-gotten wealth is too great while they're living in poverty. As he wash the dishes, a voice yells from the hallway.

"Poppa. Me and Jay about to go to the park,"

"Mijo, you know it's gangs that hang out down there. Be careful."

"No doubt, Poppa, we just be shooting hoops" D'Juan says convincingly to get out the house.

"Jay, hurry up and get your ball," he whispered.

"Yeah okay, just be in here by 10 o'clock. You keep Nana up, we have some problems okay."

"Poppa, we already know. Love you" "Yea, love you Pa'...

However, while Juelz would be at the park shooting hoops, D'Juan would be shooting craps. Cee-Lo was his game, and counting money was no thang. Half his winnings go towards a re-up pack, and the rest to the family pot. As the sun falls, the two recognized it was time to head home.

"Yo, Juan, let's go to the Deli. We can buy dinner for Nana," Juelz suggested as they approach 6th Avenue.

"A'ight, cool, but don't tell her about this money, Jay. Please." D'Juan stressed the importance of keeping this a secret.

"Come on, bro. You think she don't know? Nobody bought you this fly gear kid. Trust me she knows, she just don't care."

"Jay, you can't be so stupid. After what happened back home, how she won't care? You forget, this is Pa' and Nana we talking about." He reiterates.

"Promise kid, besides I ain't no snitch anyway. I should sock you, for even thinking that." They then locked their pinky fingers and continue on their mission. D'Juan peeled hundred dollars from a wad of twenties and bought a month's worth of food.

Once back home, they quickly loaded the refrigerator and tucked themselves in bed. "Juanie, Juelz, that's you?" Nina yells. Expecting her to enter the room any minute, they played sleep. Guessing right, she opens the door at exactly ten o'clock. Once she eases it shut, they continue on talking about the fly girls in the neighborhood.

"I'm telling you bro, the lil Rican shorty digging you. I swear, if she ask me one more time about you. I'm gone have to hit the skins for you." Juelz says with sarcasm.

"I don't know, Jay. She be around them older cats, wit mad dinero. Look at me. I'm barely copping a Q.P."

"Ahh, you ain't no playa. You think money is everything. Having paper don't mean jack, kid. It's about game, babii. Either you got it, or you don't."

D'Juan knew his brother was right, and he had to step to her. So he contemplated from that moment on, how that conversation would go.

It was September 11th, 3 p.m. He walked past the group of Rican girls sitting on their usual stoop. "What's up, Tonya? How you be?" He asks with a smile.

She looked into his hazel brown eyes and returned a gentle smile. "I'm cool. What's up?" He looks up at the sun before responding, "Its beautiful. I'm just happy to be a witness to something so pure and fresh."

"Well, thank you D'Juan. I was just thinking. Can you walk me home?" she asks politely.

"No doubt. C'mon." He smiled after throwing up the peace sign to her friends.

The two walked slowly, talking like they knew each other for years. Her accent, and bossy personality attracted the kid. Every hardship concerning her family went in one ear and out the other. He listened to her for the sake of lust. Nevertheless, she appreciates his honesty about the desire for her, and a fantasy he hopes to fulfil.

"Oh my God. Well why you never said anything?" she asks, folding her arms.

"Nah, for real. I thought you were only into older cats. Like what's up with ole boy that's always standing on the corner watching you?"

"Who? En-Rica?"

"I guess. The dude with the gold chains."

"He use to hang with my brother." She then catches what he was trying to insinuate. "Wait, you thought that was my boyfriend?"

"I don't know what to think. You mesmerize me with your beauty," he said, getting her to smile.

"Cute. But you have no worry's." She smiles while grabbing for his hand "So, you go to that charter school, Malik Shabazz?"

"No doubt. What? You been watching me or something?"

"Maybe. You got a problem with that? Yo' girlfriend gon' try to beat me up?" she said with sarcasm followed by giggles.

"Ahh, you funny now? Only girl I'm with right now is you."

"I guess you're right." She could see straight through his leather jacket into his heart. She was convinced of his sincerity, "I'll tell you what. Meet me every day after school, and we'll walk home together."

"No doubt. I'm cool wit that."

Before parting ways, they hugged and exchanged phone numbers. "So ah, now we suppose to kiss or son'thin?" He asks, licking his lips. "Ugh, not on the first date. Maybe next time Poppi." She kisses her fingers and plants them on his nose. Although he didn't get to taste her cherry lip gloss, it was the next best thing.

D'Juan knows his big brother would be proud of him so rushes to the apartment, tossing his book-bag aside in the closet. "Jay" he yells upon opening his room door. Where he saw the bare backside of a dark-complexion girl. As she motions her hips slowly on Juelz lap, passionate moans fill the room. She was a woman in a teenage body. Round black nipples compliments her D-cup breast, and a firm butt sits nice between her 36 inch hips. D'Juan was mesmerized and wanted to join desperately. But before he got caught, he quietly shuts the door and found a place on the couch. There, he leaned back and thought about Tonya.

For the next couple of weeks, they saw more of each other than anyone else. Hell, he even wanted to do her more than anything else. After school, he'd forgotten about homework, his chores, and, most nights, his curfew.

One evening, as Juelz was playing in a neighborhood three-on-three basketball tournament, D'Juan and Tonya was rooting for him in the bleachers. "Poppi, you want play a game?" she asked as his head rest between her legs.

"Definitely, it's whateva you want, ma-ma," he replied, warranting her smile.

"Yeah, you sure?"

"Why not? It's nothing crazy right?"

"Maybe a little on the wild side, but." He looked at her lips, anticipating her next words. "Okay, the game is truth or dare."

"A'ight, I'm wit' it." With her first choice she chooses dare. "A'ight, I dare you to pants that referee." He points out the one with holes in his sweat pants.

She snapped her head around. "Oh, poppi, you not right. I can't believe you."

As she complained of her dare, he interjected; "So you not gon' do it, you scared?" He taunted, he thought she was down for whatever.

"Shut up. Yeah, I'm gonna do it, get out my way."

He instantly jumped to his feet. "All yours, my señorita." She smiled as her temperature began to rise.

The referee had his back to the bleachers when she pulled his pants down to his ankles. The crowd reacted, laughing and pointing at the man as he pulls up his dirty trousers. D'Juan and Tonya ran off as fast as they could. All Juelz could think was *why? Why he had to do something so stupid?* Everyone in the neighborhood knew who they were, and it wouldn't be long before the elderly man caught up with him or even worse, sent some of his nephews or little cousins to jump him. Once he came to grips with D'Juan probably putting the young girl up to embarrass him, he looked at Juelz. Fearing he might do something to get his payback, Juelz gathered his clothes and gym bag.

"Aye, yo, yo! Tell yo' brother I'm gonna kick his little ass!" the man yelled as Juelz jogged off the court and out the gate.

Tonya finally stopped running when she reached the corner of 106th and 7th Ave. She bent over, out of breath but finding the incident to be dangerously funny. "Oh poppi, we hella wrong."

"Yo, that was crazy! You should've seen the look on his face! Ah, man, that was good!" He shared a laugh.

Once Tonya caught her breath, she got her turn. "I'm going to make this simple. I dare you to steal a pineapple from that market over there."

"Now you pushing it ma-ma. I can't steal, my family hate thrives." He proclaim

" Okay, well kiss me then. And not a baby kiss either. Kiss me like you mean it" She seduced while stepping closer.

"That's it? What's the catch?"

"Oh what, you ain't down for whateva?" She smiled while guiding his hands to her hips. "Just hold me, please." It was as if the air left her body once she fell into his arms. The sunlight got brighter for the five minutes that they locked lips. "Umm, that was amazing" she commented after licking her lips.

"Can I tell you something?" he asked.

"Anything, poppi. What?"

He inhaled deeply before confessing how his desire to have her is growing stronger by the day.

"What? You really just said that?"

"Nah, I'm just saying. I want you to be my first." After seeing he was sincere, her affection for him grew stronger.

"Wow. Well, if I told you about the dreams I've been having since we met.." She hints at her panties being wet.

"Oh word, let me touch it." They kissed again while his hands explored her Victoria Secrets. Only this time for much longer. Twenty minutes or more longer. With a promise to meet at the same time tomorrow, D'Juan couldn't wait to tell Juelz.

Tonya transformed into a little lady overnight. He gave her reason to trust and believe in a brighter future. Anytime they embraced, the pain and hardships just didn't exist. On the walk home, he received cold stares from a couple of En-Rica's crew members, but he didn't sweat it. When they mad dogged him, he just gave them a mischievous grin. Her teenage body was developing in front of their eyes, and the freshest kid in Harlem was her boyfriend. Lucky kid huh?

Juelz was waiting at the top of the steps as he walked up. "Keep yo' head up, lil bro. Somebody might take it off."

D'Juan took heed and lifted his chin. "I got my front. I know you got my back, right" They embraced with a handshake and hug.

"Yeah, but that's not gon' stop somebody from aiming at this bowling ball here. Boy," Juelz said with his hand gripping the top of D'Juan's head.

"Aye, bro, forget all that. I just finger banged Tonya, kid. Had her quivering at the hips," he said proudly.

"Yeah, yeah, whatever kid.. And I had Jamelia tasting my dick, so what. You left me in a jam today, and that's the first thing you talk about?" Juelz looked at D'Juan sideways "you buggen out fa real, you can get killed for dissen cats like that. Then what?" Juelz shakes his head with disappointment.

"My bad bro. I really wasn't trying to involve you, it was just a dare."

Juelz kept walking up the stairs, refusing to entertain such foolishness...

As they prepared for bed, Juelz socked D'Juan in the stomach, knocking the air from his body. **"Ahh,"** he groaned, clutching his stomach.

"You cost me the championship and a thousand dollars," Juelz barked.

Nina bust through the door after hearing argument between the two. She directed them to the dinner table to eat dinner and then to bed. D'Juan pouted on the way to the table. He knew a lecture from his father was coming at the very least. He socked Juelz in his back when Nina had her back turned.

"Hey, you little maleantes. I'm going to tell your poppa. He'll straighten you out. Now cool it," Nina expresses firmly.

"Okay Nana." D'Juan agreed to quit playing but immediately thereafter flips his brother off. It was only after a few bites into her Spanish rice, black beans, and grilled jumbo prawns, all was forgiven.

At four a.m., Juelz woke up from night terrors. "Ah!" he yelled.

D'Juan jumped from his sleep. "Bro, you good?"

"Yea, yeah. No doubt."

"Yo man, you can't be doing that. My heart's ponding right now." He explains

"Aye, I'm serious about what I said earlier. Always remember this if I teach you nothing else. What goes around, comes around. You living like you have no destiny. All you talk about is money and fly rides kid. You buggen out, fa'real."

"I know, Jay. I just miss home, yo. The fam, Ma, our baby brother, Lala. I think about them day and night. Tonya the only one understands. When I'm with her, my dreams has no limit kid."

Juelz listened and tried to empathize with him, but he only hopes he takes heed of the warning signs.

"You know I've been pushing, that ganja for months now. It's time to step up my hustle . Nana getting old, and Poppa always working. It's just us, Jay, and you love your basketball." He stressed how alone he felt.

"Bro, I feel the same way. Don't forget, I always put familia first. Playing ball and going to the NBA is my dream to make it better for us."

"Then that's what you do bro. We all we got"

With the same purpose in their heart that night, they made a pact. For as long as D'Juan hustled, he would take care of their Nana and send money to their mother, so Juelz could focus on going to college and if it's Allah will, to the NBA. D'Juan's only request was that the balled hard.

Juelz was now in the eighth grade, attracting several high school scouts. His crossover was Rucker's Park style, and his defense was as good as Gary Payton's in his early days. They even nicknamed him "J.P the thief." What was most impressive was his leadership and work ethic, on and off the court, with an average of 3.9 GPA and could be found tutoring underclassmen in the library afterschool. D'Juan and Tonya attended all his games, both home and away. Coach Watson made sure they were counted as being a part of the team.

It was a game against 'Leroy Heights' traveling team that made Julian Placencia a star. His coached matched him up against a top 10 prospect, for the whole game. This individual was scoring fifty and sixty points a game until that night. He was held to only nineteen points, and Juelz had a triple double—eleven rebounds, eighteen points, and fifteen assists. To make it even sweeter, the game was played at the Madison Square Garden. Juelz was on the front page of the *New York Times*, and featured in a *And One* edition magazine. – How dreams could seem so close, but reality is...

Tonya and D'Juan saw hope in each other's future as with the promise they made together—to remain in love unconditionally, no matter what happens or where in the world they may wander. She had just started high school and wanted a place they could call home. He flipped her checks making four grand every two weeks, but it still wasn't enough. They were talking about living in Manhattan someday, where it's 4-8 grand just to rent a condo on 3rd Ave. The reality is, if they dreamed big, then they would have to take big risk.

Tonya came by Nina's house while D'Juan was getting some rest. He'd recently been helping his pa' at a restaurant in Manhattan, where he was able to catch up on schoolwork as well.

"Hey, Nana, I have some groceries for you," Tonya said while stepping in the door.

"Oh, gracias, nieta." Nina thanked her with a warm smile.

D'Juan opened his eyes at the sound of Tonya's voice. He lay in bed for a few minutes, until he realized he wasn't dreaming. He quickly showered and groomed himself, getting fresh in a Mecca outfit before easing up on their conversation. "What's up, Tee? Nana?"

"Hey, boo. Come here." Tonya stopped him in route to the kitchen, "Give me a hug. I missed you." She then kissed his lips. When he didn't return the same affection, she wondered what was wrong. He hinted toward his grandmother, expecting that she wouldn't approve of their relationship. "What? You think she doesn't already know about us? *You know the streets talk CUBA*" she says loud enough for the house to hear.

When D'Juan made eye contact with his Nana, she was google-eyed with a smile; showing gold crowns over her molar teeth.

"Mi amor, kiss me now," she demanded. After he kissed her lightly on the lips, her eyes revealed her lust for more.

"Tonight, ma-ma, under the stars," he promised, getting her to switch focus to the business at hand. Once it was understood that he had the dinero to cop some real weight, she kissed Nina on the cheek. "Adios, Nana."

"Hasta luego, periquite." Nina smiles in approval as D'Juan slipped his foot in his Timberland boots.

"I love her," Tonya said, once in the hallway.

"What you do to my nana? She been acting weird since you started helping her," he asked, putting his arm around her shoulder.

She laughed and thought he was the one tripping, so he wondered what was he missing. Nina had always been strict with everyone, what's different about her; he questions.

"You really should get to know her. She's really a nice person. People have been speaking about her for years, so in return, we do favors for her," she credits the community, whom felt they owed the woman who fought for women's equality for healthcare and job pay.

"Wow. You know I heard about her and Poppa, and I do see the love they get. People stop by the restaurant often, speaking how great of a businessman my grandfather was."

"He was more than that, mi amor. He was a symbol of hope. A refugee that came to America and became a success." She described facts of his family's legacy, which he'd never known, giving him a slightly different perspective of his father's struggle...

Chapter 2

En-Rica, a Puerto Rican kid from the neighborhood, was the connect. And D'Juan thought he was just stalking Tonya while hanging on the corner of 105th. The two met him at the bodega on 104th and Lennox Ave. which was formally owned by Arnesto. D'Juan was familiar with the place. Tonya stepped up to the counter addressing the man behind the register.

"Hola, Raphael. Where's Rica?"

"Yo, mama. He in the back. He's expecting you, but aye Tee. Who's ya boy?" He motioned toward D'Juan, who was standing firm with a serious demeanor.

"Oh, you haven't heard of him. This is Cuba," she said proudly.

Raphael looked at the kid who had become quite popular in the neighborhood, and nodded his head in approval.

En-Rica was smoking a Cigarillo while watching the World Cup. As he turns in his chair, D'Juan notices a crown tattoo on his neck, same as Arnesto.

"There you are. What's up?"

Tonya's voice turned his head. She knew how much En-Rica had tried impressing her in the past and would do anything she asked.

"Aye, Tonya. What brings you down here?" he asked, cutting eyes to D'Juan.

She smacks her lips. "You remember our business from last night?" Apparently, his idea of business was something other than involving money, at least coming from her way.

"Oh, so this is the guy, huh? You know I've been seeing you around."

D'Juan extended his hand. "I'm Cuba." The name instantly rang a bell.

"Oh, one of the Shakur boys? Okay. What you need, my mans?"

D'Juan looked over to Tonya before giving his proposition. "My shorty told me you about yo' cake. I've been copping four P's of Ganja every two weeks. Now, I need some real weight. Sugar.." As D'Juan was speaking, he noticed En-Rica checking out his attire—Coogi sweatshirt, jeans, fresh Timbs, and a tapered haircut with 360 waves. His reputation befitted him.

"Yeah. Sugar huh. That's major league there my friend. Look, I don't usually do this, but I trust Tonya with my life, so I will tell you what. You buy five ounces at a grand a piece, and I'll front you five at the same price. But you only deal with me."

D'Juan looked at him in the eyes before shaking his hand. "That's a bet." He pulled two wads of small bills from his pocket and began to count it.

"It's okay little mans. Just drop it on the table." En-Rica shook his head, mumbling under his breath. He then reaches in the file cabinet and tosses D'Juan a silver package with a scorpion stamp.

D'Juan throws the package in his book bag and nodded to Tonya. "Okay, Rica. Peace." She throws up two fingers, exiting the back office.

"Aye, Tee, catch you later," En-Rica yells. D'Juan never minded the game he was trying to run. At the end of the day, the jokes were on him.

En-Rica came out his office shortly after Tonya and D'Juan left. "Aye, Ralph, I need you to keep an eye on Cuba. Make sure nothing happens to him. The kid has a bright future."

"Okay, Boss. But what about Tonya?" he asked, fully aware of En-Rica's desire to have her.

"She seems to be happy. Just worry about my investment," he reiterated.

D'Juan and Tonya had plans to hit the Uptown Movie Cinema and enjoy the rest of the night. He begins to run upstairs to stash the work when he saw his Pa' sitting on the couch with his hand on the top of his head. "Poppa, what's wrong?" He asks, dropping his book bag in the hall closet.

"It's your uncles, mijo." He shook his head and tried to explain. "Santana and Romelo have just been arrested by federal authorities. And I have a bad feeling about this."

"What, Poppa? What's going to happen?"

All Tito could do was shake his head. "We'll know soon enough. Carlosi will be here in a couple weeks." He then stood up and went to his room. D'Juan didn't know what to make of the situation, but he trusts his Pa's instincts. He retrieved his bag from the closet and burst through his room door.

"Jay," he calls out before realizing he wasn't there. He looked around, and figured he'd just missed him. He stashed the ten ounces in the broken air conditioner and grabbed a gram of ganja before heading back out the door.

Tonya could see his demeanor had changed dramatically. "Poppi, are you okay?"

He nodded his head indicating yes, but she was unconvinced. "Let's just enjoy our night."

They made one stop to a corner store for zig-zags and two Corona's. Tonya used her looks and charm to avoid having to show identification. Coming out of the store with enough on his mind, a man sleeping on the street asked for some change. When he reached in his pocket, pulling out a twenty-dollar bill, he recognized the man's face.

"Wait, I know you, young blood. You one of them Shakur boys. And you, I'm gonna show you about fucking with me," he said, gesturing toward Tonya. The stench from his breath reeked of alcohol, and his clothes looked like they hadn't been washed in weeks.

"Here, old man, and get the fuck away from her." D'Juan pushed the drunkard down, dropping the bill on his chest. They hurried into the car and smashed off.

"What was that? He ripped my shirt," Tonya said in a panic.

"Mama, calm down. I think that was the dude from Garvey Park." If his memory served correct.

"Garvey P... Who? The referee?"

"Yeah, I think so. He just looks so different without his striped shirt. I wouldn't be surprised though."

Her head snapped to the right in response to his answer. "What do you mean by that?"

"Shit, he was a bum ref, so I'm not surprised he a bum on the streets."

Tonya couldn't believe her ears. "You serious? Please tell me you joking, right?" He looked over with a firm face. "Oh my God, D'Juan. The man is homeless. Don't you see he referees in his spare time? That's his good deed to the community," she explained but D'Juan still showed no empathy. She got to speaking and cursing in Spanish and he knew what that meant.

"Okay, ma-ma. I'm sorry. When I see him again, I'll buy him some clothes or something."

"No, you gon' do more than that. You gon' buy him some food every day and give twenty dollars so he can get a motel," she demanded.

"Okay, sheesh. What you gon' do next? Volunteer to bathe him?" he said with humor. However she was not laughing. "First we embarrassed him, now you shove him to the ground, treat him like trash. No, this not right."

She made a U-turn at the next corner and searched for him the rest of the night. She warned D'Juan not to say anything else because to her he sounded inconsiderate and cruel. Well, not only did he ruin their movie night but also his chance at her sweet potato pie. Having no luck in their search, they didn't make it back to 107th until three a.m.

D'Juan crawled through the window, using the fire escape. Juelz was there, waiting with a look of concern. "Bro, where have you been? Poppa heard gunshots around the corner and came looking for you."

As if his night couldn't get any worse, he shrugged his shoulders nonchalantly and acted as if he heard nothing. He kicked off his Timbs and hopped on the top bunk, laying down while fully clothed.

"You stupid," Juelz said before finally closing his eyes.

Staring at the ceiling, he counted the stars that glowed in the dark. With that process, he imagined if he was a star, how would he feel? Did stars even feel at all? Were they alive, and where'd they get their light from was the questions he asked himself. Anticipating his father coming any minute, cracking his belt like a whip across his back, he fought his sleep. Then he thought about school and took his chances with resting his eyes for at least a couple hours. Missing one more day of school was definitely out of the question.

Tonya's soft skin rubbed against his arms. She begged for him to hold her, and when he did, she moaned from his firm grip on her bottom. "Kiss me," she whispered in his ear. So he kissed from her neck to the canary-yellow diamond navel ring, stopping just before reaching the tattoo of his name. He felt like the man when his penis made her kitty cat purr. She moaned as they made slow passionate love, kissing, and caressing her body in between movements. "Just relax," she commanded, before riding his erect penis like a seasoned veteran. Then suddenly, he was yanked out of bed by the top of his shirt.

"Mijo, wake up. Where have you been all night?" Tito yelled in his face, making his heart jump.

"Poppa, I can't breathe," he pled.

"You gonna wish you can't breathe after I'm through whooping your behind."

"What I do, Poppa?" he begged for an understanding while pleading for mercy.

"You on drugs now, mijo? I told you, we don't use or sell drugs in this house!" Tito scolded him, holding up a baggy of ganja.

Damn, he thought. With not much else to say, he took his discipline and got dressed for school.

Juelz returned to the room and smirked on the sly. "You know what Poppa always say, hermano. Hard head makes a soft ass," he said with humor.

"At least I didn't cry." As he referred to that one incident, Juelz charged like a mad bull. They wrestled and tussled until Nina broke them up.

"Aye, stop it. Why you acting like criminals? You wanna fight each other, but the government fights us all." She advises they always stay united.

"Okay, Nana. We're going to school now.. Go, punk." D'Juan pushed Juelz out the door.

Seeing Tonya that morning made D'Juan feel loved. Up until then, he felt abandonment from his closest relatives. Whether by death, incarceration, or a job keeping them busy, the recurring theme was him being alone.

"You can ride shotgun, Jay," he said with good reason to ride in the back seat.

"Yo, what's really—"

"Hey, hermano." She kissed Juelz on the cheek and cut her eyes back to D'Juan. As he suspected, she still hadn't gotten over the ordeal from last night. So he figured that would be a good time to introduce her to his world.

"Jay, did Pa tell you about our uncle Santana, and Romelo?"

Juelz looked back over his shoulder with surprise. "What's the word?"

"They just got arrested and facing a lot of jail time. I heard him telling Nana they're in serious trouble." He could feel Tonya looking through her rearview at him while he explained. Juelz began to recall the extravagant lifestyle of his uncles and the expensive gifts they received, but he could never foresee the consequences. He held his head and wiped tears from his eyes.

"Bro, you know Poppa is going to need our help. He's been drinking again." As Juelz spoke with despair, D'Juan made eye contact with Tonya. Her facial expression was saying, *I'm sorry. I didn't know.* "I know, Jay. I'm working on something big. You'll have to help at the restaurant. Me and Tonya will look after Nana."

"But you know I have practice every day at the YMCA until five o'clock."

"We gotta do what we gotta do, bro. Tonya will give you a ride. We are all in this together, and we gon' make it," he spoke with confidence.

She pulled into the Malik Shabazz students' parking lot within minutes. They had their plan together now it was just a matter of working it. "Poppi, come here." Tonya stepped outside insisting she had her morning kiss. They tongue kissed with no regard for time. "See you at two forty-five. I have a presentation for history class."

"Okay poppi. I'll be at the gym with Jay."

She nodded her head and drove off with a smile. Her confidence in 'the kid' made him feel capable of doing anything he put his mind to.

For once in the past twelve hours, he could breathe. After math and history classes, his mind drifted to his hustle. He could hear the fiends on 12th and Lennox calling him. He couldn't wait to get to work. The thought of hundred dollar sales was a distraction he endured until the school bell sounded.

At 3 p.m., Tonya dropped Juelz off at practice then picked up D'Juan. He handed her a

bundle of twenty grams, with a condom so she could stash it in a safe spot. She acted as his lookout while he handled his business. Selling two grams every ten minutes, he had a thousand dollars in less than two hours. Leaving enough time for Tonya to pick up Juelz and take him to his Pa' restaurant on Broadway. He studied in the backseat as D'Juan counted his earnings.

"A'ight brodi, tell poppa I love him. And you be easy kid."

"You already know." Juelz returned the love with his fist over his heart.

D'Juan then looked to his shorty and insisted he treat her to the cinema. She happily accepted. "But with one condition."

"Anything you desire, my queen."

"I figured you would say that. You are so cute. Okay, I seen Mr. Mitchell this morning at the park when I dropped you off," she tried to explain before he interjected.

"Who?"

"Just listen. We're inviting him to the movies and dinner as you promised."

D'Juan leaned back in his seat and contemplated how that would go. It wasn't a problem apologizing for his wrong, but to spend his hard-earned money in hopes to make a friend was just crazy. What if the man didn't want peace? Then again, he already gave his word and anything meant just that.

Mr. Mitchell was sitting on a bench at Marcus Garvey Park. Tonya flashed the high beams, signaling it was her. "Just be chill, poppi, okay?" she said, trying to get eye contact. "Look at me. I'm chilled, okay?"

"It's going to be okay. Just remember, he is a street dweller." She says as the man approach the passenger door.

"Aye, Mitch, I'm keeping it all the way real. This is not easy to do, but I respect what you did for us at the park. We had no business dissin' you, and for that, I apologize," he said, looking into his dark eyes.

"It's all fair young blood. Trust me, I know it feels to be you. I just appreciate you and your girl for making me whole again. I had to ask myself, what I do to deserve that." He shook his head, making a sigh of relief "But all is forgiven young blood."

Tonya and D'Juan looked at each other simultaneously with shame. They both felt it was Mr. Mitchell's night, no matter the expenses.

The three went into Uptown Cinema as strangers but walked out as friends. They shared laughs and Nestle's bon bons going back to the car.

"Boy that Pam Grier... She was the baddest in showbiz," Mr. Mitchell spoke highly of the main actress in *Coffee*.

D'Juan saw him in a different light after hearing him speak. The question that he would may ask at some other time, was how did a man with so much knowledge and love for people end up sleeping in the streets? There was definitely more to Mr. Mitchell than what met the eye.

For dinner, they went to Little Havana's in Manhattan. Upon seeing Tito, Mr. Mitchell saluted him with the utmost respect. "Tito, these your boys?" he asked, looking over to Juelz in his apron.

"Yeah, these mi dos mijo's. Julian is the oldest. They know who you are. I tell them stories about you."

D'Juan and Juelz looked at each other, trying to recollect which legendary tales may fit this individual.

"No, I don't think they know, my brother. But this one here, I ref him a few games. His ball handling and jump shot is butter. Remind me of a young man I once knew."

"Oh yeah? Well, that's saying a lot." The two continue to reminisce about their teenage years.

Wow, what a small world, D'Juan thought. He and Tonya conversed about their night and how good fortune came around. Once Juelz knew who the man was, he listened to his every word. Harry Mitchell was legendary, mentioned on blacktops from Holcombe Rucker in Harlem to Diamond Park in Oakland, CA. So if he said Juelz had a chance to be better than he was, he would want to believe it. Tito offered Mr. Mitchell a job and let him live in the back room of the restaurant. In return, he agreed to coach and mentor his son. When the stars shined the brightest, it seemed another blessing was received.

For the next two days, D'Juan stepped up his hustle, pushing two G-packs and an ounce of ganja at Tonya's high school. The money was coming in so fast, En-Rica feared the kid might be targeted by stick-up kids. He called Tonya at midnight,

"Hola," she answered after just getting in the bed.

"Buenas noches, señorita. I need to meet your boy tomorrow morning. Tell him it's important."

"I will, Rica. Is everything okay?"

"Si, ma-ma. I just need to give him something, that's all."

Tonya agreed to meet early, so whatever business wouldn't interfere with school.

Meanwhile, D'Juan was calling home, hoping to hear some good news concerning his uncles. Christi checked the clock and wondered who could be calling after ten o'clock.

"Hello?" she answered with a squeaky voice.

"Mama. How are you and Lala doing?"

"Oh, mijo. I'm okay, just been worried about you guys. Did your nana give you my messages?"

D'Juan was puzzled and didn't know how to answer her question. "Uhh, you know Nana is getting old. She probably forgot."

"It's okay. It's good to hear your voice. I hear you've been doing good at school and your brother's working with your poppa."

"Yes, this is true. We're doing good here, but it's nothing like home," he stressed.

"Mijo, home is where you make it. It's nothing much going on here. I wish I could send Lala out there to be with y'all."

"Yeah, Ma-ma. Why you can't both come? Me and my girlfriend are going—" He stopped midsentence after realizing his slip of the tongue.

"D'Juan, you're only twelve. What are you doing with a girlfriend?"

He could hear the tension in her voice, indicating she was upset. "Tonya helps Nana. We're just friends, Ma-ma," he plead for her understanding. "Allah knows best, I don't want you to be upset with me."

"I'm going to talk to your poppa. If he said this Tonya is a fine young lady, I'm okay with it."

"Okay, Ma-ma. Have you talked to Uncle Romie or Santana?"

"No. They don't call anyone. Their lawyers deliver messages, but that's it. My brother may spend the rest of his life in prison, hijo. It hurts my heart, and to see Lala playing outside makes me worrisome. Hijo, there's no future in playing cops and robbers," understanding that was also his favorite game, she hopes he takes heed.

D'Juan made his mind up then he had to take a trip back west. "I know Mama, but he's only a kid. I'm sure he'll grow out of it. I'll try to visit soon, okay?"

"You do that but talk to your poppa first. It's a reason why we separated, and you should know."

"Yes Ma-ma, I will. Love you."

"Love you too and tell Juelz I love him and I'm so proud of him. You be protectors of one another. Strength and courage mi hijo, always remember."

"Okay ma-ma. May peace be upon you."

"Salaam."

D'Juan bounced up and showered at seven o'clock on the nose. That morning, he was feeling more alive than the day he was born. He was ready to re-up, and after talking to his ma, he had even more motivation. Tonya was sitting in the living room talking to Nana.

"Hola, bueno días," Nana said, wishing him a good morning.

"Buenos días, Nana." He then nodded his head to Tonya, inquiring into what was going on.

"Nana, hasta luego." She kissed Nina on the cheek, promising to see her later. D'Juan was wearing a beige Karl Kani jean outfit with brown bandana tied on his head, only exposing his curly top. "You look really good poppi." Tonya complimented his B-boy style.

"Gracias, mama. So what's the drill?" he asked, knowing something had to be up. She was a whole hour early.

"En-Rica wants to see you. Is everything okay?"

"I don't know, mama. He's a funny guy. It's like every time I'm on the block, he has spies watching me and shit. I ain't feeling that, like they plottin' or son'thin'."

She looked into his eyes and got an understanding she waited all night for. "I knew it was something. He's calling me every night wanting me to be his shorti , now all of a sudden he hella cool with you? I don't buy it. Here poppi, take this in case." She handed him a .44 bulldog with an extra cylinder and a box of ammunition.

He examined the pistol and smiled, feeling the power in his hands. "Where you get this?"

"Shh, stop talking so loud and put that up." He tucked it in his belt and continued toward the car. "My brother Arnesto went to jail, so nobody knows I have it," she explained, speaking in a low tone. "Arnesto? That's your brother?" he asks, wondering if this was the same gun used to kill a man.

"Yeah, I'm sure you heard of him. Everyone still speaks of him like he's here. Everyone except..."

He looks her square in the eyes as she pauses "except who ma-ma?" anticipating an answer he cocked the hammer. "Never mind. Let's just get this over with."

With so much to consider, D'Juan's eyes were peeled when he stepped outside. The air was muggy, and the neighborhood was alive. Everyone moved with urgency to their destination. With ten grand in pocket and power in his waistband, the kid was feeling like 'the man'. Nearing the bodega, he approached with caution and pistol in hand.

The scenery was different from the last visit. Raphael wasn't behind the register, the aisles were dark, and there were no shoppers that morning. En-Rica was wearing a jumpsuit and tennis shoes as if he was going on a jog through Central Park. Tonya stepped in the room dressed in Cross Colors overalls, with the matching crop top and lady Timberland boots.

"Hey. It's good to see you." En-Rica approached, kissing her on the cheek. "And my main guy, Cuba. It's so much I want to talk about. I've been hearing a lot of good things, and honestly, I'm surprised you lasted this long down on Lennox."

"What? You spying on me?"

"My mans, you think I'll send you out of here with my product and not look after you? It's a concrete jungle out there,"

"I'm good. I can handle it." He then pulled two wads of bills from his pocket and tossed it on the table. "You wanna do business, let's talk money."

"Ahh, I like this kid. He's badass. Okay, badass, this is the business. Territory on 12th and Lennox is already being controlled by other Latino gangs. Maybe you should find some territory between 105th and 106th," he suggest.

D'Juan felt in his gut some funny shit was going to come out his mouth. "Rica, don't nobody be down there when I'm grinding, and you know these blocks around here is all sewed up."

"Well, now the block you were slinging on is sewed up. I told you when you got in it, don't expect things will be fair. However, I do have a different proposition. Work for me down on 10th and Lucas, and we can keep this thing going," he warns there may be trouble if he went back down to 12th and Lennox.

"With all due respect, I don't work for NOBODY. If I can't cop from you no more, it's good." He reached for his five grand when En-Rica grabbed his hand.

"Cuba, no one touches my money but me." He states firmly, before flipping through the bills. "If you want out, you out the heroin business for good." As he spoke from a position of authority, D'Juan imagined how one shot would make him quiver like a bitch. At the end of all that, the kid came up with a better idea.

"What about coke? It's like nobody pushing cocaine. Why is that?"

En-Rica looked over to Raphael, smiled, then back to D'Juan. "Crack kills, my man. Now pure blow we may do something with, but you have to go down to Florida for that shit." He dismissed the idea as being too risky.

"See, that's where you're wrong. You forget I'm from Cali, babii. We got kilos for the low. They don't have this though. Nah mean?" Referring to china white.

En-Rica looked at Raphael, who was the oldest of the two. He shrugged his shoulders to suggest it was maybe worth the risk. Now weighing in on D'Juan, he assesses could he be trusted, and if so, how much? "Okay, my man, and I'll be clear. Tonya speaks highly of you, so I'm doing this for her too. I'll give you eighteen ounces for uhh, say nine grand. And you owe the balance."

D'Juan's initial thought was *this motherfucker must be hard of hearing. I work for no one.* Then he does the math. Nine grand for nine ounces equals twenty-two point five thousand dollars, which he could cop a kilo and a half of blow and return to Harlem as the man.

"Yeah, that sounds like money." D'Juan agrees to the terms, optimistic he'll win in the end. Likewise, En-Rica felt his energy.

"Come see me tonight. Traveling on the weekends is always best."

"A'ight, peace." Raphael and En-Rica both smiles as he walks out.

"That's a long trip," Raphael suggested.

"Yeah, but I respect his vision. If he makes it back, he gets his block back. If he doesn't, then he loses his freedom and his girl. What we have to lose?" They shared laughs, imagining Tonya as a sex slave.

Tonya started the car and turned to D'Juan, visibly concerned. "Poppi, you sure we need to do this? I mean, between us, we're making enough dinero here. And En-Rica' is full of shit, saying he's doing this for me. He haven't done nothing for my brother since he went away, and Arnesto gave him everything."

D'Juan looked over to the door and felt eyes on them as they spoke. "Let's get away from here. I know it's something else he got up his sleeve."

Tonya merged into traffic and explained that was what she'd been saying. "Poppi, he's not trying to do nothing but get in my panties. You came up on your own. You owe him nothing." D'Juan took in everything she said. It wasn't until they were pulling into his school parking lot did he respond.

"Mama, you know this dude best. I just want you to know I'm not doing this for him. Mi madre needs to see me, and we need this score. It'll put us in the duplex ASAP," he says with conviction. She saw he wanted the best for them but was fearful of losing him. Her brother was serving prison time for smuggling drugs from Florida. And ironically, the last conversation they had was a year to the date—October 28, 1992.

Chapter 3

D'JUAN DIRECTED TONYA TO East Harlem High School. He waited on the stairs by Juelz's classroom until the bell rang. A crowd of students rush out the doors. "Yo, Jay," he called from behind the crowd.

"Yo, what's up, lil' bro? Where you was at this morning?"

"Yo, I had some business to handle."

Juelz interrupted. "I don't care about that anymore. I know you say you doing this for Ma, but you're my little brother, and I still have to take care of you. Poppa said I should be a good example for you, so I go to class. You can't keep missing school, kid. The principal is going to call Nana." Juelz gave it to him straight, and D'Juan knows how Nina feels about getting his smarts. She was convinced, it's only two places they would end up without education; the grave or the cage.

"Bro, I just came to tell you I love you, a'ight? Look, I'm gonna be in the parking lot," he said after seeing Jamelia walking up the hallway.

"Y'all, go ahead. She gon' give me a ride to the park. We'll holla later." Juelz hugged Jamelia and walked back down the hall with his arm draped over her shoulder. His six-foot-three slender frame, next to her five-foot-eight firm body, looked picture perfect. A star couple in their own right, considered to be two of the best athletes at East Harlem High.

D'Juan returned to the car with his head down. Tonya hated seeing him in that mind state. She lifted his head and reminded him their destiny lay ahead. She was his calm in the storm. His rock in the ocean. His future? Well, he didn't care what that'll look like if his family wasn't together.

With five hours until nightfall, she had the perfect date in mind, just him and her—Uptown Cinema for the Friday night special featuring Fred Williamson in *Hell in Harlem* and *Black Caesar*. She got the tickets and returned to the car. "The first show is in twenty-five minutes," she said, looking at him. He smiled briefly, indicating he was stressed. "How is your mom?" she asks, getting his attention.

"I don't know. She sounded vexed when I talked to her. Then... I don't know. What you wanna know?"

"Actually, I always wanted to know her name and why you never talk about her."

He shook his head, reluctant to speak on such a sensitive topic. "My ma's name is Christi. She's tall, brown skinned with light-brown eyes, and just beautiful. She a hustler too. She bought and sold houses for a living while Poppa had his restaurant. We lived in a five-bedroom in Clinton Hill, far from the projects. It's like the quietest place you can live in Richmond. My uncles were rich, and the familia was together. Then one night, I heard Madre and Poppa arguing. Next thing I knew, me and Juelz had to move out of there, and she took my baby brother and moved to the PJ's; just like that." He demonstrated with a snap of his finger.

"Aww, poppi. How did that make you feel?" She tried to make eye contact, but he continued to stare at the sky through the moon roof.

"I don't know how to feel. That's why I thank Allah for you," he said, finally looking at her.

"Allah? You Muslim? "

"Yeah, I was born Muslim. I don't pray as much as I use to but I know Allah is the One True God." Twenty minutes speaking of families struggle, and secrets, Tonya now understood why he carried the burden.

Ironically, without giving it any thought, the movie selection added more inspiration. The belief of being a street king was real to him. His heroes were deemed to be notorious and a threat to society by the law. While viewing the picture show, he identified with the struggle of a black man in America. In one scene, the politicians and cops were more corrupt than the murderers and bank robbers.

D'Juan left the cinema with the bright idea of being a businessman one day. So he vowed two conditions to himself with some form of discipline. Lately, he had been spending too much money on designer clothes. Although Tonya didn't mind being the recipient, she was also adamant about getting their own place. All these thoughts traveled through his mind while listening to her highlights of their movie night. Once back in the car, she just sat there. Head down with her hands on the steering wheel. After taking a few deep breaths, she finally release her thoughts,

"Pappi, I really hate the idea of you leaving. We are so close," she stressed.

"I know, ma, but we're not there yet. Look at me. Do you trust me?"

"Yeah, but what does that have to do with anything?"

"Trust has everything to do with what I feel I need to do. I love you, ma-ma. Never forget that. Unconditionally." She looked into his hazel-brown eyes and became wet in between her hips.

"Come here poppa, I want you." She grabbed his shirt, pulling him closer. When their lips and tongues touched, her body heat rises. "Let's get in the back." She directed him to the back seat.

"No doubt." He loved the spontaneous combustions. In that sense, only he could be her fireman. He pulled off his shirt while she peeled off her Apple Bottom jeans. "You have any condoms?" he asked.

"For what? Now just kiss me," she commanded while reaching for his manhood. "I like it," she said in between taking breaths. She eased on top of his lap, inserting his penis inside her. She bit his bottom lip and sucked on his neck to keep herself from moaning. He felt his temperature rising so fast he was about to bust. He grabbed her butt cheeks and pulled her closer to him. Their bodies became one as they were high in ecstasy.

"Ah, shh... shit," he moans, enticing her to release the bite on his neck and share moans in their intimate moment. As they just saw in the movie, one could never know when or where they'd take their last breath or how romantic it would be to share it together.

When she finally climaxed, her nails dug into the back of his neck as she kissed on his ear. "Don't forget me, poppi."

"Never," he assured.

They dressed and prepared for the meet with En-Rica. D'Juan still didn't know what to tell his Pa' but whatever he was going to say, it had to be that night. Tonya passed by his restaurant, but strangely, he wasn't there. In fact, the shop appeared to be closed.

"Hmm," D'Juan thought out loud. "Hold up. Pull around back. Let me see something."

She pulled to the back alleyway, where he exited the vehicle and knocked on the screen door. "Mitch! Mr. Mitchell!" he yelled repeatedly, getting no answer.

"Why do you think it's closed?" she asked, as it was out the norm.

"I don't know, ma." He scratched his head all the way to the bodega.

Tonya waited out front with the car running while D'Juan made the pickup. He clutched onto his pistol as his boots touched the ground. He nodded his head at Raphael as he walked past the cash register. En-Rica was on the phone when he entered the office.

"Yo, my mans, shut the door behind you." Upon doing so, he saw a silver package sitting on a storage locker. En-Rica signaled for him to take it while continuing his conversation. "Aye, I'll see you soon," he said before D'Juan stepped out the door.

"No doubt," he assured, followed by a smile. D'Juan returned to the car with one hand still on his pistol and the half kilo tucked under his arm. "It's good, ma." He directed Tonya to pull off, and she did so in a hurry. He leaned back in his seat, keeping one eye in the rearview mirror. His heart was pounding through his chest, and at every sight of a cop, he prayed they wouldn't follow. After making it safely back to 107th and 7th Avenue, they were finally able to exhale. Tonya looked over as she felt his eyes. "Well, we made it, poppi. The train leaves at 8:15, so I'll be here at six so we can eat and enjoy the last few hours together."

She then complained of not knowing how it'll be without him. They had grown so close in recent years. Sharing food, money, and intimate secrets over candlelight dinners. Even risking losing their freedom, all for the sake of spending an eternity with each other.

"It's gonna be good, ma. Like you said, we're almost there." They embraced with a long kiss before wishing each other a good night.

It was near midnight. D'Juan used the fire escape to enter his room without being detected and questioned of his whereabouts. "Brodi," he said with excitement.

"Shh!" Juelz demanded silence while he listened with his ear to the door. Apparently, their cousins Carlosi, Poncho a.k.a Pappi, Spider and Aunt Diana were in town for an emergency family meeting.

The boys expressed their concerns of federal indictments and their father looking at natural life. "Unc, it's hectic right now. They talking about racketeering, bribing government officials, solicitation to commit murder, and millions of dollars in property damages," Carlosi explained. Tito was sadden by the news, and simultaneously his son's could feel their hearts breaking.

"Listen to me carefully... one of you go to Atlanta, one back to Chicago, and one upstate. Your aunt Diana is going to be helping me at the restaurant and needs someone to tend to her house. You must lay low until my brother's trial, and whatever you were doing must stop. You bring attention to yourselves, and you will be indicted," he warns with sound reason. All the nephews took heed except for Carlosi.

"What's in Atlanta for us?" he asks.

"**Nothing!** That's the point. You're the key figures in mi hermano's organization. Without you, the case would be extremely weak," he advised wisely, but what they'd do with the information was out of his control. He then excused himself and went into Nana's room to share with her the disturbing news. Minutes later, her cries echoed through the apartment.

Uncertain if they'd ever live in Rich City again, Juelz put on his Sony headphones to block out the noise. He looked at D'Juan, who sat with his back to the door, staring into space, daydreaming of the streets as he remembered and what was left.

In the aftermath of the riches and Rolls Royce's, was bloodshed and life sentences in prison; hell on earth. Romelo Sr. was mentioned as Santana's lieutenant. Lyfe was on the run with international warrants, stemming from the same indictment, and Remo was already at the preliminary stages of his trail for illegal and unauthorized firearms. Out of all of them, he had the best chance of seeing daylight again.

At approximately 4:30 a.m., D'Juan walked into the kitchen. Carlosi and Pappi were stretched out on the floor and Aunt Diana on the couch. "Hey, sobrino," Aunt Diana said as he turned the kitchen lights on.

"What's up, Tia? How have you been?" he asked after not seeing her in a few years.

"All praise to Allah. I'm hanging in there. You know I'm going to be helping your poppa at the restaurant."

"Yeah? That's what's up. Where's Millian?"

"Oh, I'm so sorry honey. I meant to tell Tito, he asked about you last night."

"Word?" He ask with excitement. "I was in the room. Why you didn't come get me?"

" Well, to be honest your Tia haven't been doing well. I'm sure by now you heard about your uncle's." She briefly mentions the dire circumstances, and uncertainty of any good outcome.

D'Juan held his head and fought off tears. "I need to see Millian Tia, please. Me, him and Brutus can help."

After giving it some thought she informed him that Millan was in Nebraska with Brutis working as a club promoter. *Nebraska?* he thought. *It must be some big money involved. Nothing's in Nebraska but cornfields and nuclear warheads.* "A'ight. I'll try to be around next time you call him. Aye, I need you to do me a favor."

"Now you not going to have me in no mess with your poppa, are you?"

On second thought, it might be best he told his Pa' himself. "Nah, never. I need you to tell Millian I'll be in Chicago soon."

"Okay. I'll tell him, but you know he's talking about moving back west."

Even better, he thought. To not wake up the house, she whispered she'd talk to him later in the morning. He gave her a thumbs-up and drank his glass of orange juice while eating a handful of grapes. He then laid back in bed to rest his eyes.

"D'Juan! Julian!" Tito yelled to awaken his sons.

"Yeah, Poppa?" Juelz answered while D'Juan dreamed of better days.

"Get up, mijo. I need to talk to you now!" He then sat at the foot of D'Juan's bed. "D'Juan?" He shook him awake.

"Okay, okay, Poppa. I'm up." They both sat up in their beds with both ears open. Expecting to hear what was discussed the previous night, they felt ready.

"I want to talk to you about your madre. She's getting sick and worrisome. She asked me if one of you can come live with her for a few months. I think it would help her too." It was like destiny. D'Juan made eye contact with Juelz, having already decided who'd be going. "Julian, I know you want to see your madre, but Mitch is putting a lot of time into your training. Maybe around New Year, we all can go back West. Celebrate D'Juan's birthday as a family," he said, getting both of their hopes up.

"Yeah, Poppa. We should. Lala is getting bigger, and Ma said he's always asking about us," D'Juan said with enthusiasm. Tito's face seemed to age ten years overnight.

For the first time, Juelz looked at his father as an old, worrisome man. "I'll stay here and help you and Nana," he said, bringing comfort to Tito's heart, who then turned to D'Juan. "Mijo, you take care of your ma', and trust in the God she believes in. We'll be back together when it's his will."

"Okay poppa. I have to go now."

Meanwhile, Tonya had been sitting outside for the past fifteen minutes. "What's going on?" she thought out loud, looking down at her Donna Karen watch. After waiting another five minutes, she got out the car and walked up to the fourth floor.

"I got it." Diana opened the door and saw a pretty young face. "Hello."

"Hi. Is D'Juan home?"

"Yes, he is, and who are you?" Diana asked, standing with her hand on her hip. As Tonya got ready to introduce herself, D'Juan came to the door.

"Tia, this my girl."

"Your who? Boy, you not nothing but."

"Shut up. Move." He pushed his Aunt aside hoping she wouldn't expose his true age. She held back from cracking him upside his head, and instead asked Mrs. Shakur if she approved. He introduced Tonya to his family—from Tito to Spiciano.

Tito shook her hand gently. "I've heard so much about you. Between mi hijo and madre, you've been spoken of in high regards."

"Well, gracias, señor." She accepted with honor. Finally, Diana joined them at the kitchen table, where steak, eggs, and country fried potatoes were being served. In apologizing to Tonya for her poor hospitality, she mentioned her nephews were just kids last time she'd seen them.

"It's okay. I understand." Tonya came off to be a sweet young lady that the house adored. Carlos even saluted the kid.

Trying to enjoy breakfast with one eye on the clock became too problematic. "Poppa, Nana, familia, me and Tonya have to go. If you may, excuse me," D'Juan said, rising from the table. "Where you going, mijo?" Tito asked, causing the whole table to stop eating.

"I have a train to catch," he responded. Everyone at the table, except Juelz, erupted with laughter. "That son of yours had a good sense of humor," Diana mentioned. D'Juan nodded to Tonya, as this was their time to leave if there would ever be one.

They arrived at the train station at eight o'clock. With fifteen minutes until boarding time, he had to hurry. "Poppi, come here." She demanded a kiss.

"I'm here, ma-ma. What you got for me?" They shared a passionate French kiss for a couple minutes. He gripped her bottom with both hands as his manhood got erect.

"Okay, you have to go. I'll give you the rest when you come back." She pushes him away, leaving his pants bulging.

"Aww, that's how you do the kid? A'ight, bet that." He laughed at himself being a sucker for love.

"What? It's time for you to go unless you wanna catch the next train," she propose seductively.

"I'll catch you on the next one shorty. Peace." He threw up the peace sign as he departed.

"Peace. Love you, poppi," she yelled as he disappeared in a crowd.

First rule D'Juan learned as a transporter was to remain calm. He overheard Carlosi talk about their travels out of state—from the successful trips to the not so successful ones. "All aboard!" the conductor yelled. D'Juan boarded the Amtrak double decker and handed the conductor his ticket. "Down to the third car." He directed D'Juan to his cabin.

"Okay, thank you, sir." Now looking in the direction he was pointed in, there was a traffic jam directly in the middle of the car. "Hell with that." In frustration, he sat down until the chaos was settled. Pulling out his pencil and sketching pad, he occupied his mind. Nothing was more soothing than drawing and sculpting art. In the midst of dark thoughts, he could create something beautiful like the moonlight reflecting off of blue diamonds. As the train began to move, reality set in. "*Whoa!* he thought. *It's just me and this half a kilo. All these strange people around me that could take my book bag, and I wouldn't be able to defend myself. Why did I leave my gun? Stupid, stupid, stupid.*" He inhaled deeply and tried to remain calm. With the pencil in hand, he sketched his surroundings, starting with the young lady wearing a New York Yankees fitted cap, navy-blue overalls, and a Yankees crop top. Her attire wasn't what he would consider to be traveling gear. Maybe she was on a short trip. Then there was the lady next to her wearing a dashiki. Interestingly, she was a white woman with green eyes, freckles, and reddish-brown locs. Sketching her was fun. As he created the background, he hints at her native country and land animals. By the time he finished with the coloring and shading, it had been three hours.

"Sheesh," he thought out loud.

Seeing the coast was clear, he put his drawing kit back in his book bag and made way to cabin 14, where he'd be spending the duration of his trip. Upon entering the cabin, there was a lesbian couple hugged up and laughing. "Oh, what's up?" he said while checking the cabin number.

"Hey, lil' daddy." They sized his narrow frame up. Weighing only a hundred fifty pounds in boots, he had second thoughts about entering this small room with two heavy-set women. "We not gon' bite," they said with humor.

"Nah, I'm good." He shut the door and dug in his pocket for the key. "Nineteen," he blurted out, before locating the right cabin. He felt a few hundred pounds of pressure off his back for sure. Clutching on to his Timberland book bag, he looked out the window before dozing off...

Chapter 4

MEANWHILE, CHRISTI WAS PREPARING for D'Juan's arrival. She was in the kitchen washing dishes when gunshots rang out. The next sixty seconds of her life was in slow motion. She looked over at the dinner table, and Lala wasn't there. Steam was still rising from his plate. Then loud screams echoed through her windpipe. Naturally, she went into a state of shock. Dropping what was in her hands and running outside. There was her baby boy standing on the corner of 1st and Silver .

"Laa---laa!" she yelled.

He turned with tears in his eyes and pointed down at the eight-year-old boy. "That's my friend, Ma-ma. That's little Tim."

Christi rushed and tried to revive the child, but he was gone. "Are you hit?" She turned to Lala.

"Is he dead, Ma-ma?" he asked, just inches from being shot dead himself. She really had no response but to hug her son, for he just witnessed his best friend murdered.

By the time ambulance and paramedics arrived, Timothy Cooper Jr. was pronounced dead. His mother was on her knees screaming at the sky, asking for her baby back. Christi stood by her side while trying to console her and Lala simultaneously.

D'Juan opened his eyes as the train reaches the end of its line. *Chicago, Illinois,* he thought to himself. He immediately began to question what was going to happen next. Asking passengers made the situation even more confusing, so he hunted down the conductor. "Excuse me, Mister," he approached the Caucasian man who took his ticket.

"Yes, young lad?"

"I'm trying to get to California. The man over the speaker said this the end of the line." He appeared to be a scared teenager, riding the train for the first time.

"Oh, I got ya. See, you'll have to board another train California bound. It should be on your ticket stub."

After carefully scanning, he located the train number he should be looking to board.

"Thank you. I appreciate you." Throwing his Timberland book bag over his shoulder, he continued walking to the data center, where he could check what time his train was set to depart.

"Damn." With only ten minutes to board, he was hungry and had to use the restroom. Thinking faster than his legs can move, he chose the hot dog stand and to use the toilet once aboard. There was no way he was missing this train. Lucky for him, as he turned away, drug task force with dogs searched the bathroom. On one hand, he felt nervous, but that quickly led to adrenaline and excitement. Once he boarded the express train from Chicago to Richmond, he was good. Just sixteen more hours and it was home, sweet home.

Christi stayed up with Lala for most of the night. He had a hard time understanding why people had to die. It'd been one hardship after the next since her properties were foreclosed and family separated. Now confined to live in the Silver Street Projects, which to some was the gates of hell. Dirty needles, broken bottles, and shell casings are scattered all over the playground. By no means was this a safe environment to raise kids in. Still, she endured with faith in The Most High, that after her difficulties would come ease.

As her youngest son lay in her lap, she made dua'. "I seek protection for you in the Perfect Words of Allah from every devil and every beast and from every envious blame-worthy eye. Amen."

(Phone Rings) "Hello?" Christi answered.

"Aunty, I heard somebody was killed in front of your place. Are you and my little cousin okay?" Romelo Jr. asked.

"Yeah. He didn't get hit, but he's taking it hard. You know that boy's dad. They call him Remo."

"What? That was Little Tim?" he asked, hoping it wasn't.

"Yeah. He and Lala were God brothers, It's so sad. I just hope D'Juan gets here safe now. They been shooting all night," she explained.

"Aunty, it's gonna be some problems behind that for sure. When is Juan supposed to be here?"

After looking over at the clock, she gave her best estimation. "Should be at the train station around eight this morning."

"Thank you Aunty. Love you. If he calls you, tell him I'll pick him up."

"Okay, y'all be safe. Love you too."

At the end of a cross-country train ride, D'Juan was finally back in Rich City. He disembarked and walked through the station like a preteen returning home. His cousin Romelo Jr. a.k.a Rome was waiting out front in his candy-apple-red Malibu with caramel racing stripes. At first sight, D'Juan had to take a double look as he stepped out of the car.

"Yo, what's the drill, babii?" he expressed how happy he was to see him, for they hadn't seen each other in a few years. "Come on, fam. Let's get away from here."

"No doubt yo."

D'Juan gritted his teeth and kept both eyes in his side-view mirror. On the drive to the projects, Rome mentioned the latest casualty with grief. D'Juan was instantly saddened, "Nah, not my little dude. That's like little bro." he proclaim with watery eyes.

"I know, kid, and it's not the end." Rome assures.

D'Juan could only imagine what his little brother was going through. Ever since Remo went to jail, Little Tim was practically living with Christi. He was so distraught, he nearly forgot about the silver package in his book bag. It was good he decided to mention it before they got to the projects.

"What? Nah, we gon' have to put that up first, It's rollaz all around the PJ's." Rome immediately turned right down Market St., headed in the opposite direction of North Richmond.

"You know Ace live in Tara Hills. We can stash it up there, then go see Aunty."

D'Juan nodded his head in agreement.

"I'm gon' tell you too, kid, she stressed out the game right now."

Although it wasn't easy hearing the tale of his suffering mother, D'Juan had braced himself before leaving Harlem. Whatever condition she was in mentally, physically, or spiritually, he was now there for her.

As they wait outside Ace Boogie's crib he flew by them in his Black National doing 50 miles per hour. "That's famo?" D'Juan asked, barely recognizing his face. The last he remembered, Ace was as barefaced as he was.

"Hell yeah." Rome shook his head with the aftermath of death in mind. One thing for sure, two for certain; when Ace said it's time to ride, every soldier, and gangster affiliated with the familia would either be riding or dying that day. Rome was pretty sure he recognized his whip, and was just circling the block. Can't be too careful in the time of war.

"What's the drill, yo?" D'Juan ask as Rome shakes his head.

"You got your finger on a hair point trigger kid. Be careful cause It will go off."

"Oh, my bad. I'm just bugging out fa'real. When is this shit gone end?" he asks with frustration written on his face.

His pain could definitely be felt, so Rome got him to focus on what could be done. Santana and Romelo Sr. just blew trial, leaving nothing behind but a legacy. He uses the circumstances surrounding his Pa' getting life as motivation to succeed. The minute he stopped chasing his dreams would be the day he's dead. "Everybody has to have a dream kid. What's yours?"

"I just want my ma and baby bro out the PJ's. My family together again. I would do anything to see that happen. **ANYTHING**."

"I feel you.. You know every time I go down there, I think of how my Pa' got wrapped up. They had surveillance footage, conversations, all the shit fam. When I see my Aunty, I know she hurt. Squally in Vegas now. Who he got?"

In seeing the reality of the situation, Rome was right. The familia of kings were scattered throughout the country, and the devil was playing tricks on the minds of those living in poverty.

D'Juan listened while his mind wandered. Ace pulled up behind them and bounced out with a tight face. His jaws were locked, and demeanor was stern. He nodded his head as a signal to follow him into the house. Once inside, they embrace with familia love. Under normal circumstances, this reunion would be cause for a celebration. But, by no means were these times of normalcy. It was about money, murder, and street politics in Rich City.

"Kid, show Ace what you got," Rome suggest.

"No doubt." He pulls the silver package out his book bag and dropped it on the table. "This is the best heroin money can buy." After careful examination, they conclude it's China White.

"You know none of this been around for years." The thought instantly crossed Ace's mind—the Rodeo projects would be the perfect for business.

"What's this? A pound?"

"Nah, It's an half a kee. My mans back east got it by the tubs." He further elaborates on En-Rica's need for hustlers like him and a Cali connect. Ace and Rome looked at each other and shared thoughts.

"This will make us rich. We already movin' grams of Hop, but when this hit the market, fiends from everywhere gon' know about it."

"We gon' be famous, kid." Their vision couldn't be more clearer for D'Juan to see. His mission was to only stack fifty or sixty grand, which was nothing to them. Ace unstrapped his vest and picked up his business hat. He made a few calls to propagate this product as if it was already on the streets. His marketing strategy was simply to get people talking.

D'Juan was adamant about his east coast connect being their mill ticket, but he would need Ace and Rome's assistance. He trusted them to do what they did best and together they could move mountains. "All we need to do, is to flip this to three pounds of coke," he explains the agreement between he and En-Rica. After Ace considered the risk vs. reward for backpacking a kilo and a half back to New York, he had a more feasible idea.

"Peep, kid, I just got off the line with Joey and Jaquiz from the PJ's. They guarantee we can get twenty-five hundred per ounce. Shit, you don't need to worry about a street corner in Harlem. You and ya boy could make more loot letting us cop five or six Ps."

"A'ight. I'm gon' see what's up. I just gotta check on my ma." He then looked to Rome.

"Yeah, bro. We gotta ride. Hold on to that and see what you can do. We'll holla tonight or som'thin'," Rome said, preparing to leave.

"It's good, and trust we gon' help Aunty get out them 'jects" Ace assured. They embrace, and Rome set his destination to the Silver Street Projects.

On the highway, D'Juan got the 411 on what the rest of his familia was doing. Kaboobi's oldest sons, Hakeem and Rashaad, were hustling cocaine on 34th and Cutting. A particular hot zone where high-school dropouts did more odd jobs than the garbage man. Prince Ameere, Kaboobi's youngest, was laying low in Santa Rosa while being investigated for attempted murder and robbery. D'Juan could remember when Ameere sold two-dollar joints of Columbian Gold until he made his first thousand dollars. With his next five hundred, he copped a Diamondback GT just so he could ride him to school on the handlebars. So it was no real surprise he was now the man, flooding Rich City with Super Silver Haze and Purple Cush coming from far as Canada.

Rome parked on Third Street, and together they walked down Silver Street into the projects. The yellow tape was still stretched across the street, white chalk outlining the young boy's body, with his blood staining the

CAPO

concrete. "Damn," D'Juan thought out loud. Rome put his hand on his shoulder and assured him it was gonna be okay. Christi opened the door with stress-ridden eyes. Upon seeing his face, she extended her arms with a big smile.

"All praise to Allah. Come here, mi hijo." She squeezed his neck tightly and felt the weight of the world leave her shoulders.

"Ma-ma, I love you." Tears poured from his eyes as he became overwhelmed with his mother's love. Lala walked from the bedroom, rubbing his eyes like he had just woken up. "Hermano." He ran to hug his brother.

"Hermano, a black car killed Timmy." D'Juan and Rome looked at Lala simultaneously.

"Little brother, you seen who did this?" D'Juan asked while holding Lala by the shoulders.

"Si," he said, nodding his head. "It was his friend." D'Juan looked over to Rome, whose mind began to process.

"One of my friends?" he asked with a demand to know who. Lala didn't want his mother to hear, so he whispered in Rome's ear. "You sure?" he asks. And again, Lala nodded his head. D'Juan saw the confusion on Rome's face, but he denied talking about it. Christi didn't want to know who pulled the trigger but more so, what they were planning to do.

"Romie, I don't want you getting into trouble. I got enough on my heart losing your father to the prison system."

"Tia, I promised mi poppa I wouldn't follow his footsteps, but I also promised I would keep us safe," Rome stressed by any means necessary. Upon hearing him speak, Christi felt a sharp pain her chest. "oh Allah" she cries out, hurrying to her room.

"Ma-ma," D'Juan said, walking behind her. "Ma, you okay?"

51

"Shut the door, mijo."

He did so, then sat at the foot of her bed. She asked him to take heed to the lessons she was about to share. Only after promising he would, she explained the concept of religion. "Mijo, have you ever asked yourself what's your purpose in life?" He thought for a few seconds and shook his head, for he never thought about anything to live for outside of familia. "You need to figure that out before you make decisions that can cost another man his life. Or even your own. It'll be a day when we have to return to face Allah, and everything we've done is going to be reviewed," she further explained. "There will be some that want to return to earth for a second time. Allah doesn't grant this second time mijo. So you must make the best of your first and only time."

He nodded his head, indicating he understood. "Ma, I promise one day you gon' be proud of me. Maybe we can be a familia again." Christi smiled and put her hand on the back of his neck. She then reminded him they were a family just separated for the moment. They spent the next hour reading verses from the Holy Qur'an and making supplications that The Most High granted them patience and unity amongst other believers with true faith, striving with perseverance, and consistency in prayer.

It was just minutes after eight o'clock. Lala playing *Bill Walsh Football* on Super Nintendo. "Hermano, you not gonna leave me again, are you?" he asked as D'Juan and Rome was about to step out the front door.

"No, I'm not going to leave you, little man. I have to protect you and Ma."

"Okay." Lala continued playing his video game with the assurance his big brother would help move them out the PJ's. And as much as D'Juan loved touching and kissing on Tonya's body, home was where his heart was.

Rich City street lights made the hustlers, pimps, and macks shine like kings. With gold in their mouths or draped around their necks, it was noticeably a different era. Rome rolled through Sugar Hill, 34th and Cutting, and finally The Globe Town Projects. The kid received mad love, especially from the remaining members of the F.K org. They were now O.G's and considered by most to be Richmond's finest mobsters. Pulling into the back parking lot, D'Juan approach a trusted bodyguard in the familia. "What's really good with the V-Dopa?" he asked from the passenger's seat. Big Vain stepped off the curb with his hands in his pocket, looking at Rome first, then to him.

"D'Juan? Come here, my dude." D'Juan stepped out the vehicle and was embraced by Vain followed by other project kids. "Damn, boy, you all grown up now." Vain smiles as he is impressed by the kid's mannerism.

"No doubt. I was raised by the best." He spoke proudly

"Oh, you know I know what's up. F.K all day babii"

"Fa-real." They share a few laughs. "Aye yo, you seen my brethren?"

"They in the back at St. Nick's joint. Young Magic, Laz and Razor all of 'em" he points toward unit 3201, apartment 7 two doors down from what used to be F.K's headquarters.

"A'ight. I need to holla at you too though."

"Oh, that's for sure. I'm still in the same joint. It's all good."

"Bet."

Soon as D'Juan stepped in St. Nicks joint, all eyes were on him. He'd left as just another bad kid from the projects to return as a flamboyant hustler with money bulging in his pockets. Santonio and Young Magic were in the middle of discussing some other business with one of Arthur Moe's boys from Fifth and Barrett. D'Juan was briefly introduced to the young king who'd been running things since King Arthur went to the feds.

"Peace, king," D'Juan greeted.

"Peace" He acknowledged and appreciated the kid's blessings.

Silas and St. Nick embraced him with a shake and a hug, before returning to the business at hand. "We gon' holla, kid. Let us handle this."

With no need to say more, he stepped out the kitchen and joined Rome sitting on the couch. If he'd heard correctly, they were selling and buying three pounds of Purple Cush a month. Good indeed but the price was nearly double of that which Rome was getting it for. After Zeek left, D'Juan insisted they hear him out on some serious business.

"Aye, I overheard the conversation about how far this dro is coming from, and that's bullshit." With their undivided attention he continues; "Yeah. It's coming from Canada, but he not the one going to get it."

"We got the same strand at four g's a p." Rome adds.

Santonio looked at Young Magic and St.Nick, calculating it would be three grand less they would have to pay a month.

Rome tossed a few grams on the table "roll up"

St. Nick gutted a chocolate Phillies Blunt and stuffed it with purple cush and put fire to it. Upon inhaling and nearly coughing their dinner up, one by one, they agree to cop from Rome from that point on.

"It's gonna be good, bro. I'm back now. Tell Izzy I need to holla at him ASAP. And let Keem, Shotti Bo, and Razor know the drill." He directs at Santonio.

"They around. Probably on the One Way at the apartments.

"It's good. Just everybody be here tomorrow night if that's cool with you, Saint," D'Juan turned and asked.

"It's all good, chief. As long as I'm in." St. Nick replies while exhaling smoke.

"It's all good, little bro. Love you, boy," Silas said, followed with a brotherly hug.

The love was felt, and as he stepped out the door, he could smell money in the air. He had the connections to put The Globe back in the game, but it'd take a little more weight to be on top where they used to be...

Chapter 5

(Phone Ringing) It was three a.m. in New York. "Hola?" Tonya answered.

"What's the drill, momie? How are you?" he asked, putting a smile on her face.

"Oh my God! I was so worried about you. Everything's okay?"

"Yeah. It's good. You know, just doing what has to be done."

"Yeah, so how's momma Christi?"

"Ahh, that's a whole other story. Just holla at the delivery boy from the bodega and give him this order." When she found an ink pen, he emphasized the importance of writing every word as he said it.

"I'm starting a bakery business from my kitchen and need five pounds of sugar."

"Got it.. That's it?"

"That's it, ma-ma. And I'll see you soon." He again put a smile on her face.

"I can't wait, pappi, your dinner and dessert will be hot and ready." She enticed with seduction. They shared flirtatious humor and hopes to meet by the waterfall in one of their dreams.

Rome dropped D'Juan off at his ma's joint and met up with Ace. They had a fat cat to bag, and operation take-over was in progress. They called for a meeting at the Cotton Candy Club—a pink trailer sitting out front of one of Remo's old trap houses. Lil' Leel and Phats were amongst the few. Objective: The Rodeo Projects, which was wide open for the taken. At one point, Remo made over a half a million dollars a month in crack cocaine sales alone. All they had to do was take out the trash. Whoever wasn't working for Remo would be forced to do business elsewhere. It was the dawn of a new era, and when Remo did finally come home, he was going to be under constant surveillance. They figured he would forget about any plans to rebuild his empire if he valued freedom. Then again, mobsters like him were career criminals. By age fifty, they would either be dead or a success, but there were no retirement plans.

D'Juan was sitting in the living room, playing video games with Lala when En-Rica called back. "Yo, what's the drill?" he answered.

"Aye, my mans. I got your message, and everything is A-Okay. Make sure you come correct kid. These guys are serious," he said as a reminder.

"No doubt. It's all good."

"See you soon."

"A'ight, peace." They hung up with two different thoughts going on. D'Juan took the good news in stride, immediately paging Rome. On the other end, En-Rica wondered where he'd gotten so much cash and what he was planning to do. From the sounds of it, D'Juan wasn't thinking about returning to Harlem for long. He sat in his chair, clicking his pen, contemplating the possibilities.

Meanwhile, D'Juan was observing his little brother play video games like it was his best friend. How could he tell him, he was going back to New

York after he promised he was staying for good. And as if Lala could read his mind, he turns around bearing a face of disappointment.

"Hermano, you gonna leave us again huh?"

D'Juan sat down on the floor by his side and told him a story about the boy that ran away so he could find help.

"Sometimes, little brother, we must leave our home to come back stronger." Lala dropped his controller and ran to his room. D'Juan understand how much his brother needed him, but Lala didn't understand the threat they faced day to day by living in a danger zone. "Ah," he expressed frustration while shaking his head. Not long after, he heard the dual exhaust pipes from Rome's Malibu.

"A'ight, Ma, I'll be back!" he yelled to the back room and was gone before she could respond.

Clouds blocked the morning sunrays giving the appearance it might rain. For the kid, it was the best weather to hustle in. Feeling the raindrop hit his face made him feel alive. So yeah, some days, he prayed for rain.

"What's up, kid?" Rome asked as he adjusted the passenger's seat.

"It's good. I mean, really good. We need to get at Ace ASAP," he said with enthusiasm.

"Oh yeah. You holler at ole boy?" D'Juan nodded his head with a smile. "Well, that's what it is then."

Rome peeled rubber up the block, then passed a blunt of Purple Cush "huh, fire that up." D'Juan inhales and coughs until his eyes water and chest hurt. He looked at the blunt as if he was scared to hit it again. "That's power kid. Ain't nothing like this Back East huh?" Rome laughs while reiterating it's nothing like home.

Ace was at an apartment in the Rodeo Projects when they finally caught up with him. He was accompanied by two females, Asia and her younger cousin Passion. She instantly had a thing for Rome. Natural oil radiating from his dark skin illuminated his aura, and the open faced gold teeth complimented his swagger. Before they mentioned anything about business the ladies were excused.

Ace looked at Rome "We can fuck both of them bra. I ain't gon' front they wit it too." Rome smiled before responding "You know me nicca". They share laughs.

"Yo, I hollered at ole boy. He said it's good. We just need to come with all the cake." D'Juan put emphasis on **ALL**.

"That's nothing. We'll have that by tonight. The question is: are you ready for that trip?" Ace asked. D'Juan thought about his past experience and how nervous he was in the beginning. Now it's much more at stake and a lot more to lose. Still the reward greatly outweigh the risk. He looked confident when he told them both he was on a mission, and he should not fail even in the face of death. And that's just what they wanted to hear.

"A'ight Rome, when Joey is supposed to pick this up?" Ace asks.

"Shit. he can come get it right now" Rome assured after looking at his watch. "Do that. I'm gon' holler at fam in the meantime." Ace leans in close and told D'Juan that they're counting on him to make this happen. In the process of enforcing their will on the project residence, a few people were badly hurt, and one later died. "We'll need two more weeks to have this whole building." Ace then lays out his blueprint, with fire in his eyes. As D'Juan listened, he doesn't know how to say he wasn't in this for the long haul. He just needed fifty or sixty more grand and his mission was complete. His cousins on the other hand had already chosen their career path, and from the sounds of it there was no end. A repetitive cycle that has already separated his familia.

Rome walked back in the room confirming Joey would be to pick up the whole package for thirty-two grand. D'Juan smiled, and just that quick he regains trust in his family to aide his cause. "Lil brodi. It's gonna be okay. I told you we got you" Rome said while putting his hand on D'Juan's shoulder.

"I know brodi. That's why I'm here with y'all." They all nod their heads in agreement that ninety thousand dollars can be put towards a lot of small business ideas. Furthermore, any and all future decisions would be done together as familia.

With the more important business in the bag sitting at the foot of his bed. D'Juan chose to forego the meeting with the F.K boys. He'll catch up with them at another time if destiny permits.

(Phone Rings) "Yeah" Silas answers, waking from a marijuana induced coma.

"Yo brodi, I need you to tell Rock and Doe I'm good. I have a few more moves to make, then most likely heading back East."

"A'ight brodi, see you in a few weeks?"

"At the least. It's fam out there too nah'mean. Never know."

"I got you bro. Be cool kid, One"...

"One hunnid."

Laying in bed that night he thought about all the weight his mother had to carry in her lifetime. The guilt of her brother was so heavy to the point, her shoulders slouched. Even more motivation on why he had to do this. "If she carries the world on her shoulders, who am I not to carry five pounds." he questions himself. Then he realizes how feelings can be deceptive. First, he missed home so much, now he misses Harlem the same. "This shit's crazy" he thought out loud.

Mentally preparing for his flight in the morning he listened to "Me and against the world" and "Only Lord knows" by his distant relative Tupac Shakur. No two songs could have resonated more during those times. He opened his eyes at 5:43 a.m. after hearing his mother called the Adhan. "Allahu Akbar, la ilaha illa Allah" she translated to mean GOD is greatest and there is no deity except Allah. He and Lala waits until she's finished before they make prayer. Once completing the two prostrations for dawn prayer, they sit at the breakfast table. "I'm moving back here with you and Lala." She was comforted by his concerns, but question's if it's best for him. She'd been hearing about the recent violence associated with Lyfe's crew and the Rodeo Projects.

"Have you spoken to your Poppa about this?"

"No not yet. I mean he mentioned it but he didn't say for how long I could stay." he explained. "Yay, brother now you can take me to football practice and play catch with me." Lala blurts out in excitement.

"That's right yo."

Christi smiled seeing her sons interact for the first time in years. "Okay, you talk to him first. I'll call your grandmother after your flight leaves. What time are you leaving?"

"Rome should be here by 7:30."

"Okay mi hijo, you be safe. Remember I love you and always loved you. Tell Juelz I miss him dearly and hope to see him soon." "Yes ma-ma." He finishes his breakfast of rice cereal, scrambled eggs and biscuits, then waits for Rome to hit the horn.

By 8 o'clock D'Juan was boarding a flight to John F. Kennedy International Airport. This was his first time ever flying so he made dua (supplication) that the Most High keeps him safe. He then retrieved his trusty pencil and sketching pad from his book bag and looked out the window. Pulling thoughts from the sky, he sketch the outline of a triple deck mansion. Located in the Berkeley hills hidden by plenty of trees on a 5500 sq. Ft plot. 8 bedrooms, 2 family rooms, 6 ½ bathrooms, commercial kitchen and dining replica of a five-star restaurant. The whole basement would consist of a lounge with pool tables, a hot tub, movie theater and gym for exercising. Then a separate garage house with four car stations and a basketball court. This was a project kids dream. And seeing it on paper made him feel that much closer to it. However, before his sketch was complete, the stewardess announcement came over the p.a. System "fasten your seatbelts ladies and gentlemen. Prepare for landing. Thank you for flying Pan Am Airlines." Maybe another time; he thought to himself.

Mrs. Perez-Shakur was waiting with open arms once he cleared gate 24. "Come here Juanie" she smiled, squeezing tightly around his back. "I miss you Nana, where's mi Poppa?" He asked, looking around. "He's at work but he'll be sure to see you tonight. Your brother is here." She then pointed towards a hot dog stand. "Shhh." he said putting his finger over his lips. He then sneaks up behind Juelz as he's sinking his teeth into a turkey link with extra relish and mustard. "You don't want that" he said, slapping it out of his hands.

Juelz was shocked as he was hungry, "Come here you little." He chased D'Juan and wrestled him to the ground until Nina came to his aide. Once back on their feet they embraced with brotherly hugs. The risk and sacrifice the two were making came at a cost and neither knew when the grim reaper would cash in.

On the walk to the car D'Juan explained how their mother was doing and his plan to get her out of the projects.

Tito was waiting at the home with their Aunt Diana when they arrived. "Aww look at mi sobrino. So handsome" she says, embracing him with a hug.

"What's up Tia. You've been helping mi Poppa?"

"Yeah, you remember I used to help at the candlelight Diner? I'm so proud of mi hermano" she mentions his devotion to Little Havana's and the family business.

Tito inquires about Christi's well-being and promises to relocate the restaurant to Jack London square, Oakland CA. D'Juan's dreams were starting to become a reality. With so many reasons to celebrate, he didn't spoil the moment by announcing his scheduled flight in the next two weeks. After all his Pa' sacrificed he wanted to show his appreciation. With a bag full of hundred dollar bills, it's surely something he could slip in his pocket.

After a feast and karaoke, the boys left the grown-ups dancing the night away. Meanwhile, they counted nearly a hundred thousand dollars over and over until they got tired.

"Come on boys come get your breakfast." Nana Nina yells from the kitchen.

It was 6 a.m. rise and shine and It seemed like they just closed their eyes. "What a night" D'Juan thinks to himself, as he stumble to the kitchen table.

"Good morning Poppi" a familiar voice says with her back turned . D'Juan couldn't believe his eyes when the young Latina turned with two plates in hand "Tonya? wow. You're so beautiful ma-ma" they hugged and shared a brief kiss. "Gracias poppi. But you act like it's been years."

"Ma-ma, if you only knew. But how you been?"

"You know, just helping Nana with any odd jobs. Holding it down."

"Yes indeed, wow.. I feel like I'm dreaming right now" he steps back, glancing from her pressed hair to pedicured toes.

"No crazy. It's me." she laughs.

Without question she embraced her class and sexiness. After eating his favorite breakfast: Belgium waffles, smothered potatoes, and country fried steak, she arranged a meeting with En-Rica at the Harlem Lounge on Frederick Douglas Blvd.

Stepping in the door with pink pumps, white capri pants, with matching coat and powder pink lip gloss, D'Juan and Juelz caught En-Rica's eyes move up and down her petite frame. "Nice huh?" D'Juan commented with a mischievous grin. The two shook hands before En-Rica could respond. "This my brother Juelz he's a ball player at East Harlem High. He's going to go pro one day, watch", he expresses with confidence.

"What's up Juelz. I think I saw you around with your cousin Carlosi?"

"Yeah, no doubt. He came out here just last month.", after they shook hands, it seemed like the tension left the room.

"Is there anywhere we can count this?" D'Juan asked.

Then Tonya interjects "Poppi wait. Rica, you peeps but this a lot more than before. You got the stuff right now?"

En-Rica, laughs as if she was joking. "Yeah Tee. You know how I do business, always straight across." At the snap of his fingers Raphael dropped a duffle bag at his feet containing presumably 5 pounds. After testing the product with a Marquis reagent kit, D'Juan and En-Rica counted the money. Tonya kept her eyes peeled while Juelz stood with his hand in his pocket.

"You should know, I saw your cousin and he has a nice thing going on down in Chicago. We arranged to see each other monthly. If you can come through, it's the same deal."

"That sounds really good." D'Juan acknowledged the business proposition and continued counting. Once he reached ninety-two grand En-Rica' grabbed his wrist, "Stop there Poppa, keep the rest. It's my gift to you just came back next month." D'Juan agreed with a firm handshake.

When they returned to Mrs. Shakur's house, Juelz was asked to hold the bag. "Lil Bro, don't sweat. I'm guarding this with my life kid."

"That's right. Say, uh me and shorty about to hit mid-town."

"You need the piece?" Juelz asked pulling the 44. From his pocket.

"Never could be too safe right." D'Juan put the revolver in his coat pocket and hit the door.

The two love birds visited the Apollo for a Broadway show, shopped for ice cream, then talked in Central Park until nightfall. She knew better than to be there, that late in the evening but it wasn't by mistake.

"Ma-ma it's about that time huh?" D'Juan stood up zipping his leather jacket, "yeah you must have read my mind!" She smiles seductively. Then stands up and pushes him back down on the bench.

"What's on your mind ma?"

Easing onto his lap she whispers "you being inside of me is all I could think about." She then reaches to unbuckle his Karl Kani jeans.

"Word? Right now, right now?"

"Si, right now Poppi."

They kiss passionately for a few minutes before he picks her up and dropped her back on the grass. "Here lay on this," After handing her his jacket, he relished the moment. In fulfilling her fantasy he would share the wild and dangerous experience. "What the hell" he thought. She peels from her pants and immediately reaches for his manhood. "Shh I got you." He ensures putting two fingers over her lips. "Uh" she moans as he enters slowly. One motion of the hips caused her to moan louder. Biting on his ear and gripping his back to embrace the pleasure. He told her how it feels, fueling her fire inside. She was like a greedy nympho begging for more than she could handle. The cold air drifting between their bodies made the warmth of love more sensational. After 30 minutes of brave and careless passion, they climaxed. However, there was no water or a towel to clean themselves. So soon as their bodies separated, cum poured out of her onto his jacket. "Aww, what the fuck ma." They hurry fixing their clothes, and share laughter while reliving the experience.

With his initial plan being to catch the Greyhound back. Tonya had a better idea, to drive back to California with him. For one, she could meet his mother who she had so much love and respect for and two, she wasn't ready to let him out of her sight. After he shared his experience and hardships his mother faces with raising his little brother alone it was a great possibility he wouldn't be back for some time. They spent the next weeks with each other from sundown to sun up. Either at The Apollo, or St. Nick park, cuddled up while Juelz did his thing on the blacktop. Mr. Mitchell routine was running and then more running. His logic was, anyone can shoot or slam dunk a basketball. The one with the most endurance will be victorious...

On the day they planned to travel across the country, Tonya prepared breakfast for the house. It would be their last meal with Nana Nina for some time and she wanted it to be memorable. They shared jokes at the table and took turns feeding each other slices of an Orange. "Y'all remind me of me and your grand Papa" she describes their first few romantic dates as being simple but sweet, "Nana, you know I'm going to be back soon right", D'Juan speaks with hope.

"Um huh, I know you won't be able to stay with mi neita long." She said with a smile. D'Juan and Tonya lock eyes with no doubts about their love. After finishing their meal, they embraced her with hugs and kisses. "Aye, stop it al-ready. You're going to make me miss you before you leave, just go. And be sure to stop by your Poppa's restaurant." she said as they gather his bags. "Yes Nana."

They stopped by Little Havana's and embraced Tito before hitting the road. He was very busy that morning, but he still took time to ensure they would travel safely. He gave them specific directions to highways, and hotels, along with instructions when to fill the tank. He warned it was a dangerous road and they shouldn't stop on any dark roads or pull over for anyone that wasn't in an identified patrol car. After receiving sound advice, they embraced with kisses and hugs. Tito sent them off with a bag of shrimp tacos, chicken fajitas and tortilla chips.

Making their last stop at St. Nicks park, D'Juan approach the gated entrance admiring his brother work ethic. "Yo brodi, put that basketball down and give me a hug. We about to dip." He yells.

"Yo kid, this fo you" with perfect form , Juelz shoots hitting nothing but net. He then motions to Mr. Mitchell that he's taking a few minutes break.

The two meet at the bleachers with Tonya walking slowly behind. "It's on you kid, keep your head up, and I'm gon miss you yo" D'Juan squeezes Juelz with a brotherly hug.

"I love you brodi."

"You already know kid."

"From sun till dark it's familia till we depart." Juelz said pointing in D'Juan 's chest.

"We all we got, remember that?"

"Oh, you know I remember, You just don't forget it." They give each other dap and part ways.

"The last shot's on you kid." D'Juan mentions before stepping in the car...

Chapter 6

Finally on the road, Tonya follows Tito's instructions to the letter. She pulled into a hotel parking lot to rest, every six hours. They didn't make it to California until 8 a.m. the next morning. "Poppi we in Cali." She mentions as D'Juan opens his eyes. He stretches his arms and looked at her pretty face with admiration, "what?" She asked with an innocent smile "You are so beautiful. What I would do to spend a lifetime with you."

"That's all, just one lifetime?"

He nods his head in a jokingly manner but Tonya didn't take it kindly.

"Ah, what you hit me for?" He asked, while feeling his face for any swelling.

"Because I get tired of your smart ass. Somethings isn't funny D'Juan."

"Okay ma-ma, I'm sorry. Come here let me kiss you." He grabs for her hand

"Oh, I got something for you to kiss." She proposes with a smile.

They pulled up on the City of Vallejo at 2 p.m. He directed her to take the Tennessee off ramp and pull into a Burger King parking lot. "C'mon Ma-Ma. Get us something to eat. I have to make a call." She exits the Acura and stretches her legs.

"What do you want ?" She asked as he walks toward a payphone.

"Chicken sandwich and fries."

She looks around at all the trees and immediately feels the change of environment. Cars moving at fifty miles per hour down Tennessee as if it was a four lane highway. There were trees everywhere, the air was fresh, and It was space to breathe.

She orders their food and returned to the car where D'Juan was waiting. "Ma-ma I would be happy to just live this life with you. Was that too much?"

"Oooo, you are good. I swear D'Juan Placencia, you make my skin crawl some times. And no, that's not too much. It's not enough."

He reaches over and grabs her face. "Come here, you not tough." As she was going to complain about nothing, he put his tongue down her throat.

"That's still not enough" she seduces, reaching for his belt buckle. Within minutes, Passion pulled up next to them. "Who is that?" Tonya asked snapping her neck to where his attention goes. "That's our drop off. Hold up." He exits with his Timberland book bag draped over his shoulder.

"What's the drill Ma? They give you any instructions?"

"No. I don't know much other than I was supposed to pick up."

"A'ight, hold up" he writes down his mother's address and hands it to Tonya. "I have to deliver this personally ma. I'll be there in an hour. Love you." She looked at the address with no clue how to get there, "hello, and what's this?"

"Right... I don't know what I was thinking." He signaled to Passion he'll be behind her.

Passion led the way into the city of Rodeo. She pulled out front of a townhome near the projects and hands him a key.

"That's your key. Nobody else has one except Rome and Ace." She explained the significance in case he didn't know. Once the product was stashed in what he felt was the safest spot in the house, he locked the deadbolt and screen gate. Before rejoining Tonya in the Acura, he gives Passion a note addressed to Rome.

"Ahh sheesh"; he exhales, finally being able to lean back. They pull into Rich City and suddenly she felt the similarities to Harlem. The Silver Street projects, where legacies were made in the pursuit of blood money, but not many are left to tell the story.

Christi's face lit up when she saw Tonya. "So, you're the one."

"I guess I am momma Christi. How are you?"

"All praise to Allah. I'm good now honey, come sit with me. I heard so much about you."

"D'Juan first paged Rome then checked on Lala.

For most of the day they sat in the living room looking at baby pictures. Tonya of course found them to be cute, but D'Juan didn't care as much for his past. He's looking ahead to his future. With fresh product ready to hit the streets and a mother that's dying in front of his eyes from stress related illness, he pages Rome and Ace twice in five minutes.

Apparently, while he was on the road they were still putting pieces to their jigsaw puzzle together. They secured two Townhomes. One for the safe and guns, and the other for the stash of drugs. Their location were a secret, outside of them four individuals. When they finally made it to the stash house they unpackaged and weighed the product. Passion reminded Rome of the note D'Juan left for him was outside in the Malibu. It read "the extras are for us, with the promise we will return."

They were more than satisfied with that arrangement. Especially after selling their first ounce in grams. When word hit the Bay Area that China White was back, they'll become overnight celebrities.

"Ma. Ma-ma" D'Juan whispers. Pulling on Tonya's leg as she sleeps in his mother's bed. She kicks him away and grunts. Nonetheless he's persistent and keeps pulling and wrestling with her feet until the point it become hilarious. "What do you want? " she says loud enough to wake up the house.

"Shh" he puts one finger over his lips hoping she didn't wake his mother. Then he signals with his hands he wanted her to follow him. She fussed getting out of bed, but the nymphomaniac in her took control. Undressing from the bathroom door until being totally naked in the shower. She begged for him to squeeze her breast harder, while guiding his other hand in between her legs. The shape and firmness of her figure was amazing. "Sheesh!" he thought out loud.

She grabbed his erect penis and kissed it before licking the shaft. Then slowly, she eased it into her puss. She bit on his chest to keep herself from moaning. As he lifts, pinning her back to the wall, she wrapped her legs around his waist. "Fuck me poppi" she invites all of him inside her tight womb. In the mist of passionate strokes, cold shower water hits his back. Feeling nothing but the warmth in front, he excelled into ecstasy. "Wow" he blurts out.

It was fun while it lasted but now, they had to sneak out of the shower and back into bed. He giggled as he thought something was funny, but it was no small matter to her. To get caught while having sex in his mother's house would be the ultimate embarrassment...

Over the next few days, they went to Berkeley University, San Francisco's Pier. Pacifica's ocean side view, and Oakland Coliseum for a Thursday night Oakland Raiders game. By Sunday she admitted he was right, she didn't want to go back. "Oh my god, why do our lives have to be so difficult. You know?" He nods his head in agreement as they walk and talk through Martin Luther King Park.

"It's gone be good, I'm telling you. After Ma' get out the jects, I'm coming back. Before this shit is all over its gon be me and you. A'ight momie."

"Yeah, you promise?"

"That's my word Ma'"

He wipes a tear from her cheek as he shed one himself. Tonya was his first true love and leaving her was gut wrenching. However, sacrifice has to be made to reach their goal. And no matter how much he loved her company, he couldn't focus on his hustle until she left. Where one chapter ends a new one begins...

Chapter 7

TONYA FLEW BACK TO New York leaving him the Acura and holding on to his promise. She was his friend when he had none, introduced him to money when he needed it most, and showed him how to survive in the streets of Harlem. Turning back to the Silver Street Projects wasn't an option. He drove his maroon Acura Legend through the South Side looking for any F.K boys. He pulls up on 4th and Maine, parking outside of Silk's joint.

"Yo, Rocky" He yells across the street.

"Who dat?" Rocky edges closer with his hand behind his back.

"This Juan yo. Kaboobi nephew."

"Oh what's haddenin young money? I ain't seen you.. in a minute boi."

"Yeah I know. My Pa had to dip when all them indictments came down on my familia."

Rocky pauses while reflecting on a hectic past. "Yeah, I remember young King.." He walks around to passenger side window, "You know what's going on right now, don't you?"

D'Juan shook his head as he had not a clue. "Lyfe trying to beat that indictment so cat's dropping like flies around here. They say some body talking and it can be anyone. Lyfe is familia, so you have to be careful riding around the city right now. You feel me?"

"No doubt"

"A'ight be safe young King. Pull up to the apartments later." He then disappear as more cars began to stop on the narrow street.

D'Juan knew what he needed to now. His destination from there was an easy one to make. He pulls in the Globe and visits St.Nick. Apparently, Santonio and Silas just left and was expected to return soon. "We've been waiting to hear from you. Your cousin been keeping us lit wit this Purp."

He mention while passing a blunt. "That's what's up. But I'm telling you Saint, it's about to be mega. Fa-real. Like, this China White is a monster in the field." D'Juan explains.

"Yeah? I don't know nothing about that my G. If it's about getting more paper though, count me in."

"I already know."

Looking down at his watch, D'Juan determined it would be better to hit the streets on foot if he wanted to catch up with his crew. "I'll holla later Saint"

"Anytime Kid, you know it's good."

D'Juan walked around the corner to the apartments on the One Way. "I bet they in here." He thought out loud. (Door bell) "Who the hell at my doe" he yells from the kitchen.

"Tio, it's me D'Juan."

Upon opening the screen gate his face lit up, "Ah say it ain't so, the son of the ghost." Big Hoodie looked at his jean and leather outfit and smiled. "No Tio, I'm Tito's son" he tries to explain to the half blind old man.

"It don't matter, one brother's son or another, you all the same. Mijo, get in this house." He continues to mumble under his breath as he searches through his cabinets. "Big Hoodie, where is Dorian?"

"Who you say, Doe-boy? He in the back room playing chess wit somebody. I don't know all these sons of ....."

D'Juan left him talking to himself as he rushes to the back room. He opens door and the whole block was right there. Silas, Rocky, Santonio, Slim, Dorian, and Tydus' big brother Rico, sitting in a cloud of smoke. "What's the drilli yo?" he asked with excitement.

"Ah, the kid. Come here boy, Rock just told us you was in town" Dorian pulled him in the circle where he's embraced and showered with love.

And to think how close he was to getting robbed or merked by stick up kids in Harlem, to now being in front of his brethren was sur-real.

"Yo it's good. I heard y'all was eaten but now I see it. Cuban links, F.K pieces and shit. A'ight, I see you brodi" he directs at Santonio.

Silas and Slim laughs at his New Jack accent. "Y'all buggen, past the dro" he inhales the Purple Haze and gags. "Nah it's all good fam. We getting a couple of dollars around here, but it ain't all peaches and cream ya dig. Niccas getting clipped if they shit ain't tight." Slim mentions with a big gun sitting on his lap.

"So I hear."

D'Juan watches Rocky and Dorian playing chess, through a cloud of smoke. He was really tripping about how fast his life was moving. In contrast to chess, which is played with strategy and patience. Every move had to count. One bad one and it's a wrap, "Checkmate" Dorian announced.

Rocky leaned back and nodded his head, "Good move Doe."

"AHH Rock, what's up wit a face. Doe got you all screwed up again" Rico jokes. "Nah fool, I'm thinking about how bad yo sisters pussy stink."

While they go back and forth with insults, Silas brings D'Juan up to date. There was an all out blood feud, teenage girls coming up missing, and Israel haven't been heard from in weeks. They advised he check with his grandmother ASAP.

"Anybody talk to Capo?" D'Juan asks, changing the atmosphere.

Dorian and Rocky looked at each other, then Slim looked at Rico. "Yeah, he gon be a'ight. I met with his lawyer a few weeks ago. He looking at natural life in the Feds." Dorian explained...

Slim tapped Rocky on the shoulder indicating he and Rico had to check on some unfinished business. Rocky looked up to 'the kid' and asked him what he's going to do. There was a lot of money rolling through the fifteen block radius from 30th to 45th. The F.K organization was expanding, and his Uncle Santana was still Boss.

"No doubt, this is my crew. My familia. I was raised around y'all and if I'm gone get money it's gone be wit the familia. We all we got right" he asked, getting a definite answer.

Rocky hands him the gun off his waist "huh kid. You gone need this if you gon be around here." D'Juan took the 40. Caliber Gloc and put it in waist band. Reflecting on childhood experiences in Rich City, he refused to be a victim.

"Another thing, fill up your tank before you slide through the town. We not getting caught slippin at the gas station" Dorian advises.

"No doubt, it' s all good yo."

"Aye, you heard from Losi?"

"Nah, last time I seen him was back East. You was in the Chi' then though right?" D'Juan thoroughly recollects.

"Indeed I was."

Dorian embraced D'Juan with a five thousand dollar handshake before he hit the streets...

Grade 'A' heroin was an expensive high. Nonetheless, after fiends took their first dose they had to have it. Ace and Rome made sure Christi had thirty grand in her hand before they even thought to re-up. She found a five bed, three bathroom home, with a huge backyard in a quite community in Hilltop. She envisioned Juelz and D'Juan playing catch and basketball with Lala. Her and Tito would share a master suite with Jacuzzi, walk in shower, and two walk in closets. She shed tears of joy upon receiving the keys from the realtor.

"Mi hijo, you like it?"

"Si ma-ma, we love it." D'Juan speaks for Lala as well.

He should feel like his mission was complete, but he didn't. Within the first few weeks in Cali he had shot a man, and pistol whipped another, over a gram of smack. Yeah the money is good but the risk was too great. With so much uncertainty in this young king's life, he looks for the next best opportunity.

Leaning on the teachings of revolutionaries he focused on gaining knowledge. However, even the educational system was set up to fail. There was very little funding for books, and the teachers didn't believe in their own curriculum. The only math that made sense in his world was adding, subtracting and multiplying dividends. Which he became quite good at...

4:45a.m. Christi hands D'Juan the phone as he's barely awake. "Hello my handsome prince" Tonya's voice wakes him. "Yo, where you been ma? I've been thinking about you like crazy. You haven't spoken to Nana?"

"No, not lately. I was behind on my school work and been dealing with some things, but I'll be okay."

"Ma, please don't do that to me. What's going on with you?" He heard her take a deep breath before getting whatever off her chest. "D'Juan, I've been having nervous breakdowns. I can't stop thinking about you" she explained. "Ma, I swear to you I been feeling the same way. Can't nothing or no one replace you."

"Aww,"

"Well maybe money, but uh.." he jokes.

"Shut up stupid. And you know she ain't got nothing on all this Puerto Rican ass."

They share a few laughs and reminisce before she has to go to school.

Holiday seasons were always the hardest, because the familia didn't celebrate them. But there was one reason to celebrate New Year's Day, 1994. D'Juan's 14th birthday. Santonio and Silas woke up early that morning, calling and picking their playa potnas from J.F.K. High School. Then once Jannah got word they were going to Six Flags, she called some of her crew to join them.

Silas knock on Butch Cozie door looking for D'Juan. The old school mack opens the screen gate wearing a robe from the Hilton Hotel, and some house-shoes.

"What's up nephew, where the hoes at? Let ole Cozie spend a few dimes to have a good time."

Silas pushes pass "move out the way, you trippin."

"How be damn, lil disrespectful bastard." He yells.

D'Juan, Hakeem, Rashaad and lil Hoodie was in the dining room at the back of the house. They seem to be having a serious conversation when Silas Approached "what's up brodi?" he addresses D'Juan while pointing down at his watch. "We almost done kid, hold up."

Lil Hoodie briefs him on what they discussed so far "we was just talking about his party tonight. We gone do it at Malik's, where we can have the mics, camcorder, and all the shit."

"This lil cuz, you know we gotta represent" Hakeem said with enthusiasm with Rashaad co-signing.

"Fa sho, you know we gone do it live. But what you gon do right now kid?" Silas asked.

"Yo, I'm right behind you brodi" D'Juan shook everybody hands holding them to their promise to be at Malik's.

"Get outta here young-in. If we say we got you, we got you. Bet on that" lil Hoodie assures; and his word was bond.

Butch Cozie stands by the door with it still open as they leave, "Ah Cuba, see you's a playa. Yo poppa is a playa. But that one you wit, is a square from everywhere." he mumbles to himself even after they were gone ...

The F.K boys was dressed in the finest apparel known to teenagers. Wearing Polo Sport, Mecca, Nautica, Guess, and Karl Kani outfits, other crews took notice to how real playaz mob in fashion. Jannah and her click, were dressed in peddle-pushers, Capri pants, tank tops, and crop tops by various French designers. With their body type and natural beauty, it was no problem getting whatever they desired. Ironically, these F.K boys didn't spend a dime outside of having a good time and that's what these young divas admired. Tydus and Jannah were world class athletes, making these two crews the main attraction at any event.

Jannah approached D 'Juan while he was sipping iced lemonade. "Happy birthday playa" she jokes.

"Nah, nah, momie, I don't play no games. What 's good though?" he asked with a serious demeanor.

"What you think about Danielle?" she asked turning their attention to the yellow bone. "She cool. Down to earth, and kind of cute. Why you asked?"

"She feeling you,"

"Word? What, you a madam or som'thin?"

"No crazy man.. I'm just saying, I don 't see you talking to nobody, so what is your type?"

He looked in her eyes and gives a basic description of Tonya, and it didn't ' fit none of 'em. While they were in conversation, Tydus creeps from behind him with a small bucket of ice water, pouring it over his head.

"Ah shit. See that's why I don't trust you puta's" he barks.

They all laughed then sung happy birthday, making him feel a little better about the situation. His main man's Tydus, praised he was the champion of hustlers. Having being the first of their era to backpack drugs across the country.

The day couldn't have gone any smoother for what turned out to be a retreat. Four young men, and six young ladies removing themselves from the stresses of whatever daily life consisted of. At the same time, it was a welcome back party for the young man that they grew to love and appreciate...

Malik's House of Stylez was the place to be. The after lounge after the party. Big Vain was at the door collecting a five dollar cover charge when there was really no need. Junior and Silk teased him about ripping off the youngsters. In defense he blamed them for spiking the punch.

Young Magic, and Laz tha boy were on the mic when D'Juan stepped down into the basement.

"Shot out to the kid" Lil Hoodie shouts out as he grabs the mic, "I'm not that nicca// who-dat a blast you quicker// got a Gloc wit a thirty round snicker // I'm not to be played boy// you come around the One and you might get sprayed boy." A few bars shooting shots at his rivals.

Malik mixed the tracks, and one M.C. after the next had two minutes to do their thing. Tydus had his hand-held camcorder recording everything from the cypher, over to D'Juan, with his hands under Danielle's shirt. It seems like they drunk too much freak juice from the punch bowl.

At the end of the night, D'Juan had a hang over and his head was in the toilet screaming earl. Junior gave him a ride back to the Globe, and introduced him to Fresh Money. An O.G that was renting out his upstairs bedroom for ten dollars a night.

"Junior, what I'm supposed to do with this youngster?"

"Here, he just need to lay his head down", he said, simultaneously putting a twenty dollar bill in Fresh's hand. D'Juan was cashed out and didn't wake up until noon. He put his feet on the ground with a massive headache. "Ahh fuck. Where the hell.." Looking out the window he realizes he's in the Globe, just two doors from Silas and Santonio's joint. After a quick shower, and smoking a half of blunt he was ready to hit the streets. "Aye O.G, good looking out. I was faded"

"Yeah, you was sleep. Ole Junior brought you by. You should thank him too."

"No doubt."

"And my wife made you a egg McMuffin. You need to put something on your stomach, here."

"As long it's no pig, it's good."

"Boy, I said eggs.. Now take this and leave the whiskey to grown folks." Again, he thanks Fresh Money, and his wife Lisa for their hospitality.

For the next six months, D'Juan split shifts between the Rodeo Projects and The Globe. With the product he sold, he had no competition worth thinking about. Which in turn created some envy amongst the older hustler's in the neighborhood. He stacked a hundred grand, within that six months, aside from the 30k re-up money. He could've blew fifty grand at the Lexus auto mall, but there was no time to floss. The start of summer only meant it was time for another six month run. Ace and Rome was ready to re-up and called for a meeting at the Cotton Candy Club. Phats and Lil Leel had a nice operation on Sanford Str. on the North side, selling sixteen ounces a month. Totaling up to a little more than 90K. Once they made the collections and put ninety two grand back in the pot, D 'Juan made the call back east...

[Phone ringing], "Hola" Tonya answered.

D 'Juan uses his best show host voice "Yes, Tonya Feliciano you've been chosen to be on love connection, and we have."

"Shut up" she interrupts with laughter. "I was just dreaming about you, I swear you are mystical." She explained the power of his magic stick. "That's good ma-ma, I daydream about you even more, I'm sure."

"Are you chucky cheesing?"

"You know, you keep me smiling ma-ma, but yo dig this. I'll be there soon."

"Oh yeah, is it for personal reasons or business?"

"Maybe a little both, you have a problem with that?"

"As long as you handle your unfinished business, all is forgiven. I got my own apartment now, so I don't want to hear any more broken promises. I'll arrangement the meet, but you bring your ass to me", she long to be made whole again.

"Bet that. My word is bond and bond is life" ...

However, before he could make the trip, he was arrested in the Concord Pavilion parking lot leaving the 1994 summer jam. Intoxicated on Haze and Thug Passion, with Jannah and Danielle under his arm he felt like a king. They vowed to take full advantage of him, which was his primary focus. Totally oblivious of the extended clip bulging under his shirt. The police wrestled him to the ground causing Danielle to have a panic attack. The crowd of onlookers rallied behind him screaming "no justice, no peace."

While sitting in juvenile hall, he reflected on his life and the poor decision he'd made. He started transporting and hustling for a good cause. However, the money was so good he couldn't stop. The familia war became his and he was all in. Once he accepted that gun from Rocky, his fait was sealed. And in honesty, he was okay with riding and dying for his familia.

Tito flew back to town, immediately retaining a lawyer. Apparently, the weapon found in D'Juan's proximity under a car was linked to three homicides. Two in Richmond and another in Rodeo. Being questioned about these murders, he remembers his Pa' advice and invoked his right to remain silent.

After their first visit Tito felt it was time to move back West and open the Jack London location. Juelz was a fine role model, and he only hoped his positive influence would save his two youngest boys from the career path of Santana and Romelo. The best defense attorney in the Bay Area was Joseph Caramagno. Among the top 5 litigators in the country, he came at a pretty dime. By the second appearance in court, the murder charges were dropped to simple possession of an illegal firearm. Considering the circumstances, The Kid made out pretty well. I mean eighteen months wasn't a vacation but surely time he could do on his head.

Fresh off the bus at Preston Youth Authority he was spotted by his main man's Izreal from the weight pile. "Yo kid, what iz it boi?" Izzy yells, throwing his hands up. Recognizing his voice and stature he smiles and return the gestor "what's UP wit my dude. This where you disappeared to?" They met at the gate and embraced with a brotherly hug. "Yeah brodi, they got me for another B&E, fuckin around in the city."

"Wow... And I was looking everywhere for you kid. We was eating like kings." D'Juan explains. "I heard brodi, but we here now. This a gladiator school so keep yo guards up. You gon' be tested for sure."

"We gon give 'em hell chief. I got yours."

"No question. And you already know I got yours kid"

Within a week they were in the same dorm where they would ride their time out together.

The first piece of mail D'Juan received was from Danielle. After reading the three page letter, he felt compelled to write back. "Wow" he thought. Out of all the young ladies who said they cared, she was the first to show it. Definitely she'll be the first one he saw when the gates opened. The next letter was from Santonio telling him that Lil Hoodie was murdered.

He took this news hard and grieved for months. To make matters worse, Hakeem and Rashaad was being targeted by the FBI for the content in their music. He felt his heart turning cold, like 'fuck the Feds, fuck the D.A and whoever else believe in this Jim Crow system...

Lyfe flew a kite that would have great influence on his career path. "Peace kid, I heard you been doing well. Getting strong and reading books of knowledge. Stay focused and if you need Bella to come see you just call her. You can write me too. She'll reroute the mail. It's not too many we can trust. We all we got, remember that. I'll be in touch. One love." And it was signed Capo... P.S. 'The Globe' is yours.

Powerful words from a certified street king. Now rather this will contribute to D' Juan's destiny or demise, only God knew.

Chapter 8

A T 16 YEARS OLD 6'1" and 185 pounds solid muscle, D'Juan was left in charge of one of the most infamous projects in the San Francisco Bay Area, "The Globe." Lyfe left him in charge because he had a natural ability to lead and could be molded. Most importantly, he was loyal. A trait that's invaluable in this business. Junior and Silk would aid with the day to day operation, and all orders will still come from the top. D'Juan's duty is to enforce them.

First order of business was to organize how the product would be coming in and going out. He called for a meeting at building 3201, the old headquarters. Upon arrival, everyone checked their coats at the door except Rico, the machine treasurer. Something was odd about his demeanor especially when D' Juan spoke about their circle being infiltrated. There was also a rumor that Rico lost big at Remo's gambling shack. Either way, D'Juan smelled a rat.

"It's the middle of the month and I need to re-up 20 pounds of Super Silver Haze just came from the mountains. We need that." D'Juan states firmly. He then looked at Rico, "What we looking like Reeq?"

"We good, but we'll be better next week" Rico replies. "We don't have until next week." D'Juan insist. "Go get our money maint", he barks.

"How much, all of it?", Rico asks with attitude.

"Yeah.. All of it ma'fucka."

"Wow. Give a kid power, and a gun he's the man now. A'ight, I got you young G."

Rico says with a smerkish grin as D'Juan stares him down. Rico respected Lyfe because he knew what he had done in the past to his closest friends. However, he figured D'Juan wasn't that cold and who is this kid to give him orders. Well the kid knew he had to set an example and show how cold he could get if ever slighted.

"Rico!", he calls just before Rico opens the door. "You through wit money nicca", Bang!

One shot from D'Juan's .44 stunned Rico and everyone else in the room. He dropped to the floor gasping for air holding his abdomen. Santonio gets up to help him.

"Let him bleed!" D'Juan mumbles, gritting his teeth.

"Fuck wrong wit you, this Reeq!" Santonio attempted to bring calm to the situation.

"He ain't no good bro, this piece of shit fucked off our re-up money." D'Juan stressed, with his gun pointed toward Rico forehead. After looking into D'Juan's eyes, then down to Rico, Santonio said "Damn" like all the air had left his body. With Rico lying on the floor, seconds from death it was problematic to resume the meeting.

"From now on we calling thieves, rats, and trick willie ma'fuckaz Rico. So anytime they cross the game they'll remember, we not to be fucked wit." D' Juan stands on his position and reassures the crew of older men, he was just following orders. "Rock, Doe, we'll meet at the apartments tonight. Santonio, Silas clean this up." They all exit the building cool, calm and collected. What happen to Rico may have some consequences, but he was a liability. Dorian and Rocky couldn't do nothing but respect it.

They went to the apartments around the corner from The Globe and would lay low until night fall. Santonio and his brother wrapped the body in blankets and carried it to the dumpster. D'Juan went to the Richmond marina to gather his thoughts. He had just killed one of Lyfe's most trusted men. What would he think when he heard the news? How would Tydus react? He pondered on the endless possibilities for the rest of the night...

Rashaad and Hakeem recorded their first demo in 'the basement' at Malik's House of Styles. He was a man of many resources, so they stayed close to him as much as possible. His knowledge was invaluable and reputation as a D.J, impeccable. It would only be a matter of time before their selling cocaine and sleeping in drug infested houses days were over.

They introduced Izreal to the dope game when they were working for their pa' Kaboobi. Now six years later they control three blocks of their own. Their key to success was renting trap houses, and practically living in them. As a result, they went from making pocket change, to clocking ten grand a day.

When Santana went to the Feds everything went through Kaboobi. It was like having a direct line to Argentina. The quality was so pure, that clients came from Pittsburgh, San Francisco and the cities in between. By just purchasing two kilos a month, Hakeem and Rashaad were able to operate beneath the radar of DEA and FBI. They are just the two guys, D'Juan needs a part of his organization.

Around 6:30 p.m. D'Juan pulled up to Malik's. He parked his grand national in an alley within a few steps from the front door. He knocks on the door three times before he enters. "What's the drill champ?" Tydus asks, surprised to see him.

D 'Juan greeted him with a handshake and hug, "staying beneath the radar nah mean."

"That's mando. But brodi I have to get a message to Lyfe, can you do that for me?"

"No doubt, indeed."

As they exchange numbers, Hakeem appears through a cloud of ganja smoke. "What's haddenin wit the Kid?"

"You just who I needed to see" D'Juan continues "where's Rashaad? I'm having a meeting in the apartment, and I need y'all there", he states firmly.

"A'ight it's all good fam, but brodi in the lab, hold up," Hakeem goes to the basement and told Rashaad they have a meeting and it seemed important. Everyone who knew D'Juan took him seriously when it came to time and money.

"A'ight give me a minute" Rashaad saves the song with the intention of finishing later that night.

The three walk around the corner with guns in hand. In the danger zone, just a walk to the store could be your last. Usually when a bush moves, someone's coming out of it with their target in sight, so being quick on the draw was key for survival.

They reach the apartments on S.34th, where Rocky, Silas, Dorian and Santonio was waiting in the laundry room. They greet and get down to business. D'Juan speaks first "A'ight look, we on borrowed time so I'm a make it quick. My cousins Hakeem and Rashaad will be joining the operation and helping with the purchase of 20 pounds. Anyone in opposition?" All agreed with their body language suggesting he didn't even have to ask.

However, Hakeem and Rashaad appeared to be blindsided. They looked at each other in confusion but kept their silence. "A'ight cool, after tonight all the trees will be sold here in the apartments, the coke 35th to 37th, and The Globe will serve as our fort and base. We'll meet in 106 for now until 103 gets cleaned. Doe what you think?"

"All I been selling is grams and eighths. A Q.P is moving out just one apartment daily. We get 20 pounds we'll at least bring back 120 profit every month." Dorian Smiled and continued, "I'm wit it, we just have to stay patient and off the radar. We shouldn't buy anything flashy for at least a year straight." They all agreed.

"We gone have the young-ins directing traffic and nobody should have anything on 'em outside of a pistol and money," Rocky suggested. D' Juan quickly assured he'll get the word out first thing in the morning, that there would be no short stopping the clientele. "Also we need to talk to the store owners and assure them their businesses will be safe. Eventually we'll be in position to propose our own business ventures." D'Juan suggest, before they broke off in separate directions.

Hakeem and Rashaad went back to Butch Cozie joint and retrieved forty grand from the hidden safe. D 'Juan assures their money would be safe and apologize for putting them on the spot. Simply put, he couldn't afford them to say no.

He started the trip to Santa Rosa at midnight. He listened to music by Bob Marley as he contemplate meeting his cousin Ameere. Although they keep in touch, he haven't seen him since his pa' Santana went to the Feds, six years ago. He arrived at a little after 2 a.m. in a black Denali truck.

Ameere's girlfriend Tina meets him at the door. "What's up cousin, you know that boy nearly smoked himself into a coma waiting on y'all."

"Yea I figured that, I had to get Juelz truck, he at the tilt wit his shorty Melia". D'Juan explained.

"Oh O.k, well that explains why he didn't come. I know boo wanted to see him".

"You Know I don't involve him in my business. He gone gets us out of this shit" D'Juan continues "did cuz tell you where the bag at, I gotta hit the road". "To do what, get pulled over or fall asleep behind the wheel? Not happening, so gone over there and rest ya neck. I'll cook breakfast for y'all in the morning." Tina demands, prompting a headshake and smile.

D'Juan slept in the living room on the couch until Ameere woke him up with a chocolate philly stuffed with silver haze. "Huh, wake ya game up boi"- D'Juan inhales and coughs as he tries to sit up. "This him right here", he respects the potent indica as it brings tears to his eyes.

Tina was baking steaks, with eggs and potatoes frying on the stove top, while they discuss business and street politics in Rich City. It was hard for Ameere to picture when it seemed like only yesterday, he was standing in the back of the Globe. He occasionally visited his grandparents but after producing a few tracks for C-Bo, Spice 1, and Yukmouth, the royalty checks got too big to be coming to the P.J's mailroom.

Now with this new connect they would surely see more of each other. As Ameere counted the money, D'Juan was weighing the pounds. After the deal was complete, and bellies full, he hit the rush hour traffic blending in perfectly. He calls Dorian and Hakeem as he was pulling into his garage. It was a safe trip and they had fresh product to put on the market.

Dorian picked up a pound as it was his goal to sale one, every two days. Hakeem rolled through the south side looking for recruits, the next few days. Anyone who would join their movement had to be a hustler and have a good reputation. Every corner within a ten block radius they had locked, now they look to expand. Expansion means success in any business, so Lyfe approached his criminal enterprise with that focus. Within a weeks time there were near 30 foot soldiers from 34th to 35th. Another 20 on 37th. Their job was to direct traffic to the trap houses and bust their gun on sight of any opposition.. Which is an easy call for most, but the true test will come when tens of thousands of dollars spill over into their pockets. Money has a way of corrupting people, especially when they're young.

Heavy traffic of ladies was flowing through the South Side of Rich City. When Silver haze first hit, they only wanted purple Kush, now they're addicted and doing freaky things just to get a twenty dollar sack. Young players, and Macks circle The Globe in pursuit of a young lady that's a fiend for attention with the desire for riches. Yea, the first weekend of summer was blazing hot, and them F.K boys was keeping it lit. Hakeem and Rashaad rolled back to back in 91' highway 5.0's, Dorian and Rocky pushed T- top Iroc-Z's, and D'Juan wasn't far behind in his 92' Supra. They were dressed to impress in colorful Polo and Nautica Sport gear, Gold and diamonds shinning from fingers, up to earlobes and teeth. But aside from hysiding, there were codes to be obeyed by in the street life, and they lived up to their oath. The code of silence and loyalty being the most important.

D'Juan started his first day of summer school at John F. Kennedy High a.k.a "The K". It meant something to walk those hallways even if it's just for six weeks. The atmosphere was genuine, and the fake gets exposed in a Rich City minute. The Athletic program wasn't great by rankings but topped the charts in historical fashion. Guys like Orlando Pace, Andrew Vessel,

Rodney Webster, Mike Fielder who all played professional ball paved the way. The young ladies that attended "The K" were even a different breed. Sure they were pretty, but also loyal, down to earth, and intelligent sisters. Most of them understood what it meant to have a boyfriend and the duties that came with it. The main one of all is to support him, with all he does. Even if it means stashing a Gloc in a locker to make sure he's safe when leaving school. Yea, they were definitely cut from a different cloth.

The F.K boys, walked tall through the hallways with swag of confidence. Santonio, Izreal, Silas, and Tydus was money. Young Athletes and go-gettaz with pocket change to buy 911 Carrera's today and promised a hell of a lot more in the future.

D 'Juan' s 1st period class was history taught by Mr. Campbell who was well respected by street kids and athletes alike. D'Juan gets to his class early, as it's also the favorite choice for the ladies. The bell rings and students fill the 40 plus empty chairs within minutes. A young lady stops and stands next to his desk as he retrieves a notebook from his book bag, "Hi, D'Juan." Danielle says while touches his head. He smiles, and stands up to embrace her. While wrapping his muscular arms around her he whisper in her ear "How you been lil momma?" He squeezes tighter, thinking about the strength she provided while he was incarcerated. He could tell by the look in her eyes she wanted him. And he couldn't denied he wanted her.

"I've been ok, I guess. But we'll catch up after class." She promises planting a kiss on his cheek.

"No doubt indeed" he replies; continuing to admire her figure.

Once seated Mr. Campbell starts the lesson "young men and ladies, we will be here six weeks with each other. I'm going to make learning history fun and interesting starting with the slave trade and how most of our ancestors were treated in America." Every foreigner was glued to their seats and attentive. However for the next 50 minutes, all D'Juan could think about was how Danielle got him through those 18 months in youth authority. Her words were passionate and full of affection. While in a deep daydream, class had ended without D'Juan jotting down one note. "You ready" Danielle asks, snapping him out of a daze.

"What you mean, the Kid was born ready" he raises from a lazy position and gathers his Timberland book bag "let's rock." He put his arm around her neck and compliments her attire and physical growth. The last time he'd seen her she wore jeans and sweaters. Now, she's wearing black Capri pants, grey Manolo Timbs and a Raiderette jersey tied in the back to show her tight abs and diamond chain belly ring. As they approach her next class room he kisses her forehead. "Shorty I'll see you after school, yea?" Her face turn to curiosity "After School? where are you going?"

"I gotta focus on school, cause being around you. Sheesh... we'll be under the stairs". He smiles; looking into her eyes.

"I'll 'll be waiting" she reply with fire in her eyes.

"A'ight we'll holla"..

Walking down the hallway he could feel eyes from the shadows were starring him down. He continues to his locker and quickly retrieved his 40 cal. but the silhouette had vanished. For the rest of the day all he could think about was Danielle and how nicely shaped her body developed. He waited out front in his Silver Toyota Supra until the last bell rung. Immediately thereafter, he was approached by Angel trifling self and her jazzabell friends. "D'Juan, my cousin wants to talk to you." She then checks out his outfit from head to toe.

"Why she can't talk?" He asks, looking at Aiisha.

Angel then steps out the way, "talk to him, don't be shy now". With no shame she just spoke her heart "D'Juan I been thinking about you lately, and we really need to talk. Here take my number."

D'Juan couldn't do nothing but respect her feelings. "Aight ma. Soon as I get to the tilt, I'll hit you" He put the folded napkin in his pocket as Danielle was walking out the school doors. "Hey boo" Aiisha says in gest as she passed.

"Hey" Danielle replied with a smirk. Her focus then turned to D 'Juan as he scanned her from head to toe. Simultaneously, he could see Aiisha's diamond shaped frame through her sky-blue sundress. He smiled at that too. "Bae, I couldn't wait to see you." Danielle mention before kissing his neck.

"I told you, I'll see you later. I try to keep my promises."

As the two share smiles and words of affection, D'Juan gets a eerie feeling like he's being watched. Once seated inside his high performance sports car He handed her a gram of silver haze. "Huh, roll this". While he checks the rearview mirrors, clutching his gun, she rolls a perfect blunt, (lighter strikes) then puts it up to his lips. "Yo kid, we can get use to this" he thinks to himself.

Taking the freeway, he drove in the fast lane until turning off on San Pablo Dam Rd. " Bae, where we going?" She asks upon entering a high class community in Rich City. Nonchalantly, he looks over and held up one finger. Indicating; they'll be there in a minute and to have patience.

In the Richmond Hills there's a place, D 'Juan likes to park, smoke and overlook the city. It seemed so peaceful there. "You see?" he asks, pointing over the city toward the San Francisco Bay. She looks out and then back to him for a better understanding. "This is us on the outside looking in.

It's ugly there, but it's beautiful here." He stresses, hoping she'll realize it's more in the world to explore. She pondered on their conversation and share her plans for college, but wonder does he approve.. Nonetheless they talked until his pager vibrated for the 8th time.

"Damn ma, I gotta handle this business. Where can I take you Ms. Davis?"

"What, I ain't going home. I'm riding' wit you" she demands.

"NO.. Momie, I have some serious business to handle"

"Can I be in yo bizness D' Juan?"

He ponders on the idea before asking if she knew exactly what that would mean. Riding with him meant she would have to be willing to die with him or for him at any moment. She thought about what her duty would be all of two seconds.

"I'll do whatever for you". She says with conviction.

He knows too, she's Annabelle's niece, and he couldn't let nothing happen to her. With the gut feelings of something or someone is watching him he just can't take the chance. "Look ma-ma, I'll pick you up tomorrow. I got you okay" he then rubbed her bottom lip with his thumb. "I can't let nothing happen to my pearl, feel me?" she nodded and agreed to be dropped off at Annabelle's for the night.

After walking her to the front door, her Aunt Bella comes to the porch. "Um, so y'all kissing cousins now huh?" she inquires. "I don't know what to do Bella. She wants to live with me, and I'm in the middle of a power struggle. The familia needs me..." she interrupts before he could explain his dilemma. "Why you didn't say all that before? I know what I want, just say you don't want me and I promise never to speak to you again". Danielle shouts.

"Look, I have to go handle something. I'll see you in the a.m." He backs down off the porch, pleading for assistance from Annabelle.

"Go handle your business Cuba, I got her." As the queen of Sugar Hill, Annabelle knew the game from a hustlers view as well as the wife of a kingpin. He only hopes she tells Danielle EVERYTHING she needs to know. His life will very well depend on it...

D 'Juan meets Rocky and Dorian in the basement at Malik's. In the past 10 days nearly 6 p's were sold and only a half kilo of cocaine. Dorian suggested Hakeem sale powder at night and rock during the day. Rashaad could sale heroin at the spot on 37th. Rocky supported this idea as they obviously gave it great consideration. D 'Juan agreed it would be a power move as well but where would they get it. He could go across the tracks to the silver street projects but the feds got them under a microscope, and he haven't called back east since he'd been home. 'Maybe it was a good time. Just maybe' he thinks to himself.

As the crew discuss different possibilities, D 'Juan make mention of a possible threat...

"Dig this, I was at school today and this funny looking ma'fucka was staring at me like he knew me or som'thin " he explains.

"What he look like " Dorian asked, now sitting up in the couch.

"He was 6 feet 2 inches maybe 200 pounds, stocky, dark-skinned cat. It looked like he had a scar on his face." D'Juan continues as they ponder on the description. "Then it was a Bonneville sitting directly across from where I parked, Crazy yo." He shook his head and re-lives the experience.

"You had yo shit didn't you" Rocky asked.

"No doubt indeed".

"Then you good, just be careful boy. You somebody now." Rocky assures with a head nod.

Being careful of the endless possibilities would keep the Kid on point. He understood and no more needed to be said about that, "A'ight back to business, I'll hit Uncle Kaboobi and see about some Tar. I ain't fuckin wit the Kings-men back East right now". Dorian and Rocky nodded their heads in agreement.

"A'ight so we good?"

"No doubt. Anything is better than nothing, cause I'm surely not making that trip" Dorian confirm.

"And I'm gone need a name to that face ASAP" D'Juan mentions to Rocky before hitting the streets. See, the kid felt he knew who the fat cat was and what was his business.

It had been a long day. D 'Juan had just left the dentist copping sixteen gold teeth with diamonds and his mouth was swollen. He'd popped two Tylenol 3's and the exact moment his head hit the pillow his pager vibrates. It's Danielle "143". He closes his eyes with so many thoughts and a mischievous grin. He'd played with Danielle's mind now her heart was his. 'Silly Bambi' he thinks out loud...

Then, the weirdest thing happened that night. Aiisha shows up to his front door knocking like the police. He answered in his boxers with gun in hand, "Yo, how you know where I live?" he asks, stepping outside, looking up and down the street. There was not a soul or vehicle in sight. "Do it matter?" she entices, luring him inside while opening her blouse. He shakes his head thinking, 'this can't be real'. "Why do you question your destiny? You know you want me, stop resisting." And how right she was.

In an instant, he lifts her in his arms while placing his gun on the kitchen counter. Her legs wrapped around his waist like a python. The passion they shared was so intense they couldn't let each other go, not even to change positions. Having one orgasm after the next while she bites down on his chest. "Shh". Before he reaches ecstasy his body gets cold. Aiisha was slipping from his grips. She smiles as he tries regaining his grip. "What the fuck" he thought. Suddenly he's awakened by something vibrating on the nightstand. "Wow" he looked around for any sign of Aiisha, smell his cloths, then finally picks up his pager. "Damn" He realizes the moment he'd longed for was all a dream. Danielle had been paging for the past hour. It was nearly 8 a.m. and hopefully, she's still at Annabelle' s.

(phone ringing) "D'Juan" Annabella answered anticipating his call. "What's up Bella, where lil ma?" "You know this girl was waiting on you to take her to school". "I know, I over slept. Tell her I'm on my way". "Boy she already gone. Her cousin picked her up 15 minutes ago". He paused for a few seconds "Jannah" he thoughts to himself. "A'ight cool, I'll make it up to her", he answered. "Cuba, I love you like a son. But take this to the grave with you; never sell out for temporary satisfaction". "Umm", he thinks as the phone disconnect.

His guilt covered him. He didn't know how to treat Danielle just yet. He was a player by nature, and haven't loved anything but money for quite some time. As he slipped into some Pelle Pelle jeans he thought of his agenda. First thing First, holla at Uncle Kaboobi to discuss his plans of getting back in the heroin business. Then he'll do something special for Danielle. Stepping outside of his townhome on 9th street, the sun-rays glistened off his 360 waves and the diamonds in his teeth. His sports car was shining from turtle wax and Armor-All on the tires. Music by God-Holly,

Laz tha boy, and Doc Dolla, blast from the Bose sound system as he turn the key in the ignition.. While letting the engine rev, he puts fire to a Haze blunt. Simultaneously inhaling as he hits the gas. (Sound of rubber peeling)

He takes the back roads up to the Richmond Hills, hoping he'll catch Kaboobi before he went to work. "Walah", as he pulled into the driveway, Kaboobi was pulling up behind him. D'Juan leaps out to greet him. "The Ghost, what's good. Look like I caught you right on time."

"Yea I guess you did. I was on my way to work and forgot my pistol." Hurrying to the front door, D'Juan closely follow "Unc, I need to get work. Put me on wit yo boy." D'Juan demands with sense of urgency. "That's no problem, I needed to see him anyway. I'll be working late so I'll stop by there around midnight." Kaboobi assures while opening his front door. They go inside and discuss further details.

After listening briefly Kaboobi advises "it's never wise to buy a pound first. Build your machine, get the clients on a schedule, then go big. What if the dope is no good?"

"I'm gone get my money back" he says with conviction. After laughing at the kids response, he tries another approach "A'ight how much could you sale a week?"

"At least a Q.P. and that'll be in 20 dollar balloons."

"So first cop a half P, and sell it all in $35 Grams. This is some good dope, you gone have traffic coming from all over. But that'll get you hot too, so less traffic, more money!"

D' Juan begins to understand his Uncle's logic. There hadn't been a market set-up on the south side in some time and he could hear the money counter clicking as he spoke; loud and clear.

"Give me 4 g's, you gone be famous kid. My sons should get some of this money and get rich."

D'Juan counted out four grand while thinking to himself 'only if you knew'.

Looking down at his Locman watch, D'Juan has just enough time to make it to second period class. He went shopping at the mall where he bought some beach towels, swim trunks and bikinis from Nordstrom's. Stopping by See's candy for chocolate covered strawberries on the way out. Danielle would love what he had planned for the rest of their day. His Pa' told him about romance, but aside from extravagant trips to Paris or Miami, D'Juan could afford watching the sunset with his shorty on a warm sandy beach. He sat in his car for five minutes contemplating the beaches he knew of, finally deciding to stop by his father's restaurant after picking up Danielle.

Checking his rearview mirror, he noticed a baby blue mustang swerving in and out of lanes to keep pace with him. It took all of two seconds before he recognized the driver as Romelo Jr.. D'Juan hit his right blinker and headed off on Cutting Blvd. Both cars pulled into the gas station on South 51st. They bounce out and embrace, with shakes and hugs. "Brodie what iz it, I mean what's really good."

"You know me kid, still at it. I see you stayin on point."

D' Juan nod his head "no doubt indeed." After a few minutes, a lot of traffic began pulling in and out the gas station, getting both their attention.

"We need to put something together, hit me at the joint, same number."

"Aight, no doubt. I'm on a trip tonight but tomorrow should be good."

"Love you kid. And be careful, it's snakes slithering through this joint" Romelo warns.

"You already know" D'Juan express familia love with his fist over his heart.

They both peel out stopping incoming traffic. After two stop lights, D'Juan is at the school. 'Perfect timing' he thought. It was lunch time and only two class periods left. However, before he could park Danielle ran through the parking lot, and up to the car door. "Get in ma-ma, I have something to show you", he said with a smile. "Yea, I can't wait", she takes the passenger seat and turn up the music. Retrieving a Swisher Sweet and a bud from the console, she rolls up and aids him while on the highway.

Next stop was Little Havana's in Jack London Square, to get lunch and holler at his pa. He ordered fried Prawns, chicken tenders and fries. She opted for a beef link dinner with potato salad and baked beans. They shared a bowl of warm peach cobbler topped with French vanilla ice cream, from the same bowl eating off the same spoon. 'How romantic' Tito thinks to himself. He advise,

the two, to drive down to Half Moon Bay and guarantee they'll enjoy the experience. After eating lunch together, Tito shared his vision of them working for the family business.

Cruising down the highway D'Juan was thinking about his duty to Danielle and began to embrace the idea he was her man. In part, because that's what she believed. As they arrive to the sea side, Half Moon Bay was long as the eyes could see, and more beautiful than the mind could fathom. Sailboats, jet ski's and half naked women were everywhere. Beach volleyball was the main attraction and for other reasons than the sport itself. He looked at Danielle as she looked at him "How many girls you brought here before?"

"You are the first ma". His sincerity brings a smile to her face.

They find a spot by the water, distant from noisy elder. Danielle fires up a blunt and relaxes under the 90 degree sun rays. D'Juan lays on his back while she changes into her Baby Phat swimsuit. His face was to the clouds, and mind on his money. He raises his head while she's oiling her legs. "Let me help you with that " he asks, reaching for the oil. "Alright, but don't miss a spot", she demands.

First, he oils her back, unloosening her top, then with his firm hands massages her shoulders to her lower back. **"Ughhh"** she moans; appreciating the feeling as he kisses on her neck, and shoulders. Suddenly, she turns over and grabs his hands. Guiding them in between her legs and over a wet womb. "You feel how wet you make me?" she asks, while biting her lip.

In response, he kisses from her neck down to belly ring, gazing back up to her sandy brown eyes. Her wish was his pleasure to fulfill, and he lets it be no secret. Gently touching her with his right hand, he occupies his left hands with massaging her breast. She turned her head from side to side while stroking his fingers deeper inside. "Hold up", he tries to stop as an on-looker pass by, but her hormones increase. She begs for more as she's ready to catch fire. For nearly 15 minutes she enjoys his touch and the feeling of his manhood pulsating in her hand. Now he's ready to take it a step further, and she entices it on "Damn" he announce abruptly.

"What??"

"I'll be right back" Apparently he left the condoms in his car and didn't want the fire to go out. She was hot and ready to be busted wide open. He returned from the car with another blunt, condoms and a full length wool jacket. She smiles before biting into a chocolate covered strawberry.

"Dang, you do fly?"

"No doubt indeed, anything for you ma". He drapes the jacket over his back and lays on top of her. As he kisses her neck and bites on her nipples, she lowers his Phat Farm trunks.

"Bae, you know I haven't"

"Shh, it don't matter. Nothing matters but us right now." He ensures she's safe in his arms.

As if hypnotized by the diamonds in his teeth and heat in her puss, she loses all control. She grabs his manhood and eases it gently inside. "Uhh" she moans. With his every motion she tries pushing him out. Taking slow, rhythmic strokes, he re-position her hands to his hip and push deeper. This sex was love making, and the climax was incomparable. As her legs quivered, he stiffened up, and they both became temporarily paralyzed. Laying there with him inside for nearly 5 minutes.

When he pulled out, there was blood everywhere "Ma what the fuck" He asks in a panic "What" she looked down and jumps up "oh my God what happened?" she cries out, wrapping the bloody towel around her waist while sprinting to the showers/bathroom. He followed leaving everything, on the beach. **ONLY** thing he can think of is, it must be her period but she quickly rejects that notion.

"No stupid. This was my first time." She snaps at him "my bad ma, I didn't know. I swear I didn't" he then buried her head in his chest. After a quick shower they return to the crime scene as D'Juan referred to in a joking manner. "Shut up punk, don't make me sock you in yo face" she says while throwing a soft hook. "Okay, okay ma-ma.. I'm only trying to cheer you up. Come here." He wraps his arms around her and let her know he got her. "You ever seen anything like this?" he asks. "Only if you knew D'Juan. I never did anything like this; you my first everything" her words sent chills through his gut. She was nothing like the average girls he had sex with. To her it meant more than an orgasm, and romance. She wanted all of him and he wasn't sure if he could give her all what she wanted. He contemplate this on the drive home, often looking over as she slept peacefully. Soon as he exits on Potrero Ave., he put his gun on his lap and leaned back in his seat. "Ma" he tap her leg, getting her to wake up. "We home."

She opens her eyes and looks around, "Where we going?"

"I'm going to drop you off at", She interrupts him "NO, you taken me to yo house. I want you to hold me tonight". He looked over and thought to himself "what have I gotten myself into". He then remembers what Annabelle told him, and his promise to protect her.

"A'ight, I have to handle some important business top of the a.m. A'ight" He re-asserts his position.

"I don't have a problem with that, just remember yo business at night." Danielle states firmly.

It was midnight, and she hadn't packed any clothes. 'What she gone wear tomorrow?' He thought to leave two grand with a note instructing to drive the Acura, and cop some gear. After all, they did just share one heavenly experience...

The meeting with Kaboobi and Topaz went well, by 6 a.m. D'Juan was picking up the package and less than a hour later it was being processed and packaged in balloons. Tar, Heroin was sold a bit different than China White. It was blended for those that sniffed and kept black for the shooters. D'Juan wasted no time in opening shop at the joint on S. 37th. Who would suspect a drug operation to be aided by a respected man with a corporate salary? D'Juan paid the rent and made plans to remodel the inside. Over the weekend he spent more time on the operation than with Danielle but as long as she was sleeping in his bed and driving a 94' Acura legend she didn't complain. In fact she couldn't wait to tell her cousin Jannah and her closes friends about their beach extravaganza. How could she keep her experience a secret? For once she was happy and wanted her sisters to be happy for her. I guess Annabelle had yet to tell her that ladies should never tell!

D'Juan gets a call from Dorian on Saturday at 5 a.m. From jump, this didn't feel like business as usual.

"Yo, what's the drill?"

"This Doe, we got a problem"

"A'ight, what's good? I need the street sweeper?"

"Just meet me at Nations in 30 minutes. San Pablo"

"Say no mo"..

D'Juan quickly dressed in a sweat suit and Kevlar vest. Upon exiting on San Pablo, he pondered on the pressing matter. One, they usually meet in El Cerrito, and two Dorian and Rocky never had a problem that couldn't be fixed.

Well, this problem isn't going to be an easy fix. Apparently three teenage kids from the J.F.K. projects was gunned down on one of their blocks by some stick up kids from Ohio Ave. The news couldn't get any worse. Not only would the police interfere with business, but this is no question a act of war. They would certainly lose clientele, and this didn't set well on D'Juan's conscious. Someone would have to pay the blood money for this, and it's usually repaid in blood.

D'Juan assured Dorian he'll holler at the lieutenant from J.F.K. personally. He and Pharaoh were tight like brothers.

"IN the meantime, we need to make a trip to the storage."

"No doubt Indeed, I'm on it first thing. You know, this is not by accident, right?"

D'Juan nodded in agreement. "It is what it is. Holla in the mo'ning."

"A'ight peace" D'Juan put his fist over his heart.

He waste no time in dispelling the rumor before it would be out of his hands. He called Pharaoh and told him he'll be at his door in 20 minutes. As he pulled down 37th, he sees Pharaoh's grand national flashing the high beams. He stops and rolls down his window. "Peace bra. Aye, I just heard what happened to yo nephew, you know you have my gun". Pharaoh listens only responding by nodding his head. "Give it some time, you'll see. Aye remember Oschino?"

Pharaoh's interest peeks as he raises his head closer to the window.

"He rose from the dead bra, now I gotta finish what you started".

Pharaoh shook his head "Nah, that's all me lil bra. You know it's love kid but don't get in my way." Pharaoh then leaned back and rolled up the window. D'Juan grins as a silent agreement, but he couldn't take any chances.

The very next morning, four heavily armed men surrounded Oschino's grandmother house. Hakeem and Rashaad jumped the fence and waited in the backyard.. Slim and Dorian grew impatient after a hour and kicked in the front door. "Boom" get down, get down it's Richmond Police, "The elder lady was in shock and immediately began praying. "Aye" (Shots Fired) they shoot at a man as he ran to a back room. Another man tries to grab a kitchen knife and gets himself shot in the head. Oschino's Uncle jumped through the back window as Hakeem was standing at the back door. Rashaad walk up to the man and aimed an A.K. 47 at his face. "Please man, we didn't do nothing, Please." He hits him in the head with the stock knocking him unconscious. Hakeem, spins around the back of the house "fuck you doing", and shoots the man twice in the head, reminding Rashaad of what they came to do.

Slim slapped the elderly lady repeatedly with his, colt 45. "Where is Oschino for the last time" She was bleeding and pleading for her grandsons life. "A'ight, tell him this was for him." Bang!. Dorian had the car running as the three fled on foot. "Let's dip" He told them as the passenger door flies open. Dorian turned left on Cutting and onto the freeway ramp. It was total silence and frustration that Oschino was like a ghost. The thoughts also crossed their mind of how far he would go in avenging his family.

D'Juan and Rocky had been sitting outside his sisters joint in crescent park village for two days, still no show. What started as a protection of their business quickly turned real personal. Shoot-outs increased over the next few weeks and Ohio avenue was under fire with heat coming from two directions. Fats, the Ohio boys general agreed to give up Oschino's location when he got word. It sounded good, but still D' Juan warned Rocky and Rashaad not to trust that Fat ma'fucka.

With the exception of a couple young ladies wanting to feel the comforts of silk bedsheets, summer school haven't been too hot for the kid as. J.F.K. High, started to look more like a death trap by the day. The risk of not staying armed was too great and an off duty police named Robocop took his job way too serious. D 'Juan's attendance dropped from two classes a day to two classes a week...

It was a Thursday at around 1 p.m., he was parked in the back of the school waiting for Santonio and Silas. Aiisha approached his car with caution, looking in before speaking "D'Juan, you okay?" He open the passenger door and signals for her to get in "Yea I'm good ma, how you?"

He made eye contact, causing her to smile. "I haven't seen you around and I needed to talk to you about something." "Yeah, well talk." She rubs the inside of her legs with both hands. "I'm going to just keep it real. I always think about what could have been had you stayed." He looks over with some surprise and she doesn't understand why. "What, you don't feel nothing no more? You stone cold all of a sudden?" He shook his head and smiled "A'ight, now I'm gon keep it real. My life has been flipped upside down. I think about you yea, but that seemed like a lifetime ago." He explain.

"Well you never called. I have the same number, and I been through hell too. I'm sorry about what happened to your family but I was just as hurt. You were my best friend."

He contemplate her motives and rather or not he could trust her. Why now? "Look ma, I don't want to seem insensitive, I just been moving nah-mean", "Yes, I do now what you mean. I guess it's money over bitches huh." She said sharply. "Woe, woe be easy... M.O.B to me means money ova bullshit. Now, you wanna get some money or you wanna get fucked?"

Her first reaction was to snap, but she was in shock. Like, 'did he really just get at me like that?' She clears her throat and takes a deep breath, "look boy, I don't know who you think I am, but I ain't the one. Look on my eyes D'Juan." She demands with calm

He reaches in the ash tray grabs a half of a blunt and ponders before looking back at her.

"I use to tell myself, I'll do whatever just to see you. Now, I don't even know you."

"You know you right. So let me introduce you to the new me. I've been selling dope and hustling since I was 10. I don't have a home to go back to. My only future is in the streets making money, and not in some white man's education system. You wanta fuck wit me, you gotta be all in." Upon hearing him speak with ambition, she felt his conviction. She knew right then, she had made the right choice. "Like I said. I was will to do whatever for you before, and even more so now."

He thought about his operation and anticipated the need for transporters. Only question was could he trust her. He never trusted anyone outside of his family. Not anyone. "A'ight, I should have something up in a couple of weeks. In the meantime you can move this haze or son'thin."

"Like I said whateva." She was glued to the leather seat and was making herself lust. The sound of getting money turned her on and D'Juan made her crazy. It had been nearly 45 minutes and still no sign of Santonio or Silas. He figured they'd left with Tydus or some females, either way he'll catch 'em later.

Pulling out the parking lot he turned up the volume on "can't knock the hustle" by Jay-Z. Aiisha dropped her seat down as they rolled down Potrero Ave. She studied his movements, and admired his sense of security. He kept his eyes in the rearview mirrors, and gun in reach. "I need to ask you something." He turns down the music and continues "do you trust me?"

She nodded her head "I wouldn't be with you if I didn't"

"A'ight, I'm gone run you the drill. I 'm putting together a trip out of state. I'll need someone to travel with me." She thinks about it, and gives her full attention. "We'll be carrying 20 pounds of this haze, from Seattle to Chicago. This is too serious to be fuckin around, so if you down I need to know now."

She looked at him with a look like 'nicca you hard of hearing'. Not only did she want to be his number one, she needed the money. "I never transported before, but I'm a hustlah. I sold coke, trees, everything but my body. Just know for you it's whateva" she speaks with enthusiasm, scoring major points. "No doubt indeed".

He decides to test her hustling skills and left her with a half ounce of Heroin and a quarter pound of silver haze. She was living on 3rd and Maine St., where addicts literally hung out on her front porch. Shouldn't be a problem if she was who you say. D'Juan could tell by their conversation she'd changed some, but again, that was a lifetime ago.

D'Juan drove up to the Richmond Hills to check on his Uncle. His Pa' was worried that he was a casualty at the Chevron oil plant. Like it was an epiphany or something, he could see himself living in one of them mansions. 'In due time' he thought out loud. Pulling up to Kaboobi's he could see all three vehicles in the garage. He knocks on the door and screams his Uncle's name at the open windows. "Unc", before he knocks again, Luscious opens the door.

"Hey you, your uncle is in the back."

"A'ight" He looked over his shoulder at all that ass she had popping out her booty shorts. At first thought it was high class hoe, next maybe a model.

"Unc" D'Juan yells down the hall of the many bedrooms. "Yeah, I'm back here."

"Man, my pa heard the refinery was on fire... You good?"

"I'm in the best place sobrino, believe me when I say it. But sit, I want you to meet my boy Topaz. We call him Hop."

Finally, D'Juan gets to meet the man himself. "Peace King, it's a pleasure to meet you" They shake hands "Peace" Topaz responds with a grin.

"Me and Your Uncle goes way back we first met in North Richmond in 72, we were 12." He recalls the train heist that solidified their brotherhood. "Remember kid when I use to tell you about the Cheeba Leave-a- Posse?"

"No doubt..." D'Juan recollects, "Hop was the ringleader." They laugh at a inside joke.

Topaz Deguzman was a multi-millionaire by the mid 80's. He made his fortune selling tubs of heroin and hay bundles of Tai weed which led him into the business of managing Mexican professional boxers. The first Mexican champion boxer Roberto Doran brought hundreds of millions of dollars back to Mexico and donated 15 percent to orphans. He was their hero and loved by everyone. That is, until he went broke. He then showed D 'Juan pictures of 15 to 20 men standing in front of private planes, explaining how they flew everywhere together but now the only one's still standing was him and Kaboobi. "See, when we were running through the Silver Street Projects, Kaboobi earned the name Boo because he was like a ghost. You would often hear about him, but rarely seen him. And he never took pictures. Your uncle's a sharp dude man I swear." D'Juan listened as Topaz bragged on Kaboobi's loyalty.

At the end of a two hour trip back in time he was presented with a proposition, "D'Juan your uncle told me you have what it takes." After nonchalantly shrugging his shoulders, he proclaims, "Loyalty is royalty. Once the foundation is laid, the money will come later."

"Si indeed.. Okay this the deal. I can get you all the heroin you need, but I need guns. A.K. 47's, Machine guns, and street sweepers. It's a war going on in Mexico between the Government and the Rebels. This is why I'm here."

D'Juan gets an O.K. from Kaboobi before speaking. "When you need 'em by?"

"As soon as possible."

"They'll be military issue so give me two weeks tops, but that's not a problem." They shook hands with smiles "and I'm always on time" D'Juan added.

Danielle had been sitting at D'Juan townhome worried for a few hours. She pages him in frustration 304, 304, 304, then again. He turned his pager off and races home. This is exactly why he didn't want to deal with Danielle because she gets insecure and does crazy shit. He came to a sudden stop in the parking lot next to the Acura Legend. He bounced out with anger in his face and rage in his voice, "fuck wrong with you didn't I tell you stay out of my business?"

"You gone quit playing with me D'Juan. I haven't seen you since yesterday" she shouts with tears in her eyes. He slams the car door and walks toward the front door of his home. With a mean temper, Danielle storms behind him cursing and wishing he goes to hell. Instinctively he turned around and pointed his finger in her face "Don't fuck with me." And before he could shut the door, she pulled on his shirt begging him not to leave her. "Shut up ma, you wake the neighbors. Get in here."

Putting her on to hustle was a risk, but he'd never seen her flip like that. How could he trust someone so emotionally unstable? He smoked a blunt and relaxed his mind. Business was priority, his relationship with her was secondary. He could live without her, but money was a necessity.

Later when he turned on his pager, he had a hit from Aiisha. '510-232-1579, 411-911' "She couldn't have sold that shit already", he thought. While Danielle was busy bagging up a pound in twenty dollars sacks, D'Juan drove to the spot Aiisha had been staying. When he arrived, she was waiting by the door with a backpack and arms full of coats. D'Juan swing open his car door, "what's up Ma, you good?"

She was clearly upset and needed a shoulder to lean on. "I'm good thank you," she leaned over and kissed him on his cheek. Then handed over $2400 in a envelope "here I had to give a couple hundred to my auntie" she explained with exhaustion.

"It's all good Ma, you a'ight?"

Seeing he was the only one there for her she broke down in tears. "What did I do wrong? I don't have nobody, my life fucking sucks." "Woe ma, don't think that. I got out of bed immediately. I got you ma, just talk to me. Please."

Apparently, her aunty tried to steal her money and when she was caught, they had a fight. She was accused of being a prostitute and told her she'll be like her mother if she kept living fast. As she vented, he just listened. It was already Mid-night and Danielle would surely go crazy if he stayed away another night. He had to think fast "Ma I gotta take care of something tonight, I'm gon take you to a room and come back first thing A'ight." He lifted her chin up and kissed her forehead.

"O.K. just come back soon. I need you Habibi."

Her words were more sincere than Danielle's could ever be.

Aiisha would appreciate the luxuries, Danielle was afforded. He paid for a suite at the Hilton in Hilltop for two nights. She was left with some swisher sweets, an eighth of Haze, and two hundred dollars to order breakfast, if he didn't make it back before 10 a. m.

Walking back into his townhome, D'Juan knew something had to change. Danielle was becoming a problem. He laid with his eyes open until he daybreak for he couldn't sleep. "Danielle, I gotta make a run. It's a Half P in the bathroom weigh it out in ounces." She rolls over "then what, somebody coming?"

"Nah that's you. Take two to the Globe' and make something happen. However you move it, it's on you." He figured the only way to deal with this was keeping her busy. Then if that don't work, she would've earned her severance pay.

Aiisha was sleeping like a motherless child when he entered the room. Two pillows rested beneath her head, the covers pulled over her face, she looked so alone in the world. He sat next to her and rubbed her face "I just had a dream about you " she said opening her eyes. "Yeah, about what?" he asked then uncovers her face. "It was about me and you" she said smiling. "No bull-shitin, I did too" she demands he came close and guides his hand from her shoulders to her breast. "You want me?"

"No doubt indeed. You crazy?"

"Maybe.. But I do know I want you more" her voice intensifies with seduction.

She pulled off his shirt as he climbs on top. His sweatpants and boxers fell to his knees while he maneuvered under the covers. The passion they had for each other was undeniable. She climbs on top and rides him like a professional. Her womb was tight and felt better than in his dream. As he grows inside her, the level of passion increases, voice pitch raises, and their bodies locked like magnets. That's when he knew she was the one.

After climaxing, they relaxed in a bubbled hot tub, not even a half hour later it was time for round 2. She jumps in his arms, he catches her with both hands on her ass. "Fuck Me" she demands wrapping her legs around his waist inviting all of his manhood inside her. As sweat roll down their backs the passion increases. She lost all control as if that moment was all that mattered.

The comfort of finally holding each other felt so good they slept the whole day. It was 8 p.m. when D 'Juan rolled out of bed. He covers Aiisha' s naked body before washing his face. "I got the world in front of me and a queen got my back. Lets go get it kid." He said to the young man in the mirror. As he dresses, he told the princess of Sudan he'll be back in a couple hours. "Habibi, I wanna go to the movies."

"A'ight it's good make the arrangements. Then we'll go to Red Lobster." She appreciated the fact he remembered. Simply put, he had all she wanted in the world. "Here... Go cop some gear from the mall" He tossed a bankroll on the table.

"Be safe Habibi."

"What that mean Ma?" She smiled and proudly states "Habibi means my beloved" He pauses then smiled "Ah, Salaam Malika." She smiled pulling the sheet over her face (Door Shuts)

Rocky and Slim was standing outside the apartments with fully loaded assault rifles when D'Juan pulled up. The one way was like a military fort: soldiers with guns everywhere.

"What's up my G."

D'Juan nodded his head as he walked by. Dorian was in the middle of a high stakes with 100 grand pot. "Doe I need to holla at you, It's important." Dorian stood up evidently frustrated and walks passed D'Juan out the door, "Come on", upstairs to Big Hoodie' s joint.

Once inside, D'Juan lay out the proposition from Topaz. It initially sounded great but as they did the math, the numbers didn't add up. Which was reason to be concerned. Getting the guns wouldn't be a problem, but could they trust his people to hold up on their end! AND if was one thing Dorian didn't do was fall for the okey doke. "This what we'll do. Trade off each crate for 15 g's each, in return for 3 kees. That way we wouldn't have more dope than we could move."

"Bet." D'Juan left out the door headed to Kaboobi's crib. This was a deal of a lifetime and it couldn't slip away.

In less than 30 minutes the scene changed dramatically. There's 3 cars in the parking garage, doors open, music playing and a small crowd of 20 people. Danielle approaches him from the crowd "What's up nicca?" She was clearly intoxicated on cognac and ex-pills.

"I'm in motion momie, you good?"

"You don't have no time for me poppi", before she got too emotional D'Juan kept it movin.

"I'll holla later" leaving her with a frown on her face.

As he sat behind the wheel of his supra he noticed the Acura was nowhere in sight. He hopped out quickly in rage "bitch where is my cah?" He barked, causing her to spill her drink. "Oh that's just yours now? Fuck you D'Juan", she snaps back.

Immediately he checked his temper and didn't want to cause a bigger scene. That night she did him a favor and removed herself from the picture. He took the keys from her Gucci purse and didn't mind being the bad guy. He knew if he was soft for Danielle, she would take it for weakness.

Driving down Carlson Blvd. He spotted the Rose colored Acura Legend, shining from it's pearl gloss to the chrome rims. "Ain't this a ....." He cursed himself for trusting a snake. However, he knew the solution to this problem.

He speed races to Clinton Hill, hitting the horn as he pulled outside his Pa' joint. "Juelz " he yells as he opens the screen gate. "Yeah" he yells from the backroom.. "Brodi I need you real quick," he opens the door to find they're fully dressed to step out.

"We are about to go catch the kings of comedy at the pavilion."

"That's what's up. Me and my shorty tryna do something like that too. Come help me get the Acc right from the J.F.K projects." Juelz looked in confusion but D'Juan insisted he not ask.

They pulled the Acura in their Pa' garage and D'Juan immediately freshen up. After a 10 minute shower, he slid in some Polo jeans, button up long sleeve and laced up some Timbs. His wrist, necklace and ear-rings complimented his 16 gold and diamond teeth. Juelz had two extra tickets and the timing was perfect. Aiisha expected to go somewhere nice, so she copped a casual crop top, velour pants and suede heels from Bloomingdales.

"Juelz call this number 510-222-1005 ext. 301." Juelz dialed the number on his Motorola flip phone and handed it to D'Juan. Aiisha answered after the second ring and was told to be waiting in the front. As of no surprise, she shined bright as a Diamond. Smiling at the sight of D'Juan as he stepped out the back seat looking like a star. "Get in Ma, this our chauffeur for the night." They share smiled as he assist her into the Denali truck. "Hi" she introduced herself "My apologies, Aiisha this is Jamelia, and Jamelia this is Princess Aiisha, and you remember big head."

"Who can forget your big brother always wetting us with balloons. What's up punk?" She jokingly pushes Juelz head.

"Aye, aye, I'll take my belt off..."

They laughed and shared childhood memories all the way to the Hayward Pavilion. This being their first comedy venue no one really knew what to expect. Judging by the class of boss players and madam divas, the night would be epic.

The street was blocked off, traffic jammed around two blocks and the only available parking was a garage 4 blocks away. The night was young and warm, the stars were illuminating, and the air was fresh. Aiisha squeezed D'Juan's hand and smiled with great expectations. It was a 30 to 40 minute wait before the doorman told them what section they would be seated. The first comedian, D.L. Hughley was minutes from kicking off the show. "Y'all want something to drink?" Juelz asked.

"Just water please, me too" both ladies responded.

"Kid, lets rock" he tapped D'Juan on the shoulder before he got comfortable.

"Ahh, a'ight. You volunteering water boy. Only my brother"

"Oh you got jokes huh? nah kid, I just know how to treat a woman" D'Juan smirked and laughed inside.

Occupying the bar was Too Short, Mack Magic Mike, Calvin T and E-40 with an entourage of beautiful and provocative dressed women. "Those are Boss Playaz, nah mean. Let's holla at my peoples." D'Juan approaches a Rich City legend, "Magic what iz it?"

"Nah, not the Kid. You are always in the spotlight young mackin", they shake hands as on-lookers snap pictures.

"No doubt, I learned from the best"

The game was pure when real players played it right. And as he said, when it came down to making millions of cash money they were the best.

D'Juan leans on the bar and requests two bottles of Dom Perignon. He seized the opportunity while the bar tenders had their eyes on a dozen thoroughbred strip teasers, "Keep the change" dropping 600 dollars and pushed off in a hurry.

They returned to their seats with smiles and beverages for the ladies who were enjoying the show. One by one the Kings of comedy captivated the audience and represented. Full off two bottles of vintage champagne, D'Juan and Aiisha couldn't wait to smoke some haze and end their night at a seafood restaurant. The night was definitely still young...

Chapter 9

As hot as a summer day gets it's just as cold at night. It's 10:45 p.m. Santonio and Slim pulls in a Roscoe's Chicken and Waffles parking lot. A burgundy Yukon truck is pulling out of its parking space. It suddenly stops with the driver side obscured from Santonio's view (Door Opens). Reacting on instincts and considering the location they bounced out with weapons drawn. (Shots Fired) more than a dozen rounds were exchanged within 8 feet between Oschino and Santonio. Slim made his way around the truck and behind Oschino as he advanced on Santonio. (Shots Fired) five 45 caliber Teflon slugs pierced Oschino's vest but Santonio was down. Slim rushes to his side and helps him to the back seat "ahh" he moaned in pain. "Breathe easy brodi we gone be at the hospital in a minute" Slim alerts while maneuvering through traffic. They pulled in the E.R. slamming the brake.

"Aye I need help. My brother has been shot, he's bleeding from his face" Slim yells at a medic. The intensity in his voice gained immediate attention. Upon first glance at Santonio's wounds they rush him to emergency surgery

When the medic turned to asked questions concerning the shooting, Slim was gone. He made it back to the one way with both drivers side windows shot out and four holes in the passenger door. Rocky and Dorian seen the beat up Cadillac North Star as it pulled in the apartments. They drew their weapons and ensured he wasn't followed. With Rocky on look out, Dorian walks back to Slim "what happened to y'all?"

"We saw old boy and Lil bro got caught in a crossfire. He took one to the face and chest, but he'll be a'ight." Dorian inhales and look to the sky before letting out his frustration.

"Fuck" ...

"Ole boy up outta here though" Slim says boastfully.

Dorian looked back at Slim and told him to page D'Juan A.S.A.P.

Juelz, D'Juan, Jamelia and Aiisha was at T.G.I. Friday in Jack London Square when they seen two helicopters in the air. One was paramedic and the other was police. The high beam lights from the ghetto bird lit up the Broadway strip, looking for suspects. It was an unusual sight and a good time to lay back, enjoy the view of the Bay and feed each other fried prawns. The water was calm, and one could see clear across to San Francisco pier. A few ships, fisherman boats and seagulls were under or around the Bay Bridge. On cue "floating on your love" by the Isley Brothers plays from the juke box. D'Juan pulled Aiisha closer to his chest "ma-ma, I want you to do something for me" she looked up at him for clarity. He smiled at the smirk on her face. "Nah, not that, not now at least."

She smile and shakes her head "you crazy. But what can I do for you poppi?"

"Seriously I want you to hear my heart beating" upon request she places her ear on his chest.

"Wow, amazing. I never even heard my father's heartbeat."

He rubs her face and looked into her eyes "I'm not going out ever disappoint you, A'ight." They share eye contact followed by an intimate kiss.

"Aye lil bro, get a room." Juelz chuckles.

"Good idea it's about that time anyway." D'Juan said, reaching for his pager. Apparently it's been off since he took his keys from Danielle. "Juelz let me see yo line."

Immediately after making contact, D'Juan whole demeanor changed "What's good kid?" "Shhh" He holds one finger up while being the recipient of bad news "Give me the number...4377 Aight." D'Juan hung up before Butch Cozie could say bye. After that call, the night of laughter and romance was over.

It was 3:15 a.m. Back in the hotel, D'Juan had been laying on his back starring at the ceiling for the past hour. The uncertainty of Santonio's condition made him restless. Aiisha rubbed his chest and let him think in silence. At break of dawn, he met with Slim and got a first hand account of what happened. Interestingly enough, he heard the gunshots while dining at TGI Friday. "Wow, yo we saw the ghetto birds" D'Juan recalls the whole night.

"Shit was wild.. brodi good, but Ole boy" Slim shook his head.

"You sho, you took care of that?"

"He threw with money kid. I'll bet my gun on it" he assures.

"Yo, I saw the paramedic chopper and somebody was definitely airlifted. We gotta be sure, nah'mean."

Slim was too prideful to doubt himself but reality was a body that's dead on arrival don't get the privilege of flying anywhere. Oschino was like a fat cat with many lives. Could he have had a vest on? Did he survive a shot to the head from a 45? D'Juan couldn't sleep until those questions were answered.

Dorian met Richie, with an emergency demand for guns. The pawn shop owner was happy to see him because it always meant big business. Over a 3 year period Dorian operated as the connection from arms dealers to the gangsters in the streets. Talk about a fatal connection. They played pool discussing business "Rich, the Asians need some heavy artillery. Their family is migrating this way, so their empire is expanding." Rich walks around the table before lining up his shot. "What do they need?" He asked, straight to the point.

"5 crates." Dorian awaits his response with his pool stick resting on his shoulder.

"That sounds like war, but hell. As long as they keep that shit among their people, I don't give a shit." He ponders on so many assault rifles hitting the streets overnight. They continue, "It'll be 50 grand and they'll have to buy their own ammunition."

"Lock it in. That's a done deal." They finish their game of a 9 ball and shake hands.

Later that night Dorian and D'Juan met at Malik's. Hakeem and Rashaad were recording in the basement. It was a full house. Tydus recorded hours of footage, switching batteries into the late hours to keep the film rolling. Freestyle Saturday featured some of Richmond's hottest artists, to ever breathe on a Microphone. Flawless, D-ski Hendrix, The Jacka, Johnny Cash, Laroo, Lil Ric, Ralph Sleeze, B Dub, Fed-X, Davi Danker and Nio the Gift crammed in a room well beyond maximum capacity. The session was definitely heated but the real business was happening upstairs. D'Juan rest assured Topaz would be ready when they were.

"A'ight hit 'em and tell him next Saturday."

"Will do first thing. In the meantime we need some confirmation."

Dorian indicates with his hand he needed to say no more.

As they spoke, Rocky was at John Muir trauma unit. To nurses he was Santonio's Uncle and to the doctors he was Oschino's brother. Whatever it took, he was on the job. Fortunately Santonio made it through surgery and would just be on bed rest for a few weeks. When he opened his eyes Rocky was there. He did most of the talking, breaking the recent news.

"You lucky boi. Nurses said you was this close to no longer being amongst the living" he demonstrates less than an inch. Heavily sedated on morphine, Santonio could only grunt. "If anyone visits you, tell 'em you can't remember nothing. And oh, you ain't gotta worry about ole boy no more." Santonio tried to smile only managing a wince. Rocky walked out the hospital, passing two more gunshot victims and proclaims, "God is great.."

D'Juan and Aiisha was up first thing Monday morning looking for a place to live. The 6 month lease on the Townhome was up in less than two weeks. Considering the recent events it was no way he would rest easy on the flats. After a few open houses, and walkthroughs, Aiisha made the final decision on a penthouse in Hilltop Bayview. Not far from his Ma Christi and brother Lala. He marveled at her decision, calling her his Angel. With the thought she had in his head he could only imagine what his adversaries thought.

That Thursday Razor, Izreal, Silas and Lala helped them move. Starting at 5a.m., they had every piece of furniture and boxes in the penthouse by noon. He'd never seen Richmond as clear until he moved from the flatland. There was the good life of material wealth, extravagant trips, and wild sex on a 30th floor balcony. However the flip side was bloodshed, betrayal, and life in prison. Rich City was full of talent but very little opportunity. In the underworld, a 15 year old being raised in poverty can feel resentment. Just a matter of time before he takes what he believes is owed to him...

Chapter 10

F RIDAY MORNING D'JUAN GAVE Aiisha the keys to his Acura Legend, or tried to at least. "I'm good, I am not driven that car." She disapproved of the idea.

"Ma this my whip, I want you to drive."

"Then what? You know she gon' be illen," giving further thought she was right. He appreciated her honesty, and class. "A'ight well we gotta get you a whip after this move." Aiisha was deep in her thoughts. Then she released what was on her chest.

"D'Juan look at me" he gives her his undivided attention. "I was raped by my Uncle when I was 15. That's why I moved to Clearlake."

He was lost for words, so he did the best thing and just listened. "I wanted to kill that mother-fucker and burn him up with all his money. He got to pay for that shit."

D'Juan held her tight as her eyes watered. "I'm here now momie, don't worry about anything. I got you."

She had hostile intentions and wasn't thinking clear. He held her in his arms, kissing her forehead and wiping away tears as they rolled down her cheeks. They laid on the floor for 40 minutes in complete silence.

How could he relate to such a tragedy? She was damaged according to the Muslim tradition, in being robbed of her virginity before marriage.

Although she would never forgive her uncle, D'Juan hoped she could forgive herself. He looked down at her as she falls into a light sleep. He kisses her forehead again and held her tighter. "I don't want you to ever leave me D'Juan. Don't never let no one come in between us. You can have who you want, I'm always yo ride or die. A'ight Habibi." Although he didn't respond, how could he disagree with that. She knew her position and wasn't going to lose it by being insecure or disobedient.

However as much of a gentleman he could be at times, his focus was occupied by material things. "Momie, I wanna tell you a story. You listening?" She nodded indicating yes.

"My uncle's, Santana and Kaboobi was multi-millionaires in the 80's. They had half a million dollar homes, eighty thousand dollar sport cars, the furs, the respect. They'd lost friends and relatives to the dope game, but you know what hurt them the most?" She shook her head.

"What you saying D'Juan, is money your heart?" She asked with concern.

"No, no, no, momie you are not hearing me. You want to hurt a man full of pride. Take what he covets. He'll feel dead already." Aiisha jumped to her knees "Let's go right now." She was determined to get her revenge.

After a brief smile, they spent the next 10 minutes getting dressed. He slips on Brown Army Fatigue pants, Black Timberland hoodie and Black and Beige Timbs. She just slipped in some Jordan's, and was ready. He directed her to change into something dark but casual. "You don't wanna look like a cat burglar." He shook his head and smiled.

"Shut-up just bring yo gun." She leads the way mumbling and cursing, premeditating her first chance at revenge.

It was a short drive to Lancaster Dr. The sun was beaming, it was quiet, no kids playing in the streets and Aiisha's Uncle Omar was apparently gone to work. From where they parked they could see clear up the block. After scoping the joint he notices there was only one stoplight in between Omar's crib and Izreal's spot in Parchester Village; approximately 5 minutes flat.

Aiisha was emotional and growing impatient. What she didn't know she don't need to know. 'Ain't no banshee gone be the death of me' he thought to himself. Omar worked Tuesday through Saturday from somewhere around 4 a.m. to 4 p.m. and it was 5:30 a.m. Aiisha was asleep when D'Juan slipped out of bed and picked up Izzy. He'd left the back door of his crib unlocked so they can re-enter without waking up his Nana. Upon hopping in the Acura, it was brief smiles and the rest was business. Their minds was clear and free of intoxicants.

Izreal was no amateur when it came to burglarizing homes so D'Juan figures the job should be quick. He walks up to the backyard gate and disappears, 15-20 minutes passed. D'Juan trusts his boys skills and sat patient. The plan was to get inside and unlock the front door. As the sun rises some 45 minutes later, D'Juan walks up to the house, leaving the car running. (Sound of fence breaking) Long behold it was Izreal, running pass him with two pillowcases in hand, dropping stacks of cash with every stride. D'Juan follows his steps cleaning up the money trail and last making it to the car. He looked over to Izzy "We good?"

"Hell yeah, that's at least 100 racks" D'Juan leaned back in the passenger seat, put his Gloc 40 on his lap and watches the rearview.

They make it safely to Parchester Village just in time for breakfast. Mrs. Cartagena knocked on Izzy's door while the rubber band stacks were being counted and separated. "Izreal, honey I made you some grits, eggs, and biscuits."

"A'ight Nana, I'm just gettin up"

"Okay, come on while it's still hot." Mrs. Cartagena was a strong believer in eating a good meal to start the day. One can't be sure when they'll eat again.

"She be buzzen sometimes brodi" Izreal shook his head and continues to count. "You blessed to have her Izzy" D'Juan gave him a look of sincerity. "Yeah, I guess you right kid. But aye, who was ole boy." "Some cat named Big O, I don't know."

Izreal stopped counting. "From the triangle?"

D'Juan shrugged his shoulders. "Does it matter?"

"Hell yeah we gotta watch that shady ma'fucka."

D'Juan never heard of the name but he did acknowledge the Iron triangles sudden incline in wealth and gun violence. It was as if they came out of nowhere. He wasn't too worried though. He had a Gloc with two 30 round mags.

"Just keep yo shit and squeeze first, nah mean."

"Come on kid you know me. Everything I like is pretty. Pretty ladies with pretty pussies, pretty shoes and pretty guns." They share laughs and divide the stacks.

The split was 60/40 D'Juan taking the smaller half. He never minded breaking bread and besides, without Izzy the play wouldn't have been as smooth.

They smoked an eight of haze after eating breakfast. With a full stomach and 20 grand in each pocket D'Juan drives home thinking about what he'll do to Aiisha. She gets out a steamy hot shower and air dried before slipping into her silk robe. He watches as she dries her long, jet black curly hair, and wraps it in a silk headscarf. Her wide hips and apple bottom was complimented by a small waist. Every time D'Juan looked at her he wondered how she had grown to be so beautiful. "Um, um, um," he commented. She jumps and hits the light switch, "got's to be more careful."

"Habibi you scared me, don't do that please." He laughs. "I wasn't trying to scare you momie, I apologize. I'm just admiring your beauty." She smiled and poses with her hand on her hip. "Whatever you like, you got it King."

"Get your fine ass over here."

Her body moved to the rhythm of his heartbeat. She laid on his chest as he discuss their business in Chicago. Her focus was on getting paid, but he stressed on not getting pinched. He expected her to carry 20 pounds of Haze in her carry-on bags. She was to travel back to Seattle in the next week with his brother Juelz. Upon arrival he would get her a college I.D., Amtrak tickets, and show her how to pack her luggage. D'Juan had some business to attend to in Richmond but he promised to be with her on the trip to Chicago. She felt even more confident in being a transporter by the end of their discussion. He was sure to keep revenge at her forethoughts as motivation for a successful trip. Before walking out the door on other business, he dropped 57 grand on the bed. "Count it." He wanted her to be comfortable with seeing and counting a lot of money. It had already been proven, he could trust someone with his life but not with his money.

Dorian had his Chevy Blazer loaded with 4 crates, parked out front of Slim's spot on S.49th (lighter strikes) "I heard ole boy made it out last night." Dorian told Slim as he put fire to a backwood stuffed with haze. Slim listened in disbelief. "Wow".

"He probably in The City. I sat on him before up in Potrero Hill, I'll go check it out ASAP..."

"I'm gone let Pharaoh know too. The enemy of our enemy is our closest friend." Slim nodded in agreement. As they discussed street politics, D'Juan pulled up in his Toyota Supra. He and Dorian inventoried the artillery and headed out to meet Topaz. Slim and Silas were headed in the opposite direction, crossing the Bay bridge into San Francisco.

"Doe I was thinking about reconnecting with the China White connect back in Harlem." "Yeah we haven't had any since that last trip you made. It'll definitely make us famous again."

"Fa' real, cause I'm thinking after this drop we can't really count on Hop or his people." Dorian agreed as much.

Transporting became less popular and more dangerous over the past couple years. After giving further thought, Dorian just needed to know how he did it. D'Juan grinned then pointed to his head "I used my head kid."

Dorian leaned back, shook his head and smiled. He knew he wouldn't tell him everything, but he didn't tell him anything. The kid was sharp. He knew not to ever tell because someone could be listening and besides game is to be sold, not told.

D'Juan usually traveled to see his grandmother at the end of the summer and that time was near. Dorian thought if Santana trusted him, who was he not to. After all, Santana was still their boss. First thing first, they focused on the deal at hand. Topaz younger brother opened the gate to their backyard. Dorian backed the Blazer in, until signaled to stop. (Doors

Open.) "Aye Paso" D'Juan greeted them, and they returned the love with open arms.

"No, Pablo." Topaz directed to unlock the crate while he and D'Juan talked about his homeland in Mexico City. "You come down, it's something to see aye. Mansions of naked putahs, mountains of pot, and jungles of exotic pets." He said with pride.

"We'll see Hop." As a traveler, the kid would never turn down an invitation. "It's good Poppa." Pablo shouted. Topaz showed signs of embarrassment. "I know its good dumb asses, just put 'em in the garage like I asked you." They talked for a few more minutes, drank two shots of Tequila and the deal was finished. Fineto.

Their next stop was to Kaboobi's to pick up their 45 grand. Since Topaz met D'Juan through him he was entrusted with the money. Likewise, he would be responsible if anything went bad. So quite naturally Hakeem and Rashaad watched the deal from a far to ensure the deal went smooth.

While Dorian counted the money, D'Juan shared his idea of hooking back up with the East Coast. Kaboobi leaned in close so he could hear "listen to me nephew. My brother in the FEDS is doing a life sentence behind that China White. That's not something to take lightly. Do you not remember?" D'Juan listened carefully while acknowledging he remembers "Look it here...You got a mouth full of gold teeth with Diamonds in 'em. You look like a D-Boy. And not only that, you smell like one. What teenager you know wears Chanel #5 and not a dope dealer?"

And that's why he's the Ghost...When the kid last traveled he had the appearance of a school kid. That has changed now, so his game plan would have to be a little tighter...

"I'm going back in a few weeks to check on Nana Nina anyway. If it ain't good, I'll let it be" he assessed wisely and Kaboobi agreed on that approach.

Hakeem and Rashaad had Butch Cozie Joint rolling like a MGM Casino. They sold nothing less than 35 dollars grams, making a thousand dollars every hour. Izreal was the general of the foot soldiers. He brought energy back to the streets. From S.35th to 39, he kept it lit. The hustler moving the product was just as important as the product itself. Drug addicts wanted a good fix, but most important Izzy related to their struggle. With a junky for a mother and father doing life in prison, he was raised by half his clientele.

Hakeem and Rashaad parked their candy coated Cutlass and SS Monte Carlo on Cutting Blvd. attracting more traffic. The Globe' expanded to a 20 block radius within a year.

Rocky and Silas had been back and forth to the city and still no sighting of Oschino. They spent their days in the shade and nights hiding in bushes or under cars. Who could sleep with murder on their minds? A question was left unanswered, but for how long only time will tell...

Aiisha called her cousin Angle inquiring about their uncle. Ever since her old wounds were re-opened she'd convinced herself there was only one way to heal them. To close that chapter permanently. Angel advised her to see a counselor or get some therapy and don't even sweat it. Reasoning one day he'll rape a girl with AIDS or go to prison and be raped himself. They joked and laughed at the image of Omar being bent over, sleeping a long T-Shirt and made to be somebodies fuck boy. In all seriousness the idea of sending him to hell first class was even better. D'Juan could tell she was troubled, so he spent more time with her than usual. All week it was her world with him just living in it. They enjoyed bowling, Ice Skating, a movie at drive in theater, picnic at Golden Gate Park, whatever she wanted. It was his pleasure to please her. They spent the weekend shopping at the Lexus auto mall, Victoria Secret and Christian Dior outlets. With qualities of a boss lady, she must look up to par. Besides, she earned it.

It was Friday, the last day of summer school. Aiisha pulled up to Kennedy High in a 95' a coke white LS 450. She stepped out in a red Prada dress with black Jimmy Choo open toe heels. Early morning gossip circulated like a Rich City minute. It was no secret who was D'Juan's number one, and the more Danielle thought about it, the more her emotions took control. Jannah was the first to be cursed out, being the bearer of bad news. Tears rolled down her check as she waited for the first period class to end. The bell couldn't have rung soon enough. She was ashamed and angry but the sad part was she could only blame herself. A reality she wasn't going to accept. (Bell rang out)

Danielle went mad, bursting through Mr. Campbell's door with rage, she rushes Aiisha "Bitch!" She yells, leaping and grabbing at her face. They tussled falling over desks and pulling at each other cloths. Danielle had a mean right cross, causing damage to the left side of Aiisha's face. However, Aiisha's long powerful legs and one horse kick to the stomach was the deciding blow. Danielle buckled, gasping for air. Aiisha spit blood in her face and taunted, while pressing six inch stiletto heels in her jaw. "Don't you ever in yo life you bitch."

Schools security saved Danielle from further humiliation. As they were being separated, multiple idle threats were made against Aiisha's life. She just laughed, "Take ya ponytail with you lil momma." Spectators got a show worth paying for. A bloody fight and a lot of stripping.

The school's principal Mrs. Cheney tried counseling the two young ladies. They were both good students and expected to have promising futures. She'd known D'Juan Placencia since Verde Elementary school and her opinion of him hadn't changed. He was just trouble, and there she was again cleaning up his mess. She was adamantly clear, that if they continued to be interested in guys like D'Juan, they'll both be dead or pregnant by the end of the year. One thing Mrs. Cheney said resonated with a lot of truth: the love for money and this material world has our young men chasing dreams and getting high to escape reality. An education is the only way to make it in the real world.

Aiisha was committed to ride with D'Juan through thick and thin. The true question, was she really ready to die before experiencing the quality of life?

Jannah paged D'Juan 911, 911. He and Izzy were in the Globe cooking and weighing cocaine. After the process was complete he returned the page.

(Phone Rings) "Hello,"

"Peace and blessings Jannah"

"Peace and Blessings sir. You need to get it together." She said with resentment

"Speak, what's on your mind."

"You know them girls were fighting over you today. You wrong brother" obviously he didn't know what was really going on but not hearing from Aiisha definitely had him concerned. "What are you talkin bout?"

"You know Danielle is fucking crazy. She straight up flipped when she seen Aiisha pull up in a new Lexus." She then explained the drama that followed

After hearing a brief lecture he interrupted her, "with all due respect ma, my bizness is my bizness. I don't fuck with Danielle and Aiisha a be a'ight." He said with aggression.

"I just don't understand, what do you see in those kinds of girls?"

'Walah' the real issue became evident. She was really feeling the kid. "Look ma, I'm in the middle of something... I might tell you later just keep that thought on ya mind. Peace" She giggles before responding "Peace" ...

Immediately after, he'd received a page from Aiisha "look at this shit here brodi. I'm out". He then holstered his Glock 40. under his arm.

"All is well?" Izzy asked, momentarily putting down his cigarillo.

"Yeah it's good, Danielle and my shorty cat fighting at the K"

"Good luck with that one buddy." Izzy said sarcastically while shaking his head.

Juelz was packing for the drive to Seattle. He enjoyed Jamelia's company and made living arrangements for them both. It seems Mr. tender below the zipper couldn't sleep without her by his side. She just graduated from with a 3.8 GPA, 4 star recruit for track and field committed to Washington State University on a full ride. It brought joy to the family in knowing he at least had a chance to escape the dangerous consequences of the street life. Only the most high knew the grief their family had to endure over the past decade.

Tito sat down with his boys and explained some valuable lessons "get your smarts, no one can ever take that away from you. Use your talents to open doors of opportunity and remember knowledge will expand your perception." "Yes poppa. Sometimes, I wish mi Hermano stayed in Harlem. Maybe he'll be going to college too." Juelz then looks over to D'Juan.

"Don't do that to yourself Mijo. You've been an excellent role model. D'Juan will be fine, I'm sure of it. He has his destiny and you yours, It's just how life is Mijo." He explains.

Anytime their father spoke it was words of wisdom. Even when it appeared D'Juan wasn't listening he was. After playing a few games of chess, Tito locked himself in his office, and Juelz continued packing. "I love you big brother. I got to check on shorty, peace king." D'Juan announced before walking out the door. "Peace."

Aiisha met him at the door with fire in her heart "Where the fuck you been? Didn't you get my messages?"

"Breathe easy momie I missed you." He looked into her eyes captivating her soul. "How was your day?" He asked cool, calm and collected.

"Ooh" she stomps the floor then storms into the bedroom, with him not far behind. "shorty what's wrong?" Taking a few deep breaths she responded as if exhausted, "I had to beat that little crazy bitch ass today D'Juan." He then pulled her to his chest in attempts to console her. "Yeah, talk to poppa."

"She punched me a few times, but you should see her though." He listened as she shared her version of events, only laughing when she explained how scarring Danielle's jaw made her feel. She taunted her not being worthy of king in dominant fashion. After she was done venting he brought smiles to her face and massaged her shoulders to ease tension.

Hot water filled the bath tub of African Fantasy scented oils and bubbles. She compliment his mannerism, appreciating how he made her feel special (cork popping) "The night is still young my queen." He handed her a box of See's chocolate covered strawberries and poured Dom Perignon into two champagne glasses.

"Indeed it is my king" she responded with a seductive smile. Sitting opposite ends of the tub, he admired her unselfishness, "Let's toast to this journey" she proposed..

"No doubt indeed" (Glasses Clink). After licking the chocolate with the tip of her tongue she shared the first strawberry. On cue he pressed play on the stereo systems remote control, "A mission to please by the Isley Brothers featuring Ron Isley set off the fireworks. His best kept surprise was the 5 karat tennis bracelet hidden in the box.

As D'Juan and Aiisha's romance heated up practically overnight, Omar was hot on the trail of the Rican kids that burglarized his crib. The surveillance footage showed a clear shot of Izzy's head as he climbed through a bathroom window. The sound of the gate breaking didn't help either. Awakening neighbors who provided detailed descriptions of two Latinos fleeing on feet. Only a few experienced house bandits fit those descriptions so the process of elimination would be quick and simple.

He first figured to call in a favor from a well-respected, young hustler from the North side. He pulled up on Sanford Ave. against the flow of traffic "Phats, check it out for a minute." He was signaled to pull over.

"You know it's hot out here right now, what's good?" Phats asked with his head on a swivel. "Aye you seen little Le'el lately?"

"Huh?" He was reluctant to give any information, seeing Omar was heated about something.

"Somebody broke in my joint and took something I want back"

"Ahh, Nah I ain't seen him. He probably in the jects" then Phats back onto the sidewalk focusing on oncoming traffic. Omar leans out the window asking one last question,

"Do he still have braids?"

Phats remembers when he lost all his money in a raid and Omar fronted a kilo with no interest, so as a favor he spared Omar his life. "Like I said, I ain't seen him. But I know he didn't have nothing to do with that." Phats then waved his hand jesting Omar to keep it moving. He processed the information as he drove across the train tracks and into Central Richmond...

The nickel block had been hot all summer, with squad cars parked from 1st and McDonald to 4th and Ripley. So when Omar pulled alongside two of Author Moe's soldiers they were on high alert, "what's up wit this ma'fucka?" Rico thought out loud before rolling down the window. Zeek grips the Mac-10 on his lap. "What iz it?" Rico ask.

Simultaneously, Omar had his finger on an A.K 47. "Where's Rio?" He asked sharply.

"Mario? He been in Y.A. for a year now."

"Tell him I said keep his head up and see me when he come home."

"A'ight fasho" Rico said nodding his head, while Zeek clinched his teeth. Omar showed a mischievous grin before cruising off in his Grey Chevelle. From there his focus became Young Magic and Izzy, both from the same neighborhood. The F.K boys had the Globe' locked down like a fortress. Without help from the inside, that would be a dead end.

Sunday morning, birds chirping and air so fresh D'Juan could taste it. Aiisha's Louis Vuitton luggage was packed, and she was ever ready. Juelz and Jamelia pulled out front hitting the horn twice.

"Be with you shortly my queen." D'Juan kisses her forehead and sends her out the door with a slap on her apple bottom "sheesh." He compliments the bounce. She smiled walking into the morning sun rays wearing pink Prada pajama pants, grey tank top, grey and pink Air Max tennis shoes. They had a 12 hour drive ahead, which seemed like an eternity without her beloved.

D'Juan and Dorian had little time to organize. So, first order of business was keeping security tight. Rocky and Slim assigned a dozen foot soldiers to guard the trap houses. Then armed every F.K affiliate. Hakeem, Rashaad and Izzy copped 5 kilos with just half the profits. Selling grams for $35 dollars and ounces for $600 was great for business. The last order of operations concerned the specifics of how they would import and export. Starting with the 20 pounds awaiting in Seattle, WA. Ten would be exported to Chicago and the other ten going back to Rich City. They stood to make 300% profit from the mid-west trip alone, leaving open several other business ventures.

Chapter 11

CARLOS HAD BUSINESS IN order on his end. So soon as the product land, Aiisha would be on the first thing smoking with money in the bag. "Why you not with her?" Rocky and Rashaad expressed their concerns. "No offense little bra, but we don't trust no bitch with our doe."

"You don't need to trust her, you trust me. I got other business to tend to back East a'ight. It's good don't sweat it." After expressing their displeasure, they had another dilemma, similar in nature. Dorian needed a woman to accompany him on the 12 hour drive back, and not just any woman but one who's game tight and had nothing to look forward to. At least for the next 5 to 10 years anyway. The table was open for suggestions, "why not Juicy?" referring to his sister. "She solid, got license, and could be trusted." A few mention with a vote of confidence.

"Nah I can't listen to her mouth for twenty minutes left alone twelve hours."

"Shadonje is the only one left brodi. She young, but she a hustla from the neighborhood." Hakeem suggest, adding she could be coached by Juicy while taking all the risk.

Dorian pondered on the idea, "Keemi Bo, get her on the phone. Tell her to be ready in an hour."

"A'ight I'm on it." Hakeem returned after a couple minutes. "She say it's good, just give her a Grand up front and two zips when y'all get back."

"Tell her I'm on my way now."

"And I just got word Lil Tone came home this morning. He requested to see you." Sharing a brief smile, Dorian rest his hand on D'Juan shoulder. "A'ight, I'll swing by there before we dip out. You and Rock, put something together for him; gifts, and whatever else. Just keep it private." He emphasize only familia..

"Fa sure."

By 7:50 p.m. D'Juan, Dorian and Shadonje were pulling into Oakland International Airport parking lot, listening to Jay-Z's 'Can't Knock The Hustle.'

Meanwhile Danielle was bitter as an old lemon. She threw bricks busting the windows out of the Townhome, before realizing it was vacant. D'Juan changed his pager number and was seldom seen in Rich City. She was desperately seeking attention from a ghost. Jannah even tried taking her on double dates with educated young gentlemen, star athletes, and fly by the night playas. No matter how many men entered her bedroom, she still felt jaded.

Tydus was walking out of Ron's liquor store to his car as Danielle crossed the street. "What are you doing out here so late?" Looking at his guess watch, then back at her.

"I'm about to get some swisher's, what's up?" She asked walking up to his chest.

"It's my birthday and I want you to have a drink with me. You'll be the first I celebrate with." He offers a party package as well.

"Um, I guess I'm cool with that. You have always been my folks." She returned a smile then follows him back into the store. "What do you want now my friend?" Akmed asked. "Give me a 'Beautiful' for the young lady" he then looked at Danielle "a box of swishers."

Akmed complete this transaction then jokingly throws a box of condoms on the counter. "On the house" he smiled at Tydus who was feeling like the man. He'd Just copped a Grand National super sport sitting on 21' chrome rims and stacked a half a million dollars. Finding humor in Akmed joke, he entertained the idea. "Never know right." They share laughs.

It was 1 a.m. and Dru Hill's 12 step was in the deck. Danielle was enjoying the comforts of the heated passenger seat, while rolling a blunt and sipping the 'beautiful'. An alcoholic beverage of Remy Martin, Grand Marnier, and Peach liqueur. After turning off Carlson Blvd. They were in front of his spot behind Crescent Park Village. It was no question what his intentions were, but Danielle was no fool. "I'm feeling it" indicating she was passed tipsy.

"Danny I heard that pum is tight."

"It is, it's wet too. You want to taste it?" She teases; unbuttoning her pants watching his eyes as they were keyed on her c- cups."

"6ty 9?" He suggests.

"I'm down."

She felt the wad of bills in his front pocket while pulling his pants down. Motivation for given him a sensation only a professional deep throat could fulfil. He would cum less than 5 minutes, then she sat up and rode his face for another 10 minutes. She had multiple orgasms as he maneuvered his tongue from her booty to pussy hole. When blood rushes back to his manhood, she rode him from back to front. As he was ready to cum she timed it perfectly. With a sudden movement, she had his penis in hand, ejaculating it onto his stomach and shirt. His first instinct was to toss her out and into the street. But being the player he was, he laughed about it and promised to get her back on the next one..

Full of liquor and the taste of Danielle sweetness, it was a hell of a start to his special day. He returned home and hit the bed like a brick. 'The darker the berry the sweeter the juice' he thought to himself bringing a smile. Not waking up until noon with a mad headache and nearly four grand lighter. "Aww, wow" slapping himself as the big willie player that got played...

Seattle, Washington. Home of the Seahawks and Supersonics to most. Then to others it's the underworld of Pot Farmers and College life. The atmosphere was beautiful. With old fashioned homes being a staple of peaceful suburban areas, and giant trees being the cause of fresh air.

Juelz had a Duplex within 5 miles from Washington University. Shadonje pulled the 1995 Intrepid, a rental from the Airport into his garage port at 9 a.m.

"Ahhh" one by one they exited stretching their limbs. "We not gone be long. Shadonje, shower, eat and get a couple hours of rest. By noon we want to be hittin the road" Dorian instructed.

"Yes sir boss" sarcastically speaking.

They followed D'Juan up the stairs. Three knocks on the door echoed throughout the house. "Habibi" Aiisha opens the door and literally jumps into his arms "I missed you already yo" she said, squeezing tightly around his neck.

He carried her to the kitchen enjoying the warmth of her body. "I missed you even more my queen. Where is brodi?" He gestures it wasn't the time for pleasure .

"He'll be back in a minute. Ameere out here or something like that. He said you'll know who I'm talking about and where to find him."

"A'ight cool we right on point. Did you eat anything yet?"

"Habibi I just woke up" she could sense the urgency in his voice.

"Show her where the shower is. Me and Doe gotta run. Be ready by noon we gotta train to catch."

"Okay, come on Donje."

While they freshened up and prepared mentally, Dorian and D'Juan headed off to Ameere's spot. He had a four bedroom home with a barn and shed in the backyard just outside of Tacoma. His Cadillac North Star and Lincoln Navigator were parked out front. Juelz was in the kitchen making fried eggs and beef sausage with Swiss and Jack cheese sandwiches when he heard two taps on the window, "Who dat?" Ameere asked.

"It's The Kid, you know the drill" Ameere opened the door with a proper greeting of peace and blessing. "Ahh, just on time boi. I had a move up for 13 p's of Jack, but I know y'all wanted first bid" they followed him into the lounge a.k.a. the don room. "No doubt indeed, this what we came for" D'Juan picked up a bud smell.

"Fire some of that shit up. Let me see how it burn." Dorian requested, reaching for his backwood cigars.

"Huh" Ameere tossed and eighth onto the coffee table. "Come on Juan" then he led the way to get 12 pounds of silver haze from the barn. D'Juan couldn't even fathom how many plants he had growing under Godzilla lights. At least 80, standing 7ft. tall, each weighing up to 2 pounds. While admiring a hundred grand stock in equipment, his most valuable asset was the vacuum sealer. No question the smartest investment he could have made. They stopped by the small shed for 8 pounds of Jack Herrera, where Ameere educated him on the cloning process.

Back in the don room they weighed and sealed each pound. The Kings-men specifically ordered silver haze so Dorian would have the privilege in introducing Jack Herrera to Rich City. "How many of these sandwiches y'all want?" Juelz yelled back .

"Aye fam, we need to get moving" Dorian suggested while checking his guess watch. "Indeed y'all set to go. You'll beat the dogs just do the speed limit in town" Ameere advise. Four breakfast sandwiches were hot and wrapped on the table for the taking. "The love is eternal fam. Be careful on that road" Juelz announced before they walked out the door.

D'Juan looked back with the eye of a panther, "I'm gonna survive by any means necessary".

"I know hermano" Juelz admired D'Juan for his courage and ambition...

Aiisha dressed in a Washington Huskies pull over hoodie and sweatpants. Her hair was in a ponytail and her aura shined like a College freshman. With an Eddie Bauer book-bag of contraband over one shoulder and Luggage in the other hand she was in motion. D'Juan stood by her side awaiting their escort to Amtrak. He wore blue and yellow Polo jeans, a matching shirt, a drawback polo hat, and suitcases were his travel luggage. He was out on business and his father taught him well. The most valuable lesson being the ethics of a business man 101.

They arrived at the train station at or around 5 p.m. with less than a hour to burn, Aiisha pulled a Norton's Reader from her book bag and began reading. The autobiographies of famous writers such as Frederick Douglass 'Learning to read' Sherman Alexie 'Superman and me' and Langston Hughes 'salvation', opened her eyes to a realm of new possibilities. She began to believe in herself as D'Juan always told her, she could do anything she put her mind to. She looked up catching eye contact and they shared a smile of admiration.

As the train arrives she gathers her bag and half of a sandwich. The double decker train stopped and released only a handful of passengers.

"All aboard..."

She stepped aboard handing the conductor a ticket for stagecoach. "Okay thank you, I see you'll be stationed in the third coach it seems. Have a pleasant ride." "I hope so thank you" she replied with a smile. D'Juan was stationed in the fourth coach, and with no company was finally able to relax. After an hour or so he decided to check on her.

(Knock on the door) An elder Chinese man answered "excuse me sir I was wondering where the dining car is" D'Juan asked politely

"ahh, I not sure, but I think two cars that way" pointing toward the back of the train. "Thank you peace"

"yeah peace on you too; good bye." The elder man shuts the door complimenting the young man's mannerisms to his wife. Aiisha overheard their conversation and waited a few minutes before heading out toward the dinning coach.

Upon entering the next coach she feels a muscular arm grab her by the neck. Before she could scream, her mouth was covered "ahh, I got you my little bird" D'Juan is humored by her reaction, until she slapped the smile off his face. "That ain't funny. I was really scared."

"A'ight, a'ight, my bad but you need to learn how to reverse a arm bar or something. Never know what monsters you'll face in the world. It's dangerous out there." He stressed.

"ah whatever. You must be lonely. You miss me huh" she smiled seductively,

"No doubt and I'm not gon' be alone the whole ride, so slide through first thing."

"I don't know, I'll think about it" she said, making her butt jiggle while departing.

Aiisha guarded her book-bag with her life, even using it as a pillow. As convenient it may seem to sleep for the next 8 hours, the Asian couple was too energetic for that. They insisted she play a game with them. She didn't mind learning anything new, especially when involving other cultures. Thirty minutes into it she began having fun.

"Hold on okay, I met this boy in the dining coach. I'll be right back" she then ran to D'Juan station and drug him by his sleeve. He had no interest in playing games with strangers, but he wanted her to be comfortable and happy. The Asian couple smiled at the sight of his face "hello" they greeted.

"This is Mr. and Mrs. Chiu, and this is Julian" Aiisha pleasantly introduce, and D'Juan followed suit "It's my pleasure to meet you, so what game is it that has this young lady so excited?" He asked.

"This is checkers, come. Real fun let me show you." He'd never played Chinese checkers before, but it turned out to be a fascinating game. Two and a half hours flew by seeming like it was no more than 30 minutes. "Well excuse me but I have to get some rest, I really appreciate you for inviting me. It's been fun, thank you."

"Okay Julian. Come back anytime." They were all smiles as he exited. Aiisha joined him shortly after, falling right into his arms. Their bodies fit perfect when together, like they were made for each other.

At first he thought he wanted to relieve some tension then his big head gained control, business first. "Listen to what I'm telling you, it's important. Auntie Monese will be waiting in the plaza at McDonald's. She has a thing for fries and milkshakes. You'll embrace her like you're her daughter. If you're hungry order to go. If I don't follow you, just continue as instructed. Now, repeat what I just said" Stressing the importance of maintaining a calm genuine demeanor. And to his delight she repeated him word for word with a smile "I always listen to Habibi."

"As you should my queen. I would never mislead you. Auntie well-seasoned too. Had a lot of success in her transporting days" he explained. Then gave her a forehead kiss assuring he'll be with her soon. She went back to her coach and rested her eyes.

D'Juan leaned back looking out at the Colorado Rocky Mountains. In his reflection was a young man who has yet to find purpose. Although he travels, his destination was uncertain. He dozes off with his head against the window until a woman with two children opens the station door. "Hola I'm Gabriella. Sorry to wake you" she introduced herself kindly.

"Hola madam, I'm Julian. I was just taking a nap out of boredom. Please never mind.. I needed the company," he returned a friendly smile and offers assistance.

The Children dropped their guards after being aided by this young man. Not taking offense as he and their beautiful mother was holding a pleasant conversation. Attracted by her eloquent speech, it was her hazel green eyes flickering warning signs. If he didn't know any better it seemed too much like right. "Where are you from Julian?"

"Washington. I go to the University too." He speaks briefly on his athletic career.

"Oh okay I go to Columbia." She said leaning closer.

"That's what's up, you headed back now?"

"Yeah but first I'm visiting family in Chicago." She speaks of her ill grandmother. He nodded his head and continues to listen. "Do you have family in Chicago?"

"huh?" He hesitated before answering "Well if you consider my Muslim brothers as family. Yeah, a whole lot of family" he expressed with humor.

Kaboobi and Carlosi warned of how undercover agents would be deceptive. What were the odds of this beautiful woman entering his station asking so many questions? Starting with them piercing eyes like she already knew the answers. Her body language coupled with her intuition exposed her true identity as DEA. By talking less and listening more, D'Juan pretends to be into her. At times she was flirtatious and tempting to his lower desire. This sexy Latina in her early thirties was definitely a test of discipline.

Thinking ahead, Aiisha would follow instructions to the letter, and he marveled his preparations. Once Gabrielle felt he was travelling alone, he'll be the only focus. Finally, three hours of pretending to enjoy a fictitious conversation was over.

"Attention all Amtrak passengers, we've reached the end of the line. Downtown Chicago, home of the six time Champion Bulls and 85 Champion Bears. Watch your step upon exit and thank you for traveling with Amtrak. Lights, Cameras and Magic."

He exited walking away from the plaza with the feeling of hazel green eyes burning his back. Awaiting his luggage to be pulled, he wrestled with the thoughts of either buying a one way to New York or visiting the Mosque Downtown. Monese knew something was wrong when she didn't see his face. They did as planned and awaited his call..

It Was approximately 11:25 p.m. when he checked his luggage in a locker. Within the first hour of isolating himself, it became evident his suspicion was correct. As he used the urinal, D.E.A agents were searching his luggage. No worries. He walked with confidence into the plaza to buy an Apple Cinnamon Bagel, cup of coffee and the Chicago Tribune. Preparing for a long night, any entertainment coupled with caffeine was essential. The first departure to New York wasn't until 4:05 a.m.

Leaning back in his seat D'Juan contemplated calling his Aunt. She and Aiisha would probably be restless until hearing his voice. With them in mind there was a story in the Tribune he found interesting. Nearly 50 people were killed in that month alone within four square miles. Apparently the Latino and Italians were having power a struggle, turning the west side into a danger zone.

Trying to fathom the chaos in the City he observed his surrounding's. Young adults were rude and inconsiderate. Children throwing toys, jumping on chairs like it was play time at daycare. Families bundling under coats to keep warm. As heavy his eyes were, how can anyone sleep in an environment so hostile? "Fuck this" he thought out loud. Rising from his seat in search of a pay phone.

(Phone Ringing) "Hello" Monese voice was weak.

"Yeah I'll be late. I caught a flat tire. Can you call me a tow truck?"

"Yeah hold on" she rolled out of bed grabbing a pen and paper "where too?"

"The Union Station, but it'll be around 4:30"

"I got it sweetie, you'll see him in a black truck okay. Be safe, and Auntie loves you."

"Love you too Peace." Returning to his seat he was encountered with a happy K-9 putting his nose in other people's personal business. After a brief exchange of words with a crooked nose pig, barring stripes and the last name Flanagan, D'Juan sat patiently reading anything he could get his hands on. If it wasn't steam coming from his ears then the seat behind him must have been on fire.

"Aiisha, Aiisha" Monese pulled on her blanket "huh" she jumps from a dead sleep. "I just talked to your king. He'll be with us for breakfast."

"Okay thank you aunt Nesse." Aiisha was liberated from her worries. Monese then relayed the information to Carlosi explaining the situation. D'Juan purchased a ticket to Syracuse, New York for a hundred dollars on student discount. Occasionally taking a short walk with the feeling of being a moving target, he smiled as the train arrived.

It was 4:15 a.m. approaching the Springfield stop.. "Passengers, we'll be stopping momentarily for 10 minutes. If you leave for any reason please be on board by 4:27."

That was D'Juan's cue. He immediately began walking toward the dining coach, with the intention of buying someone's jacket off their back. Once there, an Amtrak employee was kind enough to leave his jacket at a table while taking a bathroom break. "Shit, even better" he thought out loud. Moving quickly, he continued walking towards the back of the train putting on the uniforms jacket and hat.

Immediately exiting the next coach with his head down, he puts fire to a cigarillo. Casually blending in with the passengers as they formed a small crowd, "I hope you're enjoying your trip." He said in passing. As people begin boarding the train he took long strides in the opposite direction. Through the station and into the parking lot without looking back. He disappeared into a residential district, hiding beside the first house on the corner. He was finally able to see what was behind him, and everything approaching.

Ten minutes after the train departed, a black Chevy Tahoe parked a block from the station. D'Juan had no question it was Carlos. As he crept along the passenger door, it opened, "how was the trip Kid?"

"Sheesh. We'll I'm here now. I see you staying on point."

"Don't forget kid. I am King" They shook hands with firm grips "missed you lil brodi. The familia is good. I got a surprise for you" Carlos hints, then pulled onto Tennessee Ave.

"Yo it's good to see you too brodi. Fa' real, fa' real. I'm good on surprises though." D'Juan leans back in the warm leather seats looking out the passenger side window. Carlos took the long route home to ensure he wasn't being followed. Besides, they had a lot to discuss between the street politics back home as well as in Harlem.

Chapter 12

Carlos spot was in the Robert Taylor projects on 51st & State side. 'I guess it's true what they say, like father like son.' D'Juan thought to himself. As long as his ma' was living comfortably in a luxury condo he was good with living in the projects. Their brotherhood 'La Familia of Kings', were now nearly ten thousand strong and expanding. They have their hands in the small business sector, real estate and the black market. Basically anything that was profitable. When the kid stepped out of the truck he was surrounded by projects towering eighteen to twenty stories high. "Jo you remember how we used to sit in Sugar Hill and dream about pulling up in a Rolls Royce like pops and Sonny?"

"No doubt indeed. More like I was dreaming, and you were right there"

"Yeah but I learned a lot since then. See Pops was right about there being more money to be gained legally than illegal. Especially for a bonafide hustler." D'Juan takes heed as he continues to listen "Jo, I bought moms a condo for 800 grand. The markets are bigger here. More money, more opportunities. You don't have to dream no more kid. This is real Babii." Carlos then toss him a key ring with six car keys. One for a Mercedes Benz, Dodge, Hummer, Ferrari and two Cadillac's. D'Juan looked at him, then

156

back to the Chevy truck sitting on 32' rims. "Fa'real huh" he thought to himself .

Carlos leads the way into 5132 building and up 18 flight of stairs "Damn y'all don't have elevators?" D'Juan gasp from fatigue. "Nobody uses the elevator unless you're an elder. It's like a curse or some shit. Go in it alive by the time it stops you're dead and ain't nobody seen jack." There were adolescents as nine years old smoking joints and shooting craps with a fist full of fifty and twenty dollar bills. Upon opening the door to the 18th floor you can smell the fresh paint. New carpet lined the hallway and silver door knobs distinguished this floor from the seventeen below it. And the difference was the 10 units occupying the same space as the standard 50 units. "We call this the kings quarters. That's Pappi joint, Spiders two doors down, Brutis, Millian and Jaylen's at the end of the hall." Pointing to the different units remodeled into luxury penthouse suites.

Opening his door sounded like unlocking a vault. There was steel reinforcement one foot on each side of the doorway. A burglar would have a better chance taking a sledgehammer and trying to knock through the 10 inch walls, reinforced with steel rods.

D'Juan stepped inside and no wonder. There was marble floor every inch of the 3500 sq. ft. Ebony wood furniture, a great deal of ancient South American artifacts. The most recognizable was the gold and silver crown sitting on his own sculpture. He felt the weight and didn't bother asking how much it was worth.

After an hour tour to the crib, they sat down to negotiate business. Seventy grand for the whole ten pounds was fair. Why bother selling ounce for ounce, when Carlos had the team and the perfect market to move it.

Besides, it's been four years since last seeing each other, and as many night clubs as ladies with secret lovers.

Aiisha was wide awake at dawn anticipating the arrival of the love of her life. Monese informed her he'll be there in less than an hour with his cousins. They began cooking breakfast minutes after they met in the kitchen. "You want some coffee honey?"

"Yes please I could hardly sleep last night." Aiisha sounded exhausted.

"Yeah me neither, I swear them boys gonna be the death of me. As much I worry, oh Allah knows best."

"I know right.. I don't know what I'll do without D'Juan. He changed my life and made me feel so alive." She said smiling. Monese looked at the young lady visibly in love. She only hoped she wasn't naïve to the facts of life. D'Juan lived a dangerous lifestyle, that could cost him everything in the blink on an eye.

"You know the fastest way to a man's heart?" Monese asked.

"Actually I do. It's through his stomach."

"Oh so you know. Well honey get to cooking." They shared laughter and family recipes while preparing the special meal.

The young men walked through the door spreading their peace and blessings. The kitchen table was spread nicely; A Pyrex baking pan of country fried potatoes, 16 baked chicken breast, 24 eggs over easy and a bread basket of Grandma Nina's biscuits. Monese greeted them with peace and blessings. "Habibi" Aiisha wrapped her arms around D'Juan's neck kissing on his face.

"So Aiisha these are my boy's Poncho, Carlos, Spiciano and my nephew Brutis."

"Assalamu Aleikum Malika" They greeted with the upmost respect.

"Wa Aleikum Assalam wah Rahman Tu'allahi." She smiled feeling affection from her boyfriend and acceptance from his family.

D'Juan put his arm around her shoulder and compliments her mannerism. "This my shorty right here, a true ride or die nah'mean."

One by one they complimented her humility, cooking and the fact she was Muslim. The perfect lady for a young man with a troubled past. She smiled, then expressed how they were more of a family than she ever had.

D'Juan was first to reach for seconds. "You high on that happy grass, huh" Monese said followed by a lecture. Example of why a king shouldn't get high was his greasy hands and face.

"Come here my king" Aiisha wiped his mouth with a table cloth. They shared humor and memories while enjoying the rest of their meal. "Man, sis gotta cook dinner" Brutis suggested. She smiled then looked at D'Juan for approval. "She wouldn't mind that. Just Auntie might feel some type of way about using her kitchen." "Not even honey, its fine with me. I can use the help." Apparently Monese took a liking to Aiisha. Cause EVERYONE knows she don't share her kitchen.

"Excuse me I have to go to the restroom." D'Juan excused himself and signaled for Aiisha to follow him. Once in the hallway he questioned the whereabouts of the back pack. "It's in the closet of this room right here" she opened the room door and retrieved the product. After a brief examination everything was in order "tell Losi to holla at me and give us a minute." Before she walked out the door, he grabbed hold of her arm "Ma-ma, I couldn't have done this without you." They then embrace with a hug and passionate French kiss. "Umm" she comments with a smile.

Carlos enters the room and examines the handy work. "Jo what's this?" he asked with a puzzling look.

"10 books, 10 pounds." D'Juan explained "I guarantee you, they gone call this super silver haze?" Carlos nodded his head highly impressed. When he'd left California they used gas tanks and diesel tires to smuggle drugs. "This is really, really good, let me go get yo cake."

Carlos returned with seven stacks of hundred dollar bills in a Bank of America money bag. D'Juan immediately began stashing the money in Aiisha luggage. "Yo, Lil brodi you not gone count it?" Carlos asked.

D'Juan was obviously confused. "Fa what, I know it's good." He continued stuffing the ten grand stacks in hidden pouches. After a few seconds of silence he turned his head back to Carlos "Should I count it?"

"Always count yo cake kid. Good business is hand to hand. You weigh your product and keep things straight on your end. Then count your cake to ensure its right from their end. It's never personal." Carlos explains the principalities.

After counting out seventy two grand he sat aside the last two and recounted. When Carlos returned he asked was it all there. D'Juan smiled and tried handing him two grand. "That's fo ya shorty. Moms like her. Keep her close to ya rib nah'mean."

"Indeed." D'Juan couldn't agree with him more. Hell, after considering the elegant lifestyle she'd become accustomed to, two grand was hardly enough.

"Aiisha come here for a few tics." He yelled down the hall. "A'ight big bro. I'll be with you all in a minute. Let me lace her tennis shoes on a few things."

"Handle your business." Carlos excused himself before Aiisha entered the room. "Yes, my beloved." She asked with a warm smile.

"Sit with me. Here is 2 g's, a little pocket change. The rest is in the Lui bag. You'll take the greyhound home. Keep this bag in your sight at all times." He said with emphasis.

"Okay, okay, I got this. Ride or die right." She leans in for a brief kiss. "Aye Habibi me and Auntie going sightseeing tonight. Cool?"

"Yea, why not? Learn from her she has a lot to show you. Just be out in two days. Doe is expecting you."

"Dude, I swear.. One more order from you. You know I got you don't even sweat." As she smiled, D'Juan looked into her eyes with all seriousness. Leaving no questions to how important her job was. "I'll be back before you leave. I want to give you something to remember me by." She was hypnotized by all the diamonds when he smiled. "I'll be waiting Habibi." He walked out of the room signaling to his brethren, it was time to roll out.

Kissing Monese on the cheek, "Love you Auntie. Take care of my queen."

"Oh she is my sweetie. Don't worry about her. She'll probably be back out here before you will." He looked back over his shoulder and shook his head upon seeing her smiled.

The night ahead was intended for D'Juan to get acquainted with his family of kings. Carlos and Brutis took him on a tour through the neighborhoods out North, and surrounding locations of family businesses. Their money was tied into several establishments, but he was still waiting to see the criminal empire. Where are the trap houses and block machines? He thought to himself.

Pipe A.K.A Viper was a multi club owner, Pepper A.K.A Peep show was a video director, venue promoter and responsible for a few major artists career. The two worked together at Mystery Street recording, a 5 star rated venue. So when an artist came to or ascended into stardom from the Chi, they were the somebody's that made it happen. D'Juan's understanding grew within those few hours. Having the best dro in town was only to increase business relationships. When an artist flew in, or High Rollers hit the club they wanted the best. Who had the reputation, finest top shelf, most entertaining D.J's, etc. In the business sector it was important to identify what made them different from the competition. What follows is the sexy but classy women who attracts the bosses, captains, along with their crews.

As the inheritor of the legendary Mr. Silks, Viper's reputation exceeded other Chi-town club owners. Drawing in thousands of jezebel diva's for the annual player balls. 'Yeah, Mr. Silks. Where players could continue to play, and hustlers could shine like platinum.' D'Juan was embraced as a king that has risen from the ashes. He brought the same Cali swag, Carlos hopped off the greyhound within 89'. Hustle and Muscle babii. Never mind his age, at 17 years old he was a Capo and transporter. In his wicked thinking it wasn't about where he was from but where he was at.

Chicago had the beautiful landscape and sophisticated skyscrapers downtown, but the Chi was the ghetto. As they cruised through the North and South Side streets he was in his comfort zone. It wasn't until 3:20 a.m. when they pulled into the Robert Taylors. Upon stepping out the Tahoe he remembered his suitcases and Marc Jacob leather jackets. "Fuck brodi, my luggage at the station." Carlos turned his head with a tired expression. "It's good don't even sweat it. Give me the key, I'll have Tut pick it up tonight."

"That's what's up" D'Juan was able to exhale.

Carlos continues walking up the stairs to the 5th floor. Stopping by Tut spot to introduce the kid as his little brother. (Knock on the door) "Jo leave a message" He answered while clutching a Mac-11.

"This Losi fool"

"Oh, why you ain't say so " he opened the door gun in hand, and butt naked woman on the couch. "Jo, this Cuban D'Juan. My lil bro." Both nod their heads "peace king."

"Peace" They then embraced with a shake and hug. "Jo kid, big bro told me a lot about you, it's a pleasure."

"It's all love."

"I see you busy, I need you handle this fo me though ASAP." He demands

"Its good, but only cause it's fo the young king."

D'Juan put his fist over his heart before stepping out. "Yep, no doubt."

D'Juan rested his eyes for a few hours. Carlos was wide awake listening to music "What's the drilli?"

"What up Kid. Ah, I'm just vibing to Wicked Streets." he then unplugged the headphones letting the speakers bump. The artist and voice sounded very familiar "who dat?" D'Juan asked while bobbing his head.

Carlos smiled "this Lil Ric, one of Rich City's finest no doubt."

"Aww yeah. Ole boy from J.F.K. projects. He dope but wait until Hakeem and Rashaad drop their demo" D'Juan depicted the freestyle session and how they murdered it. "Get me that demo A.S.A.P Just know these cats out here are serious. If the lil folks are dedicated, I'll take 'em to the top." he assured.

Carlos played a few tracks by his artists, in between expressing his love for music dating back to real hip-hop and rhythm and blues . "You had

Slick Rick, Rakim, Ice Cube, The Gap Band, Manhattans, Miles Davis. They had a message kid," he goes on. And the main reason he invested in recording studios and clubs, is so he could bring that real sound back.

Carlos transformed from the vicious criminally minded individual that D'Juan once knew. It seem too good to be true, "How do you do all this and hustle? Isn't that a conflict?"

"To the contrary young soldier it's a benefit. For one I don't do anything illegal. My hustle is tied into businesses now. Some of our brothers still do their thing but not here." Carlos strongly emphasizes. They don't shit where they sleep. That's how they could live like the Kings they are. "In fact this is a prime example, you listening?"

"No doubt, speak on it." D'Juan is all ears as Carlos demeanor changes.

"Spider met Jaylen and Millian in Natti last week. They set up nice operations in some little apartments they call the bricks. All's going well. Mad cake rolling in, they low key, and nobody no jack. Then they slide through a little titty bar with hammers cocked, raider jackets and pro fitted tilted Ace-Deuce, showing no respect to the establishment. Turns out, some God-body's running the joint." D'Juan shook his head in anticipation of the aftermath. Carlos continues the story. "So you know Milli, a straight live wire. He slaps a stripper on the ass, bouncers try to show muscle, shit happens, guns blazed, and a few bodies laid after the smoke cleared. End result, million dollar operation fineto, done. And we're still paying for the damages. Understand something Kid, we can't have that here." As the message could get no clearer, the two seen eye to eye on that point. Just from what he saw, there was a lot to lose.

Looking up at the grandfather clock it was 10 a.m. "Aye brodi I gotta see Aiisha before she dip nah'mean." Carlos took a few seconds before responding "Lil Brodi, I know that's your shorty. She feels you, probably would ride for you even die for you but bro, that's a lot of cake. You know that right?"

"No doubt indeed. It's not something I haven't contemplated trust me. The difference is, I can give her what she desires most." Carlos folds his arms and leans back. "What can you give her that seventy g's can't buy?"

"Revenge, babii. The secrets which lie beneath the surface can influence a person to do things they never thought they could." D'Juan then showed a mischievous grin. Carlos shook his head, grabs the car keys and walks towards the door. "Oh, Tut brought your bags. They're in the hall closet."

"A'ight give me a minute to hop in the water and dip myself in Polo."

"Yep, I would expect nothing less."

Aiisha was anticipating the last day she'll see D'Juan for the next few months. She was in the shower rubbing soap over her body imaging it was his hands. Reminiscing how he would hold her from behind. She washed her hair thoroughly with African Fantasy shampoo. By the time she was done making love to herself, D'Juan was knocking on the door.

"Yes" she asked while turning the water off.

"Salaam Queen" they both smiled simultaneously. She opened the door and jumps in his arms, wet and naked. He stepped into the steamy room shutting the door behind him. His Polo Jeans and boxers hit the Ivory floor within seconds. She pulled him out of his Polo shirt and bites down on his chest. He sat her on the sink and eases his manhood inside her wet and steamy womb. It was her desire to have it rough and it was his pleasure to fulfill it. Switching positions after ten minutes, she gripped the bathtub while he pulled her hair and moved his hips slowly, "Ah, Ah." She bites her lip to keep from moaning loudly. He proceeded in giving her every inch of thug passion. After he'd cum inside her, neither of them felt guilty. He kept a slow motion until his knees buckled. "Sheesh!"

"Habibi, that was amazing. Wow. Come were, let me kiss it." Before he could react she grabbed his manhood licking and sucking it clean. The sensation was so pleasing it crippled him. Fighting with pushing her head away he thought, 'fuck it you only live once.'

Carlos and Monese were walking in the door from getting breakfast as D'Juan and Aiisha laid on the leather sofa, watching Love and Basketball. "Hey, you little love birds, y'all want some Belgium waffles and turkey sausage?" Monese asked.

"Yes ma'am." Her timing couldn't have been better for they worked up a mean appetite. Eating their meal and looking out the window over Lake Michigan reflected their love. Pure, beautiful and never ending.

Meanwhile Carlos and Monese were in discussion concerning whether it would be best for her to travel back with Aiisha. She agreed for two reasons. One, there was a lot at stake and two, the time to visit family was long overdue. Carlos gave her $1800, and $1200 strictly for gas. Her Cadillac 1995 Seville still had brand new times and needed some road miles. Before they headed out they made Salah (prayer) together with Carlos leading, D'Juan by his side, Monese and Aiisha following. D'Juan admired the discipline Muslim men and women had. No matter what business they had in the day Salah was made on time.

Aiisha and Monese hit the road heading west, D'Juan and Carlos headed back to the South Side of Chicago. "Brodi, let me see yo line" D'Juan asked. He dialed Butch Cozie joint (Phone Ringing) "Hello" he answered.

"Unc, telegram this message."

"You know I keep my pen and tablet kiddo, talk to me."

"Tell Doe, Lil ma gon' meet him at the restaurant tomorrow at 10 p.m. Got it?"

"10 p.m. restaurant."

"Indeed, a'ight peace O.G."

Thinking about it he felt better about sending Aiisha with the money now. For one, he knew it was safe, two she could see how it's done. D'Juan was daydreaming and stuck in a daze.

"Jo kid she is gone. Yo cake is all you should be concerned with, and that's good nah'mean. I need you focused."

"It's good Losi. My head got so much going on in there."

Chapter 13

CARLOS LOOKED OVER AND could understand the young man's plight. He'd been there before "don't even sweat it lil bro. Whatever's in the rich is back there, you here now." D'Juan couldn't begin to explain the trouble he'd caused.

Carlos pulled up to Caribbean Liquor store copped some Garcia Vegas, then stopped in front of a record store the size of a warehouse.

"This is where hits are made kid." Rightfully so, they called it the hit factory. "Come on" Carlos said, leading the way. If an artist came to Chicago they would have to stop there for autograph signing or just to visit no question. D'Juan was introduced to Indian Joe the store manager, on the walk to the studio. Stepping through double pane glass doors, he entered a session with Twista and Do or Die. Instantly feeling the Mob music as it vibrated his chest.

He was impressed with the gold and platinum plaques on the walls. "Kid roll up" Carlos tossed him a quarter ounce and a box of Vega's. He split them with a razor, crushed the haze down real fine and packed tight as he rolled. "Huh, fire up" D'Juan handed him back two nicely rolled Vega's while he continued to roll. As the room blanketed with smoke, the engineer stopped recording. "Jo what's that Hydro or Cali?"

Carlos let him taste it before proclaiming "Super Silver Haze babii, Canada's finest." The engineer and Super Producer Rob lo coughed up fluid from his lungs nearly throwing up on his 64 track mixing board.

"Ooo wee, this power, Cho come taste this." Rob put the session to an halt allowing the artist to smoke. "My folks here say this waking the Chi up"

"Woe, yeah this definitely from out of orbit. Huh" one of the artist said while passing the blunt around to his crew.

"You know I need as much of this I can get."

"No doubt, let's talk."

While Carlos discussed business, D'Juan got a closer look of who recorded and produced those plaques. "Jo, Lil mans you know how to rock the mic?" Rob lo asks. "Nah I just appreciate music. My cousins do though. Dope as Heroin too" D'Juan represents proudly.

"Yo brother good people, we need to get them on wax if they are truly hot. It's a huge market for artists here. In Cali you gotta go to L.A. if you want to reach superstar status." D'Juan nodded his head in agreement.

"Yeah the Independent market in the Yay is a'ight. Ain't no real cake through." They continue to talk while D'Juan was soaking up game. The more he learned how local artists blew up to mega stars, the more he became inspired.

With the knowledge D'Juan acquired in just that little time he'd identified the problem with Bay Area artists. They lacked the network and benefits of having major labels in the Area. To even get a label deal they would have to sign with Def jam, Universal Records, Sony or Interscope.

"I appreciate the game folks," D'Juan handed Rob lo the remaining grams in the sandwich bag. Good game was invaluable.

Twista and the Do or die crew embraced D'Juan as a young king and invited them to the next show. Carlos assured they'll be there.

"A'ight jo we out," Carlos put his arm around D'Juan neck and spoke in a low tone, "you a key figure kid. Your personality and demeanor is powerful, use it. Get out of that military mind state. Trust me kid, you'll get rich but most importantly, be alive."

Again D'Juan felt where he was coming from but how could he leave his brothers in a struggle. At the front of his mind was the day Carlos and his brothers left. His whole family separated, making the winter a season of dread and summers colder. Juelz, Hakeem, Rashaad, Romelo Jr., and Ameere crowded on bunk beds sleeping head to feet. Selling crack as adolescence, renting trap houses, fighting for survival was his life story. Nothing was promised, but he vowed to never leave a comrade behind.

Carlos sped through the neighborhood in his 95' Dodge Viper only stopping at red lights. D'Juan watched as he popped the clutch and shifted only using three of the six gears.

"Jo kid, you know how to drive a stick?"

"What you ill in the head or something? I'm a ridah bra."

"Ridah huh. A'ight let see ." Carlos pulled over to switch seats. "Now this is nothing like a fifty or Supra kid. This is double the horse power and five times the expenses. Don't wreck my cah."

"You gon' talk or let me drive?" He popped the clutch in first gear and peeled rubber, fish tailing half the block. Chirping while shifting into second. "Woe" realizing how powerful the machine was he eased off the gas. He wanted to get comfortable behind the wheel before showing Carlos how to drive without caution. Again his mentality was you only live once.

"Yeah you a lil ridah." Carlos commends proudly. His little mans had grown up and could barely ride a bike last he'd seen him, now handling the wheel of a hundred thousand dollar sports car.

As they pulled into the Taylors D'Juan alerted Carlos of the Z28 Camaro following. "Don't sweat that. It looked like Tut. Besides, nobody gon' come in here with that anyway." Still Carlos retrieved his 50 caliber desert eagle from the stash box. Tut made himself visible after they parked "jo you got the fly gangsta behind the wheel?" Tut seemed to be surprised.

"Jo, this kid got mad handles. What's good?"

"Tomorrow night it's gonna be thick at Mr. Silks. I know the kid need to get out and see how we do it."

"We already ahead of you playboy. Just be retchi" Carlos said with a smile.

(Door Open) They proceed walking up to the 5th floor to Tut's joint with him boasting about the new artillery he'd copped. "Y'all got the Haze, but these joints is what move the crowds, nah'mean" he pulled a crate of new sub machine guns, and Sig Sauer's from the closet. A baldhead nut fa real. He played with guns more than his shorty's clitoris.

Carlos told D'Juan about the importance of having someone like that around. Reasoning you can't be all hustle and no muscle. "Jo, these 380 joints could fit in the back holsters. Strictly fa when we step out ya dig?" Carlos chuckles as Tut fits the holster.

"What? We can't carry a fucking dessert eagle in the joint all the time. Jo kid, big bro be in the joint posted with this big ass canon. It hit the floor on New Year's Eve and everybody shook." Tut described the scene with humor.

"Fuckin right, I hold big shit in the joint. Now they know, don't wanna get shot stay the fuck from around me." They all laugh.

"See he crazy. Jo, you a bad influence fa real."

"All bull aside, these some nice joints."

"Yeah fresh from the ship."

D'Juan was busy fitting a holster on his belt while why cracked jokes and christened the joint with Silver Haze.

"Tut you got ammo?" He asked while inspecting the 380 Sig Sauer.

"No question, what's a gat with no ammo?" He went to the back room and came back with a box of shells and hollow points. D'Juan chose the hollow points.

"Got some garlic?"

"Garlic? Yeah look in the cabinet. Should be some Olive Oil in there too."

"A'ight."

"Oh I forgot it's some chicken in the freezer." Tut jokes; unaware of what he was doing.

D'Juan first peeled then boiled the garlic for 10 minutes. He used a spoon to scoop it out of the water then let it dry.

"Where you learn how to do that?" Tut ask while inspecting the handy work.

"An old assassin back in the Rich. See, when Garlic oil gets in your bloodstream it turns lethal. So even if the bullet don't kill you, you still through.." He explains.

Tut tapped Carlos in his chest. "We gotta keep around. He's a mad scientist."

Carlos chuckled and didn't seem surprised. "I told you the kid is a ridah!"

Late in the evening, D'Juan and Tut walked and talked about Chi-town and Rich City in comparison. To some degree they believed the ghetto is the ghetto, no matter in America or China. A place where intelligence and talent is often overlooked. The Super heroes are Dope dealers and the staple for success was being a multi-millionaire. The ladies aren't much different. Some are educated, humble, well-mannered with morals and others are just sack chasers.

"No question if shorty thick with just a little bit of class, she gone be popular amongst the D-Boys nah mean." D'Juan explained.

"No doubt. I got a lil freak up right now. I mean, straight nympho. She'll even pay us to run her."

"no shit?"

"Come on Kid, don't tell me you hard of hearing now. Nicca, her and her sister on the 12th floor right now."

"You ain't saying nothing, but maybe some other time. I got a lot of shit going on up here." He demonstrate by pointing to his head. "I feel you Jo, but I'm about to get some head. Fuck what you going thru..."

As they were walking back to the 5135 building they heard screams "help, help" Coming from the streets. "Jo, you hear that.. come on" they ran toward federal Street and as they got closer they saw a kid getting beat with billy clubs. An old lady watched helplessly as her screams echoes through the night. "Aww hell naw" D'Juan thought out loud, simultaneously drawing his gun **(Shots Fired).** The cops duck and look for cover as semi-automatic rounds whistle pass their ears. Not even two minutes later, more shots were fired from the shadows of darkness. Under rapid fire, all the pigs could do was take cover and call for backup.

As the smoke cleared, the old lady helped her grandson up and into the Taylor projects. D'Juan and Tut jogged back to the building and walked calmly up to Tut's spot.

"That shit was crazy. Ma'fucka just gon' beat the young-in like that" D'Juan blurts out expressing his anger.

"The pigs were going to kill that kid, in front of his grandmother Jo." Tut spoke as if he'd witnessed police brutality on a regular.

(Knocking on the door) "Grab the Mac " they arm themselves with sub machine guns and take cover behind a couch. (Three knocks on the door again) "Jo" Tut hollers.

"This Brutis." Tut opens the door.. "We to kings quarter, come on."

They hurried with the sound of sirens getting near. Carlos, Viper, and Pappi were waiting in the safe house. Once all together they discussed the situation that will surely bring more heat to the Taylors. Although they agree it's their duty to protect their own, the matter was, Chicago's Mayor didn't take kindly to cop killers. They were told to lay low for a few days. No women, no visitors, nothing until the news media gets the full story. Tut's only request was his artillery be in arms reach.

Carlos talked to D'Juan through the midnight hours in his crib. "Doe made the pickup and inquired about the N.Y. thing."

"Yeah, I plan to reconnect with En-Rica." D'Juan explained further details.

"You know most of the Kings-men from L.E.S, under indictment. I don't know if that'll be wise considering." Carlos advised; not ruling out still traveling to see their Nana. "Jo, remember shorty you had, uh what's her name?" Carlos tried to recollect.

"Ahh, that's Tonya sexy ass, my lil Rican momie."

"Yeah, that's her. She had you wrapped around her finger kid" Carlos said, breaking the young player balls. For the rest of the night they reminisce on summer's spent in Harlem.

By noon the next day Carlos copped D'Juan a Motorola flip phone. He wasted no time in reconnecting with Aiisha. She told him how much she misses him and not to worry, she'll be holding it down until he came home. They also discuss the possibility of her moving to Chicago to go to college. Something she would only consider if he was there with her. Sounded good but he couldn't make any commitments. He lived like a rolling stone with the fear if he stopped moving, his past would catch up to him.

She brought him up to speed with the latest news; that her uncle Omar's crib was broken into a money and jewelry was taken. Came to no real surprise but the bounty on two Rican kids had the streets buzzing. And he knew for the right price, Izzy was a dead man.

He immediately dialed Butch Cozie joint. "Hello" Butch answered.

"Unc I need you to write this down. This for either Rock or Doe. Keep Izzy next to you at all times."

"Yeah I got it, Izzy. Who you talkin about the light skinned curly head youngster?"

D'Juan tenses up "Yeah." "Okay yeah, he and Rashaad just left here suited and booted. They were talking about club Jefferies over there Downtown Oakland." He explained with enthusiasm.

"A'ight make sure they get that **ASAP** and tell them to hit me on this line #402-689-7002."

"Alright now, you be careful."

"Peace" D'Juan hung up with an eerie feeling. All night he tossed and turned waiting on a call from back home.

It was 5 a.m. Central time, lights were off, yet the Taylor residents never slept. "Five-O" someone yelled from a 10th floor window. Coppers in all black uniforms were everywhere like bats in the dark. All four blocks from 44th and state to 51st and Federal were cornered by Task Force. Their attempt to raid documented gang members were derailed by angry residents throwing bricks, buckets of urine, and scolding hot water from their windows.

Just the night before, the grandmother of the boy that was beaten half crippled gave her accounts of police brutality on 60 minutes. Stressing the officers duty is to serve and protect, but there was no protection for her grandson who was an honor student at George Washington Carver High School. What would have happened had them shadows in the dark not been there? Task force literally ran out the Robert Taylor Projects in less than 45 minutes.

It would be 7p.m Eastern time. He thought about Tonya and wondered if she had the same number. She should be around nineteen now, and probably got her own crib. He called his grandmother Nina P., Whom he hadn't spoken to in a while..

[Phone Ringing]

"Hola" she answers.

"Nana, this D'Juan. How are you?"

"Ohh, mi nieto. It's so good to hear your voice. Tonya just asked about you."

"Yeah, how is she?"

"Hold on.. She left a number for you to call and you can ask yourself. Wow, now that's something." Nina believed in signs and hinted at Tonya being apart of his destiny.

"Nana, I'm thinking about seeing you soon okay. Probably in the next few days."

"Come on, I'll be here. You know I don't do much traveling any more. Your nana getting old" (she laughs) "love you nana, I saw a picture of you from mi poppa. You still look young and restless." He said, putting a smile on her face.

"Well thank you honey. Now you get here and see your Tonya. That girl loves you."

His Nana had a beautiful sense of humor, and was always on point. With respect for her intuition, he immediately called Tonya (phone ringing) voicemail pick up.

"Yo, what's really good momie? This the kid holla back, 402-689-7002." Before he could sit the phone down she was calling back.

"What's up stranger" he smiled anticipating the sound of an Angel's voice.

"Hello poppi, how are you man?" She asked while embracing the dream felt moment.

"I'm good, you know.. movin with the wind."

"Yo, I missed you like craa-zy. I've been thinking about coming to Cali to get my king." she laughs "no doubt indeed, I feel you ma. I miss you even more."

"Yeah?" she asked with excitement.

"No doubt, and the crazy thing is I'm on my way to get my wife ret now" suddenly the phone was muted as all breath leaves her lungs "wait what?" She asked sharply.

"I'll be in Harlem really soon ma."

"Oh shit don't fucking play with me D'Juan Shakur. You made me nervous." They caught up on old times and talked until the phones battery went dead. He needed a getaway, and it couldn't have been a better time.

Carlos came back around 8 p.m. "Yo kid, it's Mr. Silks tonight, be ready in two hours."

"A'ight, you know I can't wait to break jail."

"I gotta bust a few moves before we leave. The folks Twista and Do or Die performing tonight. I got somebody I want you to meet too." He said smiling, stepping out the door. D'Juan bounced up, showered for 30 minutes and laid out 3 of his 4 shirts. Colors represented who you were with or what side of town you were from, so to avoid misconceptions he chose the white and black Phasage suit. White pants white black and gold shit, black loafers, white coat. After brushing and shining his teeth for 10 minutes he was near perfection. French braids a week old but he wasn't sweaten that. As he sat in the lazy boy rolling Garcia Vegas for the night, it hit him. 'Jewelry box.' He opted for his gold Rolex set; chain, bracelet and ring.

(phone ringing) He tried calling Aiisha, getting no answer. (phone ringing) He and Tonya had a pleasant conversation about how they made each other better. In times when Harlem was in chaos they found peace walking through Central Park. Only thing they didn't do was commit armed robbery. She would fight over him and not tell him directly, why she was fighting. She'll just hiss at whoever was getting too close. Her fear was that she loved D'Juan more than he could appreciate. The thought wasn't far from the truth. Soon as Carlos keys hit the door he cut their conversation short and told her to hold that thought and he'll holla back...

Carlos threw on his white Ferragamo blazer with black Ferragamo loafers and was headed back out the door "lets dip kid." With no further due, it was time to roll.. Brutis pulled out his white on white Cadillac Fleetwood, waxed down with butter on the tires. Mr. Silks hosted the biggest event in the Chi that night. The kings rolled through forty to fifty deep suited and booted with hundred dollar bills folded in bank rolls. Viper reserved 6 tables in the V.I.P. lounge. On each table were two bottles of Dom Perignon on Ice. D'Juan dropped a box of rolled Vegas on each table. The young fly gangster had all eyes on him no question.

"Jo kid" Carlos signaled for him while having a conversation with two beautiful dark skinned ladies. They were smiling and staring at D'Juan head to feet as he approached.

"What it is bra." Giving dap then looking at potential company for the night. This is Megan and she's Keyana.

"Peace Queen " he greeted them with a kiss on their hands. "Ooo I got a handsome Prince. Come-on love, let's get to know each other better."

Megan looked back over her shoulder, smiling at Keyana before disappearing in the crowd. She was nearly 6 feet in heels, jet black hair past shoulder length, bright smile and a fast tongue. They danced and sipped from chilled champagne glasses.

"Where are you from?" She asked. "I'm from Cali, Rich City babii." He said with a smile.

"I'm from August Town, Jamaica. You been in Chicago long?"

"Not even. I just got here at the start of the summer. Hopefully, we can make each other's night worth remembering." He said with conviction.

"Oh, well okay rude boy. I'm going to uphold my end." She said before turning around popping her lower bottom. D'Juan knew Jamaicans were either freaky, crazy or both. Only time will tell about this one.

After dancing five songs, they returned to the V.I.P. tables "here let me get that for you." She poured him another glass of champagne and put fire to the blunt hanging from his mouth. (Inhale) she was mesmerized watching him inhaling smoke through his nose. "You like the ganja smoke rude boy?" She asked, biting her bottom lip, and moving her hands up and down his muscular frame.

Meanwhile, Twista took the stage, and the tables were cleared. D'Juan was hazy and in Mack mode. "I could be a rude boy. The question is you a rude girl?" He hypnotizes her with his smile. She leans towards him under his command. He grabs her head "show me rude and unpredictable." He lays back and enjoys intoxicating himself while she gets drunk on his love. Carlos looked over and smiled then took Keyana to the stage area to enjoy the show.

"It's coming you gon' take it" Megan nodded her head and hums while slurping the spit from his penis.

"A'ight, you better take it all." The last thing he needed was cum stains, on his two thousand dollar suit.

"Ahhh shit" he blurts out, slipping down on the couch seat. The ending was even more pleasing than the licking and slow sucking.

"Sheesh" he complimented; her head game was super.

She wrote her number on a napkin, stuffing it in his pants pocket. "Call me tonight. I want to get rude boy now." She smiled looking down at his manhood.

"A'ight, we'll see." He said non nonchalantly. Wrapping his arm around her shoulder as they joined Carlos and Keyana. Looking around, he was impressed by how many people were dancing and genuinely there to have a good night. It was the first club he'd been inside without his gun.

The show was over at 2 a.m. but doors didn't open until 3. The last hour was where the mingling and networking took place. For Carlos it was a business deal. The loud smell of Silver Haze along with the celebrity treatment he sold 5 pounds that night alone. D'Juan was busy with his hand under Megan's dress. She had a nice bubble bottom, and he couldn't wait to make it pop. Doors opened and Carlos led to their fleet of luxury cars.

"Keep it wet Momie." D'Juan then slaps her on the hip and pushed through the crowded streets with his shirt half buttoned exposing his abs and chest. No question, he was feeling on top of his game. Once backseat of the Cadillac, Carlos reluctantly relayed a message from back home. "Aye kid you need to holla at doe, Asap." He passed the phone with a disturbing look. "What's good?" Carlos just shook his head indicating it wasn't good.

(Phone Ringing) "Yeah", Dorian answered with anger and frustration. "Speak to me?"

"You need to get out here ASAP. Izzy gone lil cuz. He just was with uh…" D'Juan slipped into a daze after hearing his firsthand man, little globe town playa was dead. He dropped the phone in his lap.

"Hello… Hello." He could hear Dorian saying something, but he didn't have the words or energy to respond. He looked up and made eye contact with Pappi. "You a'ight lil brodi?" D'Juan had this blank expression and couldn't speak. Putting his hand on his forehead he rested on the door. Next time he opened his eyes he was in Pappi's guest room. The whole night was surreal he felt like it was a crazy dream. "So this how it feel huh?" For the first time he had to bury one of his own. His head was pounding, his body was weak, his eyes were heavy, he could do nothing but sleep, with the bitter taste of death on his tongue.

12:30 p.m. Pappi, Carlos, Spider and Brutis were meeting at the living room table. D'Juan stumbled out of bed into the bathroom and freshened up. A 45 minute shower, and a gram of haze rectified his equilibrium.

"Peace King" he said stumbling to the table in his bathrobe holding a pint of orange juice and a cinnamon raisin bagel.

"What's the drill?".

"Our concern is you lil brodi. Aye, believe me when I tell you, I know how you feel. Nobody likes to lose their folks. Hear me on this No-body. You our lil folks and we don't want you to get caught up in no fuck shit." Brutis said loud and clear.

D'Juan finished his breakfast and waited a few minutes to respond. "Losi do you know what I would do if somebody harmed a tiny hair on our head? That's what I do for my brother's."

Carlos figured it would be difficult getting him to understand, that the game is not what they say it is. Instead, he let him make his own choices as long as he could accept the consequences.

"Yeah I know, that's why I got you a 9 o'clock first class. We love you Lil bra."

"That was my main man's bro. This shirt hurt."

They tried their best to console him and enjoy their last few hours together. Brutis was a natural comedian, and his entertainment eased the tension in the room, **NO QUESTION!**

Before D'Juan's flight he made it clear his mission was no point of return, Kamikazi style. The world they created for themselves was beautiful and seemed promising. Still it remained he had a kingdom of his own and with it came duties and responsibilities, which his honor wouldn't allow him to neglect. See, in the real world there is no free lunch. The only thing guaranteed in life is death...

Chapter 14

ROCKY AND SILAS WERE outside Oakland International at 1:27 a.m. D'Juan could taste the bitter, sweetness of revenge in the air. The three briefly embraced before entering Rocky's Iroc.

"Rocko what's the play?" D'Juan asked for directions.

"I don't know, you gotta holla at ya cousins. One of 'em fell asleep on the job." D'Juan looked toward Silas for understanding. "They slid through Jefferies, then dropped him off in Parchester That night. The next morning his Grandma found him dead in the living room."

"Wow", D'Juan leaned back contemplating the possibilities,

"huh" Silas handed him a Colt 45 with a pearl handle. There wasn't much more to talk about. No one had an idea who was next to die, but one thing for certain war was declared.

"Take me to a Cozie joint." D'Juan requested before passing 34th and Cutting.

It was a full house when they arrived. Hakeem and Dorian were in the backyard going over details from the time of leaving the club to dropping Izreal off. They weren't followed nor was it any beef at the club. However, he was sloppy drunk, stumbling into his crib and careless. Even dropped

184

his chrome piece on the back seat floor. Nothing about the scenario sat well with D'Juan.

One theory was one of the twins from 43rd Ave. Retaliated from when Izzy and Razor robbed the dice game earlier in the week. Another and more likely one, was someone closer than most collected the 50 grand bounty Omar put on his head. D'Juan expressed the process of elimination would be quite simple. Start somewhere and end wherever. Eventually there would be nobody left.

Rocky had questions concerning this cat they were calling Big O. He'd heard his name in the recent weeks but couldn't put a face with the name, "who's this fucking guy?" Rocky asked, turning in circles.

"You know that cat Rock. Myron cousin, had the Grey Chevelle with red racing stripes." Dorian explained.

"Nah, not the cat use to rock the funny haircuts and sell Bean pies?"

"That's who we talking bout"

"Fuck outta here, you sure?" Rocky ask in doubt.

"He just been over there in the Iron Triangle, out of sight out of mind" Dorian gave the best detailed description and warned he wasn't to be underestimated.

Then with precise timing, Malik suggested, "before you make new enemies be sure your own house is clean." The wisest words of the hour. D'Juan had his suspicion so he trusted his instincts,

"yo I gotta check on something."

"Rock, go wit him." Dorian commanded.

"Nah, I gotta do this by myself."

He left the circle in search of Izreal's Nana, Mrs. Cartagena. He knocked on the doors of known relatives, even her church. Until finding her, at the last place he expected; her house.

(Knock on door) "Hello, Mrs. Cartagena this is D'Juan." She opened the door eyes puffy and heavy. "They killed my baby. What he could've done?" D'Juan rushed to hug and console her. He had done enough crying but the pain definitely intensified seeing her in defeat. They sat in the living room where she questioned her lack of supervision. "Nana, you done nothing wrong. You were the best for him. I'm going to find out who did this, you here me? I promise."

She lifted her head from his shoulder "and what you going to do? Get yourself killed?"

"No Nana, I'm going to bring them justice."

"I always told him. Baby, these people not your friends. Now they killed him" she shook her head in disappointment. Then went on about different girls running in and out the house, calling them by name. "Hold up, did you just say Danielle?"

"Yeah she came over Wednesday in a truck." She vaguely recollects.

Upon hearing this, D'Juan scoots closer and held her hand." Nana, this is important. What color was the truck?"

She searches her memory bank. "I don't know baby. It was night time. But it's one of them new trucks." He raised up and kissed his forehead.

"Thank You, here's my pager number call anytime for anything. Don't worry about the funeral expenses." She took the number and hugged him. "Okay thank you. Cuba. Wait, don't you get into any trouble."

Before he left he looked around the scattered clothing in Izzy's room. His stash spot was a hole in the wooden floor under the carpet. He moved the dresser and his money, drugs, the mac-10 with extra clips was still there. Bullet holes were in the back door coming from the inside 'somebody was waiting in this ma'fucka.' Trusting his instincts he checked the door, and the lock was still broken. He'd told Izzy to stop leaving the back door unlocked. It was no question in his mind that he was betrayed.

D'Juan separated the drugs and artillery from the money. Izzy would've wanted his grandmother to have the money if anything happened but in the state she was in, she wouldn't have accepted it. So D'Juan left it in the stash and would tell her where it was after the funeral. He cleaned the room in orderly fashion putting things in their respective place.

On the drive to his Bayview penthouse. D'Juan had a vision of leaving Danielle and Omar in the bed together resting in piss and horse manure. That backstabbing whore, who else could have known about the back door? NO one would ever suspect her neither. Making Izzy's death just another unsolved mystery. "Perfect crime" he thought.

Aiisha jumped when she heard keys hit the lock "Habibi." She ran to the door jumping on D'Juan as he stepped inside. "Hold on ma-ma let me put this bag down." She had a way of easing his mental state. No matter what obstacle he faced she would help him through it. "I didn't expect to see you so soon. I miss you so much." She sat on his lap hugging and kissing his face. You know I couldn't stay away from you for two months. Just too damn long. She strips him from his clothes, and they make passionate love on the couch.

It's at or around 1 a.m. Rocky and Silas was walking toward 43rd Ave with Chinese A.K. 47's and more than two hundred rounds. As they approached the alley leading to Wall Street, a shopping cart with blankets and clothing was in their path. Rocky signals for Silas to wait at the end of the alley.

"I'm gone push the cart. After I get half down the block follow me" he whispered. Rocky wrapped himself in the blanket, to obscure his assault rifle. He could hear voices coming from a backyard, so he walked slower. The street lights were dim, aiding the sneak attack. Then suddenly, five rival crew members walked from a backyard behind Rocky. (Shots Fired) In one motion he dropped to one knee lifting and squeezing the trigger of his fully automatic assault rifle.

Silas had them in his sights and let off rapid fire before they could draw. Four fell flat, crawling on the front lawn. Rocky stood over each one of them ensuring the mission was complete. **'BANG, BANG, BANG, BANG!** As neighbors lights came on, they ran fast as they could until crossing 37th Street. Out of breath, and evading police, they hid on the side of a duplex home.

When the ghetto bird joined the search they unarmed themselves, separated and walked in opposite directions. Rocky made it to McDonalds and called his kids mother to pick him up. Dressed in army fatigue, Silas was held up outside of 7 eleven.

"Keep your hands up, walk backwards slow, very slow." The policeman commanded. His first thought was, he was just two blocks from the Clinton Hill Estates, where he could surely lose them. Then he thought no witness, no trace, no case. He did as asked, speaking proper and acting confused.

"Drop to your knees." Two police then approached him with guns aimed at his head "lay on the ground," One fat ass cop put his knee in his back.

"Ah" he yells out.. He was handcuffed, stood up and searched aggressively. "Aye what's going on?" Silas asks loud enough so any on-lookers could hear.

"I'll tell you in a second." A cop returns after searching his wallet. "Okay Mr. Sosa, you fit the description of a shooting suspect."

"What.. Are you serious? I just came from my uncle's house in the Clinton Hills."

"Shut the fuck up. Frankly, I don't give a shit what you say. You look guilty" said the fat cop. "Just hold on sir. If what you're telling us checks out you'll be released." said Officer Diaz. As he sat on the hood, another police vehicle passed with someone sitting behind the dark tents "Negative. No ID" came over the radio. "Sorry sir for the inconvenience. Seems like you have no warrants and they have found the suspect." He was un-cuffed, and demanded to find shelter within the next hour. As bad as he wanted to spit in the coppers face, he just decided to get the hell out of dodge.

The police made several arrest that night for possession of firearms, but none were the murder weapons. Overnight, word hit the street that rival crews were paying witnesses to fabricate statements, implicating Rocky and Slim. What a cold game!

Chapter 15

Aiisha was hot and wide open. She was so excited to see D'Juan in bed when she opened her eyes. She rubbed on his chest, kissed his lips and face as he was in a deep sleep. Throwing back the sheets she examined his naked body. Then commenced to kissing and licking every inch of his manhood. Blood rushed through his body as he awoke. "You like" she asks with a smile.

"No doubt indeed." He rubbed his fingers through her hair, while releasing some stress. Lyfe used to tell him 'before you make a tough decision make love to your woman. You'll think better.' He knew she was hungry for revenge, but was she ready?

She brushed her teeth and went to the kitchen to prepare breakfast. "Let me get my ass up" he said to himself, putting his feet to the floor. After hearing the shower water running she joined him "Habibi, I'm coming in."

"A'ight come on" seeing her naked body appear through the steam was like envisioning his queen in Paradise. She rested in his arms feeling secure as she'd ever been.

"My queen I've been thinking about something you told me. It's really bugging me." she looked back over her shoulder "What?"

"When's the last you talked to Angel?" Instantly her body language changed. She wondered if he knew her plot to kill Omar.

"I haven't heard from her since she was telling me about the money and all that."

"Yeah that's what I'm talking about. I wanna watch you kill that fat ma'fucka." She turned around and looked him in the eyes.

"I want to soo bad, but I never shot a gun. You gon' show me?" She asked on her tippy toes. "No doubt, but you can't freeze up" To her, his words were fatally romantic.

"You trust me with your life don't you."

"That's what I'm telling you."

They enjoyed breakfast, then shared the next few hours playing NBA Jams on Super Nintendo. "Come here let me show you something, "she sat between his legs. He handed her his gun using the men on T.V. as a target.

"You aim with the sights. Concentrate, take a deep breath and squeeze."

(**BANG**). The shot rang through the penthouse.

"What the fuck ma" he barks, snatching the gun away. "You said squeeze " she replies smiling.

All he could do was shake his head and smile. "You shoot him like our T.V. he a dead ma'fucka." They both shared laughs and a bottle of his favorite Champagne.

Slim had been in San Francisco since Izzy's death. He had his sights locked on Oschino, just waiting until he came outside for a newspaper, to empty the garbage or even showing his head through a window. The AR-15 and 9 mm Taurus were both equip with silencers.

A dark skinned woman presumed to be Oschino's old lady had been coming and going, non-stop for the past few days. Growing impatient he followed her Green S.U.V. to the store, where she came out with a bag of diapers. However, upon looking in the truck there were no car seats, or any signs of a daycare at the apartment.

The next day he took a ride down to Harbor Road and waited for a mailman. Walah, with one in sight he made his move. "Aye, excuse me sir. You delivered this package to my address, but this isn't for me."

As the mailman looked down at the package he saw a gun pointed at his stomach "you want to live?" He nodded his head indicating yes. "Just walk over here. All I need is your uniform and mail bag."

"You can have all this just please."

They disappeared behind some apartments where the man handed over his clothes and mail bag before being knocked unconscious.

Slim returned to Potrero Hill with a special delivery. In full uniform he exited the mail truck meeting Tameka at the door. "Excuse me ma'am are you Tameka Vaughn?" She hesitated before answering. "Uh yes" she recognized Slims face, but the uniform was a perfect disguise. "Okay good I have something for you. This will only take a minute."

He approached the door step with a box in one hand and gun resting beneath it "okay" She went to sit her bags down inside the door when he pushed her inside (**screams**) "Bitch shut up." She is silenced with a slap over the head. Wasting no time he searched room after room. Hearing sounds coming from a television, he opened the door slowly leading with the silencer of his 9mm.

Oschino laid in a bed with tubes running from his body to a monitor. Slim smiled at the sight of him in a vegetable state "look at ya now." He then snatched the breathing tube from his throat, the I.V. from his arms, and watched as his body struggled with the angel of death.

Screams from downstairs alerted the neighbors. "Shit" Slim hurried down the stairs chasing Tameka outside. She screamed for help stopping traffic pointing back in his direction. He collected himself and hurried around the corner to his truck. He drove a few blocks before discarding the uniform and handgun in a recycling bin.

It was rush hour, and bumper to bumper traffic on the Bay Bridge. The thought of catching Bart transit back to Rich City crossed his mind. And it may have been his best chance at a swift escape. Then again he had no reason to panic.

It wasn't until he was across the Bay bridge he was flagged by Highway Patrol. Remaining cool, he handed the patrolman his license and registration. Slim did his best, explaining he'd just got a call from his daughters school, and was in a hurry. What he hoped would be a simple traffic stop turned into a 30 minute wait. Minutes later, four more cars and CHP bikes were lined up on each side of the freeway. "This is how it's gonna end huh" he thought out loud.

As his fate was inevitable, his mindset was no surrender, no retreat. Taking aim from behind tinted windows he waited for a clear shot. After inhaling and exhaling twice, he squeezed the trigger of an AR-15, hitting two officers. He then put the pedal to the metal with two patrol cars on his tail. They reached high speeds of 110 miles per hour swerving through lanes until finally exiting at the Hagenburger turn off. Oakland Police department (OPD) joined the chase and began maneuvering behind the truck.

Suddenly, Slim slammed on the brakes coming to an abrupt stop. He swung the door open with one hand, rifle in the other, he jumped out and charged (shots fired) 30 to 40 rounds were shot into the squad cars. Officers fired back forcing Slim to take cover in front of the truck. All he had to do was run one city block and through the park, he would be home free.

Unfortunately, the swat team arrived surrounding him with a tactical position. He smiled and looked up to the sky before saying "Izzy, I'm on my way my G." Living up to his promise, he tried shooting his way out. (**Bang**) he was dropped with one shot.

"Stay down mother-fucker" were the last words he heard before losing consciousness. A tear rolled from his eyes as the rifle laid just 3 feet from his outstretched arms...

[**BACK IN RICH CITY**] D'Juan told Aiisha he had to make a few runs. When he made promises he kept them and all he could think about was Izzy's funeral. How a man lived is how he should be buried, he reasoned. A Globe Town Playa no question, and heartbreaker he may have been depending on who you asked.

From earlier days, D'Juan remembered them representing in house parties, leaving stories to be told the next day. The young ladies kept their names at the tip of their tongues. It's painful to relive those memories knowing that's where they ended. They shared dreams and ambitions to buy land in Puerto Rico, Atlanta, Ga. and Ghana, Africa. Opening restaurants and food markets until eventually having enough capital and clout to getting a stake in the import and export business. As twelve year old runaways their dream seemed far as the stars in the sky. Still they dealt with their present situation as Orphans vowing to protect each other and once successful, help other refugees. Nothing was impossible. Old timers had a saying that skies were the limits. Izzy's vision was beyond that. Now it was D'Juan mission to see it through.

Chapter 16

MANY THOUGHTS CROSSED HIS mind on the drive to Malik's. Dorian, Santonio and Junior sat in the lounge area in deep discussion.

"What iz it?" D'Juan asked, catching them by surprise. "What's the drill? Y'all act like you saw a ghost or something." He then saw the long look on their faces and the Newspaper sitting on the table.

"It's Slim bra" Santonio said shaking his head. D'Juan looked toward Dorian for answers, then to Junior.

"What the fuck happened?" He asked in frustration,

"Sit down little cousin. Understand this, Slim knew better than anybody that when you ride sometimes you die."

They handed him the Oakland Tribune and it was unbelievable. If he made it from ICU, he'll surely be facing the death penalty. He dropped the newspaper on the crystal glass table and slipped into deep thought. "What about his son, lil Man? Damn, I know Juicy is goin through it. Fuck me man." He shakes his head trying to fathom the recent drama.

It was if their crew was cut in half overnight. Rocky and Silas were laying low with heat from homicide detectives breathing down their necks,

Hakeem and Rashaad shut down shop and were recording in Oakland with Harm from the Rich and Keek The Sneak.

"A'ight look, This is all fucked up." After exhaling Haze smoke, he focuses on one issue at a time.

"First Priority is Izzy Funeral. Doe, I need 15 g's. His Nana is expecting me in the next hour." D'Juan speaks as if he's in a daze.

"A'ight let me hit sis." Dorian left the room to make the call.

Malik entered the room and sat on the arm of the couch. "Aye let me ask you something kid." D'Juan looked into his eyes with a blank expression. "Did you know Danielle was fucking around with them cats in the Iron Triangle?"

D'Juan shrugged his shoulders as if it was of no concern.

"A'ight look at it this way. Who knew where Izzy laid his head and was cold enough to betray him? Cause you do realize he was set up right?" Malik had made the connection but D'Juan acted dumb, and blind.

"Brodi, she just Copt a Lex Coupe, and been seen everywhere except in the Globe." Santonio interjected. D'Juan listened while taking mental notes. Although he didn't agree verbally he knew their suspicions were dead on.

"Little cuz, juicy waiting on you." Dorian announced

"A'ight. Aye, let me handle this I'll holla later." D'Juan exits with cenacle thoughts and an itch to scratch.

Juicy was waiting out in front of the apartments on S. 34th. She handed him an envelope and pleaded he be careful. In that year she'd buried her cousin Little Hoodie and the father of her two kids. At only 30 years old her eyes were stress ridden.

Mrs. Cartagena was sitting in the living room looking at family pictures when someone knocked on the door. "Hold on, just a minute" she yelled, making way to the door.

"It's D'Juan Nana." She opened the door and greeted him with a warm hug.

"Oh, it's so good to see you. I was just flipping through photo albums. Pictures of Ameere, Izreal and you at the daycare."

"Oh yeah, let me see what you talkin bout." He took a seat on the couch with tears in his eyes as she flipped page after page, recalling memory after memory. And if the walls could talk, that would explain Izzy's voice echoing through the halls.

Two hours flew by, checking his Rolex timepiece and D'Juan had other arrangements to make.

"Nana I need you to call Rolling Hills and reserve a plot. Then call Fuller Funeral Homes. Put them on notice your grandson is in route with whatever funds are needed." He then opened the envelope of large bills. She nodded her head in agreement.

As painful the process was, it had to be done. He kissed her on the cheek and took one step out the door before dropping to his knees. The energy of the house was gone. Mrs. Cartagena was slipping into depression, and he was partly to blame. The burden was like having an elephant on his back. He held his hands in front of his face and made a Dua (supplication) "Oh most High, all praise be to you Lord of the worlds, most gracious most merciful. Master of the day of judgement, you I worship and only your aid do I seek, show me the straight path of those who have gained your favor and not the path of those who have earned your wrath or went astray. Ameen."

Aiisha paged him with the emergency code more than 5 times. Whatever it was would have to wait. Nothing was more important than the business at hand. Next stop was Fullers Funeral home on 30th and Cutting Blvd. Chills ran up his sleeve as he stepped in the place. A lady named Chyna was the manager and offered great assistance. For 10 grand she agreed to order a Custom Gucci casket and prepare the body with any barber of choice. Another five g's to secure a spot in the Garden of Paradise. Solid Marble was chosen for the headstone with a sculpture of his face above his name. D'Juan took care of those who looked after his people. Besides, he never knew when it would be his time.

Immediately after receiving a hefty tip, Chyna called the Richmond Coroner and requested the body of Izreal Cisneros.

Aiisha was pacing back and forth, phone in hand cursing every 5 minutes. The sound of D'Juan keys hitting the door eased her tension.

(Door Opens) "Habibi where you been? I was stressed out the game. Ugh" She was obviously irritated.

"It's good ma-ma, I'm here now.. I got you." He held her in his arms. "Talk to me my queen."

"I just talked to Angel, and she said he asked about me, and if she can get me back to work. I swear, this fagot got nerves." She held her breath anticipating his response.

"Ma-ma, why you got her in your business?"

"I didn't want to tell you but she got eyes on him for me. I knew she was still working for that bitch." She then threw the phone.

"Calm yo nerves Ma. You'll get yo shot at his crown. Maybe tomorrow but you have to be cool. Never do anything while you're angry." He advised, rubbing her face as she leaned on his shoulder. It was total silence as they both premeditated murder.

"Angel knows where he keep his money too." She nicely reminded.

"A'ight, call and tell her to get here **ASAP**." Whatever the risk, he figured it'll be worth it.

Angel was at the front door less than an hour later. By that time D'Juan was dead tired and closed his eyes.

"Baby, I got a surprise for you." Aiisha whispered in his ear. Her lips were painted with cherry smooches lipstick, her hair was pressed hanging down her back and she was completely naked. She stood over him, dancing to slow grooves as he relaxed his head on pillows.

Angel entered the room in Victoria Secrets Lingerie, asking Aiisha if she could have some. It was as if his hands were tied behind his head. He couldn't move nor did he want to. Angel unfastened her bra strap, placing it over his eyes. The feeling of a sharp fingernail scratches from his chest to below his belt line. In an instant his manhood was being blown and sucked on like a popsicle. Her mouth was cold, her throat was deeper than he's ever felt before and she sucked harder and harder. Aiisha giggled and watched as he seemed to be pleased.

"You like habibi?"

When he nodded his head indicating yes, she started choking him.

"Oh you don't like how I do it? You like when she sucks your dick. Do you know who she is? huh do you?"

The feeling turned from sensation to pain and he wanted Angel to stop. Aiisha continued choking and taunting him. "You still don't know? She's death baby."

"Ahh" he jumped from his sleep feeling of this chest then down to his manhood. "What the fuck was that about?" He questioned himself.

As if the night couldn't get weirder. Angel and Aiisha were on the couch watching S&M pornographic videos. He grabbed a bottle of Moet and quart of orange juice from the refrigerator. "What the hell y'all watching?" he asked while pouring a glass of mimosas.

They started giggling then Angel replied "Aiisha wants to learn how to dominate your ass." D'Juan didn't see any humor in the joke and turned the T.V. off. He then looked at them both with a serious demeanor. "You know why you here?" He ask.

"Oh cousin, tell my beloved what you told me about the money." Angel took a deep breath before speaking. "Well, I needed to borrow a few g's until I get my settlement from Chevron, then I'll pay him back or whatever. He told me it's good, I just have to do a job for him. So I went to his crib and he got a pile of bills on the living room floor. Do you know, I stayed up hours counting that shit and he only gave me $250." She complains maliciously.

"How much was it?"

"Um, four hundred and ninety thousand dollars. I wanted to take it all and run out the door." She demonstrates, followed by laughter.

"Listen this is not a game. He hurt someone dear to me, now we gon' hit him where it hurt the most." He demonstrate by a tight closed fist.

"I understand completely. I just wanna hurt that bitch. He doesn't have a safe though he put all the money in the trunk of a Chevelle in his garage." D'Juan pondered on the information. 'Clever,' he thought. Who would have the time or inclination to look there?

"A'ight look, this all I need you to do. Go to the house and leave the front door unlocked."

"That's it?" She then looked at Aiisha for clarity.

He regained her attention by clapping his hands twice. "Aye. Quit looking at her. Focus on the job. That's it, got it?"

"Yeah I got it."

He had a good mind to get some rest and put the play in motion the next day. However, the burden he'd carried from Mrs. Cartagena was too heavy to sleep on. He threw back the covers and told Aiisha it was time, no more waiting. Angel called Omar and told him she needed something. Due to her insisting it was big money involved he agreed to meet after business hours.

1:40 a.m. D'Juan and Aiisha laid under the Cadillac Escalade parked out front a three story home. Angel rings the doorbell. Omar opened the door in his pajama robe, with gun in hand. He takes a look outside before shutting and locking the door. After 5 minutes, D'Juan leads to the front door (door open). They immediately heard voices coming from the kitchen. "You don't know if they want a half pound or half kee?"

"They said they wanna spend 8 g's what's that?" Angel asks with a stutter. Omar senses something was sketchy as she was obviously nervous. "Fuck wrong wit you" he asks, slapping her face. D'Juan's arm swung around the wall, with his 45. Aimed chest high. "Fuck boy" (shots fired)

"Ahhh" Angel screams as two shots sizzle past her ear and into Omar's large frame.

"The money in the car," he squealed in a plea for his life.

"This is not about the money putah."

D'Juan picked up the 44 bulldog laying by his feet, then hands it to Aiisha. She dropped the hood from her head, boiling with rage "remember when you called me bitch" **BANG, BANG, BANG**. Three shots to the face from close range left a bloody mess. And like she'd been longing for this day, she exhaled as a sign of relief. Angel panicked and ran out the door screaming and hollering, surely waking up neighbors.

There was a little more than 30 ounces of powder cocaine bagged up on the counter. "Get that" he told Aiisha while struggling with unlocking the trunk. Time was ticking and with the thought of Angel pulling off in the getaway vehicle, he decided to abandon his big score. Cursing and blaming himself for not going with his first mind..

They make it to the get away car, but Angel was nowhere to be found. He hopped behind the wheel and slowly drove down College Park Ave.

"We gotta put this shit up, then look for this stupid bitch." He changed clothes and vehicles, leaving Aiisha at the penthouse. She had seen enough for the night.

Not returning home until 5 a.m. his shorty was worried sick. "Habibi, forget it. As long as we are safe I am so done with her."

He couldn't agree more. "No doubt, let's get some rest."

(Pager vibrating on night stand) 7 a.m. D'Juan jumps to his feet responding to an emergency page. He slipped on some polo jeans, sports coat and Nike Airmax's. "Peace queen." He kisses shorty on the forehead and left quite as possible.

Dorian was on the corner of S. 35th and Beck when he pulled up. He had the house phone in his hand signaling for D'Juan to come in the house (Door opened) "What's the drill?"

"Lyfe is going to call back within the next 15 to 20 minutes, here." Dorian hands him the phone and put fire to a nicely stuffed Backwood. (Lighter strikes) As the house filled with Haze smoke they discussed plans to open up another joint.

From night fall until sunrise they formulated solid blue prints for the operation. Word from Hakeem was 4th street were getting all their clientele. Heroin addicts are only loyal to the man with the dope and recent bloodshed was bad for business. D'Juan has a remedy but who will be on board "Does this mean we need to holla at Hop's people?"

Dorian thought about it. "You know what, that's what we might have to do. This haze will eventually sale itself."

They agreed, the profit margins from Heroin and powder cocaine would be much greater. (Phone rings) "Hello" D'Juan answered in his best old man voice.

"What's up with the kid?" Lyfe asked. They both laugh.

"What's good with a King?"

"Getting ready to get out of here. They got me in this half-way house in the T.L.'s"

"That's what's up, it's good timing too" D'Juan emphasizes.

"I heard, but aye the name of the game is survival. Dead man ain't shit nah mean." Lyfe reiterates.

"No doubt indeed."

"Aye, I gotta sign these papers to get my home passes. I'll send a word soon as I touch."

"A'ight, I'll be there first thing. You already know."

"Indeed stay down young King, 100."

"One."

D'Juan and Dorian felt better now that Lyfe was finally home. No question he would get things back in order. "Doe, get with The Ghost first chance and tell him what's up. Those his people he'll be able to tie us in." Dorian nodded his head indicating that was the first order of business.

D'Juan planned to take Aiisha to breakfast, then on a couple errands. When he stepped in his front door he smelled blueberries and potatoes. Shorty was preparing a breakfast better than any local restaurant. She smiled as he watched her butter the blueberry pancakes.

"I thought you'll be hungry.. You look like you lost weight." She opened the oven releasing an aroma. "Baked steak, country fried potatoes. Oh yeah, you think you know me don't you?" He picked her up from behind causing her to giggle. They sat down and enjoyed a tall glass of Mimosas with a wholesome breakfast. There was still no word from Angel and when asked, Aiisha shrugged her shoulders with no concern or care at all.

By noon they were in San Francisco, splurging in the Prada and Escada stores while shopping for Izzy at the Gucci store. Their next stop was Precious Beauty salon, where shorty opted for a unique style of African braids. Her hair was long and thick enough to do anything she wished. Meanwhile, D'Juan swung by Fullers Funeral Home, to drop off Izzy's gear to Chyna.

"You know it's not many young men care about anything other than themselves." She said complimenting his mannerism.

"I guess I'm one of a kind" he replies, smiling at the older, attractive woman. He hands her Malik's number and assured her he would come at the drop of a dime to cut Izzy's hair.

"Ok. tell him to be here next Thursday at 2:30. The casket should be here Wednesday."

"Will do." They shared smiled and it was apparent she was digging the young king.

"Oh here's my card, call me." He glanced at it, then back into her eyes "is this business or personal?"

"It could be business, but I'd rather it be personal."

He nodded and smiled as she strutted off in her thigh high dress. "Niiice" he thought.

Stepping outside, approaching his car he saw Danielle crossing the tracks on Cutting Blvd. He took a long look at the cherry red SC 400 Lexus Coupe. He hurried to get on her trail and followed slowly. She made a right on Carlson Blvd, and a left on Potrero Ave. stopping at one of Pharaoh's joints. Out of respect he let her breathe. "Maybe next time," he thought.

Aiisha walked out the door as he pulled up to the salon. Her hair was braided in zig zag tiny cornrows, into a bun in the back. Jet black and shining from the juices and berries radiating from her scalp.

(Door Open) "Looks excellent momie." He compliments.

She smiled and sat quietly for a few minutes indicating something was on her mind. "Ma you good?" She paused then squinted her eyes before speaking. "I just heard they found Angel." She again looked at him with eyes that could pierce through his soul.

"Oh yeah where they find that putah?" He asked with a lack of concern.

"They found her by the train tracks in North Richmond, with a bullet in her head."

"She's dead?"

"Yeah D'Juan don't play stupid." She then pushes his face prompting an immediate response.

"Aye" he frowned up and pulled over with a sudden turn of the wheel. "Don't ever fucking touch me like that, and most importantly, don't doubt me." Lifting her chin to eye level he wanted to be sure she understood. "I don't know what happened to her. I really went looking for her dumb ass, all that morning. Now I told you she was your responsibility." He calls to mind.

"Alright, forget it. I just know her momma is going to be asking me what happened."

D'Juan merges into traffic pondering on how that conversation would go, "so what happened?" She put her head in her hands before responding "I don't know what to tell that lady. I really don't."

He chooses his next words very carefully. She was having a nervous break down, and the pressure would only get heavier in days to come. "Ma-ma, I'm gone give it to you straight. We have to convince ourselves, that night never existed." He makes eye contact to ensure she's listening. "Angel stopped by the house, made a call and was picked up around midnight. That's the script, don't change it, don't hide it. Okay." She nodded her head indicating she understood. As well as the consequences they would all face, had Angel got arrested. Shorty learned that night what was behind the scenes of the street life. With sharing romance, and bottles of expensive Champagne, there came hangover's and nightmares.

To reflect on life from outside their little ole city D'Juan took Aiisha to his favorite spot in the Richmond Hills. "Baby have you ever thought about a Diamond?"

She looked at him with a smile "What do you mean, like a diamond ring?"

"Well, more so just the Diamond itself and the process it goes through before it's shaped to be the gem we love."

"I never thought about it, but where are you going with this?"

He looked out into the City lights, then over to her "if you could pick one gem to represent your quality, what would it be and why?"

"I guess a canary yellow one, because it's so rare." She explained.

He nodded his head in agreement "Your personality and demeanor is rare for sure. There is also this transparency about you, making your beauty radiate from your heart. A pure gift that illuminates your body. That's why I'm so attracted to you." he adds, aside from her sex appeal. "I understand that. Thank you my beloved. I love how you break things down for me."

He stroked her face with the back of his hand. "It's my duty so trust me and let me lead you." She grabbed his hand and put it over her heart. "I trust you with my heart, without it I can't live." Her words were felt deeply, penetrating his stone cold heart. He knew the true test will testify to her love and loyalty.

The next few days they spent with each other away from Richmond. Santa Cruz Boardwalk was the perfect getaway. Walking the beach holding hands and kicking seashells was mental stimulation. Smelling the Ocean, feeling it's coldness wash up on their feet, helped them realize they were free. Free to go wherever in the world they wished. Watching the sailboats tact with the North West winds, and the Brown Pelicans who migrated from the gulf of Mexico, was all the evidence needed.

Aiisha was out of high school and considering the drama from the past summer. More reason why D'Juan was less likely to be returning anytime soon. Making matters worse, Angel's mother had been leaving disturbing messages, to contact her immediately.

Returning to Richmond was like locking a 10 pound ball and chain on his ankle. For the past four days they felt peace and freedom to do whatever, whenever. To forget the last time she saw Angel would be difficult when the reality was she was her cousin and going to the funeral service was mandatory. How ironic was it that her service was the same day as Izzy's?

"Habibi my aunt wants me to spend the night and go to the service with her in the morning. Can you come please?" she pleaded, stressing his presence by her side was needed.

"What time will it be?"

"It starts at 10 o'clock" she said holding his hands. (He exhales) "Wow, a'ight. One of my comrades' funeral is tomorrow. I'll try ma." She rubs his face, look in his light brown eyes and saw resentment. "I'll always love you." She kissed him on the forehead with a tear rolling down her cheek.

D'Juan called Chyna to verify the time of the services and if anything else was needed. She confirmed the viewing time was at 11 a.m. and gave her sincere condolences. Upon request from Santana a horse chariot would be escorting the casket to Rolling Hills.

"One last ride through the Rich huh," D'Juan thought.

He spent the rest of the day in the Globe with some neighborhood rappers, the A.O.B (All Out Boys) and Players on Green. Liters of Hennessy, Alize, and cases of Heineken and Corona were distributed throughout the back of the projects. Izzy lived life and represented his crew to the fullest. A F.K boy and Globe Town Playa fa' sho.

Music by 2 Pac "how long will they mourn me", Richie Rich "Do G's get to go to heaven', Coolie-O "Gangster Paradise" and Bone Thugs-n-Harmony 'Cross roads' banged from home size audio speakers outside St. Nick's joint. Laotians from the Globe, spray painted a mural of Izzy standing in front of Shacks liquor. With his hat to the back, Mickey's beer in one hand and chronic stuffed Garcia Vega in the other. Big Vain and Young Magic fired off 21 rounds from A.K. 47's in solute...

It was 8 a.m. D'Juan woke up at Santonio's crib slightly hungover. "Ah shit" he mumbled while stumbling to the bathroom. "Aye Silence."

"What's up brodi?"

"I need you to get my bags from the Supra. The keys are in my coat."

"A'ight got you bro."

D'Juan showered for 30 minutes letting the water run off his head down his back. Preparing for funerals was something he vowed to forever dislike. Silas placed his bags on the sinks countertop, he exited the shower, drying off and getting dressed as fast as possible. Stepping out in a black V-Neck Gucci sweater matching down to his canvas shoes, he shed a tear. He couldn't stand the thought of seeing his main man laid up in a casket. However, a true brother would be there no question.

A twenty car caravan rolled out the Globe with another ten to fifteen cars joining from S.34th and Cutting Blvd. Women from all walks of life attended the service rather they knew Izzy personally or not. After the pass weeks of homicides and drama stemming from his love affairs, curiosity led to interest in paying homage. All eyes focused on the Young King resting in plush wearing a white Gucci V-neck sweater, button up shirt, slacks and a green tie, complimented by a Rolex chain resting on his chest.

One by one, ex-girlfriends and mistresses kissed his face. D'Juan stood in observance, being the last to pay his respect.

"I got him brodi." He leaned near the casket and whispered.

Santonio, Silas, Dorian, Hakeem, Rashaad and Rocky joined him for a moment of silence before the undertaker sealed the casket.

The Horse Chariot ride through Rich City was like an out of body experience for D'Juan. He knew it could have easily been him in that box. All the talk about being untouchable, or real niccas don't die wasn't reality. In real life, there was nothing anyone could do or say to avoid the reaper.

At the burial site, nineteen doves were release, followed up with a song by the Playaz on Green titled "It's the dank." It was one of Izzy's favorite records, and would rather have it no other way. His crew accompanied Mrs. Cartagena and other family members sharing their childhood memories. Apparently, they knew him better than anyone of his distant relatives.

Chapter 17

*I*T WAS 10 P.M. Danielle pulled up to the gas station on 10th and Pennsylvania Ave. She stepped out of her Lexus Coupe on 20' inch rims with Mary J. Blige 'what's the 411' blasting from her sound system. Original brown Manalo Blahnic Timberlands complimented her Army fatigue outfit. D'Juan spotted her as he passed by Pennsylvania Ave, coming from the Rumrill Garden complex "look at this shit here." He thought out loud. He hit a U-turn and parked on 9th street where he was able to appear from the darkness. With swishers sweets and a Mango Snapple in hand, she strutted back to her car "A yo, lil momma you missed me" he asked from within 4 feet.

She turned around in shock and after looking into his dark eyes, became terrified. Unable to say a word, she walked backwards "What's wrong with you ma, you good?" He asked; edging closer, maintaining eye contact. The guilt in her eyes suddenly turned into tears. "I don't remember seeing you at Izzy funeral. What happened? You forget the code?" As he got within a step she kicked him in the shin and turned to run. Before she could shut the car door he snatched her by her collar. "I told you never cross me."

"Leave me alone. Please D'Juan, just let me go. I' didn't do nothing, I swear " she pleaded with tears rolling down her face.

"Taste this you little nasty bitch." He jammed his Gloc 40., in her mouth, tormenting her until she begged to die. He then wiped the slob from the barrel onto her shirt and shot two slugs into the engine block. The music muffled and her cries rang out.

"Why you didn't kill me" she screamed from her knees.

"You already dead to me."

Realizing the camera over his head and store clerk on the phone he quickly left the scene. He knew it was just a matter of time before the police came knocking.

Pulling up to the Bayview penthouse it was obvious, Aiisha hadn't been there. Her Lexus LS 450 haven't moved, and the house felt empty. It was an eerie feeling making him draw his weapon and began searching room to room. Thereafter, he sat with his back to the bedroom wall. "What the fuck" he questioned himself. How could he let his temper jeopardize everything he had going? Usually when he had done some hot headed shit, Aiisha would be the cool one. She was his rock. In being optimistic, he hoped she'll come home by morning. "Insha'Allah", he thought out loud before closing his eyes.

With trouble on his mind, the Angel of Death haunted him. His dream of Angel and Aiisha manifested into virtual reality. Shorty finally found Angel walking along San Pablo Blvd. They came home late into the night with intentions to fulfill their fantasy. D'Juan was in a deep sleep laying on his back as they entered the room. She crawled under the bedspread, pulled his boxers down, and began massaging his manhood as it became erect. He was bounded by ropes made from money, enticed by sexual pleasure, and duped by his own dreams.

Angel whispered in his ear "You want it poppi?" While easing his manhood inside her cold womb. Her nails was sharp as razor blades up around his throat, "Is it good to you huh?" She rotates her hips faster while Aiisha massaged his scrotums.

"Damn" he thought out loud.

If Angel climaxed she'll slice his throat. Aiisha grabbed his face demanding attention, "you seem to be surprised poppi. You didn't think I would find her?" She tormented him then smiled seductively. Her thirty two teeth turned razor sharp. Angel then lifted up allowing his manhood to fall into Aiisha's hands. While carving a cross on his forehead she stared into his soul with fire red eyes.

"Come with me," she demanded. Simultaneously Aiisha opened her mouth.

"Ah" he jumped from the nightmare.

In cold sweat, and conscience stained with Angel's blood he called his ma Christi. (**Phone Ringing**) "Hello" she'd awakened from a deep sleep. "Ma I'm sorry to wake you but I've been having troubled thoughts and nightmares again. Someone is always dying around me." hearing the stress in his voice, she rose from the covers.

"Oh my son, usually that's how The Most High speaks to us. You need to pray." She emphasized."

I do pray ma, this is something else." He explained further "It's like the people closest to me are dying because of me."

"Sometimes prayer alone, just isn't enough. Read some verses in the Qur'an. Ponder on them and try to understand the meaning. The last time I had dreams like that your uncle was taken away from me. So you see?"

"Wow I never thought about it like that. I love you ma."

"I love you too, mijo."

Christi always had the right message for any trial he'd encountered. She heard of all the chaos his name was associated with and anticipated that call. She only hoped he understood his divine purpose before it's too late.

7:00 a.m. D'Juan hadn't been back to sleep. He showered and got fitted in some casual polo sport apparel, navy blue shorts, matching shirt, socks and drawback hat. He started the Lexus with a craving for waffles. He turned onto the freeway in route for downtown Oakland. Upon reaching in the center console for a swisher sweet he saw Chyna's business card. He tossed it on the passenger's seat and proceeded to split the swisher while floating in cruise control. The closer he got to the waffle house the more he thought about Chyna. After all, she was feeling the kid. "Why the hell not?" He thought out loud.

He veered off on the next exit and pulled up to a pay phone.

(**phone ringing**) "Yes Hello"

"Chyna this D'Juan. I didn't mean to call so early but I was considering breakfast and thought about you." She giggled bringing a smile to his face. "Well don't I feel special" They shared laughs. "I mean I would love for you to join me."

"I don't see a problem with that. Where are you now?"

"I'm in Emeryville at the shell station by the freeway."

"Okay you'll have to get on the freeway and exit on Ashby." She continued giving directions to her home in Kensington Hills. "Give me about twenty minutes."

"I'll be ready." She assures.

He arrived in front of her luxurious home less than twenty minutes later. It was apparent by her career choice she was a bonafide hustler. The three car garage with a S500 Mercedes Benz and 4.6 Range Rover parked in the driveway were just fruits of her labor. As he reached the last step of a flight of stairs she opened the door.

"Peace Queen." He greeted her with a smile.

"Hey there handsome." She stepped out in black hills by Jimmy Choo with a white and black skin tight dress by Dolce & Gabbana. French manicure and pedicure highlighted by the diamond tennis bracelets on her wrist and ankle. Her lips were glossy and reflected off the morning sunrays. She was sexy as the elegant words that spilled from her mouth. He took her hand and ushered her down the stairs and into the passenger seat.

"I see you got a good taste to go with your gentle mannerism." She complimented, as he closed the door behind her. Once sitting behind the wheel, he looked over and smiled. "What?" She asks bashfully.

"You look in the mirror lately? I only prefer the best" he smiled and expressed appreciation for her natural beauty. "Um, is that so.."

Chapter 18

B REAKFAST WAS FULFILLING AS could be. They both enjoyed Belgium waffles topped with whip cream and strawberries, baked chicken breast and large orange juice. As good as the meal was, their conversation was even better. She made it clear she wasn't interested in fling. She had real goals and he wouldn't be a hindrance.

"Chyna takes care of Chyna. I don't need a man to take care of me, but when he has me, he has all of me. That's the only way I can trust again." She explained in proclaiming her standards.

"I understand completely. Everybody has to have dreams, babii." He smiled captivating her charm.

"How old are you?" She asked.

"Do it matter?"

"Not really. I like your demeanor but I need you to know you legal." She says followed by giggles. "Oh, you got jokes. I'm 18 ma." He assured.

Thereafter, she told him she was a realtor and who her family were. Likewise, he introduced her to the Shakur family history. From Cuba, to the Candlelight, to Harlem. She was intrigued by his will to survive. Interested in his dreams and inspired by his ambitions. She wondered, will he be the one to make her empire a happy kingdom...

The drive back to her home was the start of something beautiful. She was relaxed and comfortable with him behind the wheel. For many years she'd been in total control of her life, so sitting in the passenger seat for a change was definitely something she appreciated. "Can you be here for dinner?" She asked before exiting the vehicle.

"Indeed what you have in mind?"

"It'll be a surprise just be here around five okay" she demanded.

"Since you put it that way I'll definitely clear my schedule." They shared smiles as she shut the door.

"Um, um, um" he thought out loud as she strutted up the stairs.

Traffic was moving like clockwork through the twenty block radius surrounding the Globe. Dorian worked the night shift at the 37th street joint with grams and eight balls of tar heroin. Rocky, Silas and Santonio held the fort, anticipating retaliation from the recent weeks of bloodshed. Hakeem and Rashaad engineered the money flow, while D'Juan campaign their product as if it was a legal drug and their trap houses were the poor man pharmacy. They figured by selling five ounces a day between their two joints that'll equal a kilo per week a hundred grand a month. Not a bad approach to reactivating a million dollar machine.

D'Juan walked into Malik's House of Stylez while Dorian was getting a triple fade.

"Aye, what up wit the kid?" Malik sat down the clippers wiping his hands clean of hair.

"You know me babii, hitting and missing."

They laugh, shake hands and embrace with a hug. Dorian passed a rolled backwood of Naide. D'Juan inhaled then nearly coughed up his breakfast "what's this boi?" he ask, wiping slob from his mouth.

"Naidene there boi." Dorian smiled while telling him about the new strain of dark haze.

The demand for Silver Haze was great but going back and forth to Washington involved huge risk. Naide was exotic indica which they could label Dark Haze and their business would only increase.

Santonio linked up with his cousin Bishop, from San Fran who had barrels of Naide. Word was, he was the front man for the Jamaican Posse, and with the feds watching their every move, he needed all the help he could get.

The machine was back in motion and D'Juan could definitely make use of the two pounds of cocaine he had tuck at his crib. After all, time was ticking and opportunity waits for no man. Look at slim, a straight ridah, always first on the scene. Now paralyzed from the neck down in a comatose state. D'Juan began evaluating the risk verse reward factors with his hustle. In all honesty, he didn't want to die without being a multi-millionaire, nor spend the rest of his life in prison before traveling the world.

After a month of not seeing or speaking to each other. D'Juan and Aiisha agreed to meet at the International House of Pancakes (IHOP) in Hilltop. He hated to believe he couldn't trust her but he had more than one reason not to. He parked the Lexus in plain view then walked across the street to the Nissan dealership awaiting her arrival. "Huh" D'Juan was in a state of confusion when she arrived with his Pa'. He jogged to the parking lot and walked up behind her as she headed to the restaurant "What's good ma-ma?" He greeted her with a smile.

"Habibi" she turned around in excitement, embracing with a hug and passionate kiss. She had a look of worry in her eyes yet was happy to see him. They chose the far left corner to sit, where everything was in front of them.

"Where you been my queen?" He asked humbly.

"D'Juan I'm scared. I've been hearing a lot of stuff since I been with you. I never cared before but", She struggled to express herself.

He lifted her chin up "Well what changed?"

"I hate to question you so I don't. Angel was my cousin but what I fear is I'll do anything for you, anything." He grabbed her hands and put one finger over her lips indicating she needed to say no more. "What you want to eat?" He asked as the waitress approached.

"How are you two doing today, can I help you with something?"

"Oh I'll get whatever he gets." Shorty replied with a smile.

"In-deed, yes mam. We'll get turkey sausage, fried eggs with country style potatoes."

"Yes sir and would you like pancakes or waffles?"

"We only come to IHOP for the cakes babii," he said, drawing a smile from the elder woman. Aiisha then tossed a dirty napkin in his face "do you always have to be so charming?"

"Word? Don't tell me you feeling some type of way about..." Jesting at the waiter who was old enough to be his grandma.

"You know what?" She asked pointing a knife with a skirmish grin. "It's okay, but I've been thinking about going to college in Chicago. Aunt Monese is going to help me enroll in Marquette. I'll work at pa' restaurant until your birthday. She said, I need to there by the third if I want to start spring semester." It was clear she had her mind made up so all he could do was support her decision.

"That's a beautiful thing ma. I'll be out there soon, you know that right?" They shared smiles.

"Well my hope is sooner than later."

"Insha'Allah right." "Yes Habibi. Insha'Allah."

She loved the sound of him leaving Rich City and the danger that haunted him. And although she loved him, she wasn't naive. She wanted more for herself than being abandoned on some train tracks with a bullet to the head. His life was full of uncertainty. He'd become accustomed to being a ghost, sleeping from pillow to post. She wanted a home. He knew, after all was said she was right. Yet and still nothing was more important than being rich, not even her.

After brunch he dropped her off at his Pa's house where she'd been living for the past month. He assured her he'll be there if and whenever she needed him. She agreed with the feeling of security but overnight her heart was at war with itself. With the phone in hand she contemplated calling for the passion she so much desired. But with pleasure lies the question "is it worth dying for?"

D'Juan and Dorian played chess, chimney smoking dark haze at the 37th street joint. All night it was one and two hundred dollar sales, every few minutes. Damn good, considering it was the middle of the month. In the middle of an intense game, Chyna paged D'Juan leaving the code 1311 (I **want you**) prompting him to smile. Meanwhile, Dorian moved his night in position to take his queen. "check".

"Good Move," he acknowledged looking back to the board. However, Dorian did not agree "nah kid, what's on ya mind? You are playing bad chess."

D'Juan couldn't agree more, "shit just mani. I got shorty at pops joint telling me I'm dangerous, materialistic and inconsiderate to her feelings. I don't know fam. Sometimes I get overwhelmed." As he shook his head, Dorian looked at him and smiled "Kid, come on man. Anybody who knows you, will tell you the same,"

"Fuck outta here, I ain't materialistic. I just like to buy nice shit."

With the next move Dorian takes his queen and told him "When you slippin on ya game you lose your most valuable piece!"

Made D'Juan further asses some things. Dorian always shared knowledge with his younger cousins, rather they wanted it or not. Raw and uncut...

It was 4 a.m. when D'Juan pulled up to Chyna's crib. Every night he'd come around the same time, liquored up with a lot of energy to burn. She answered the door naked and a desire to be fucked until sunrise. Her Chanel perfume is dominated by his X.O. and marijuana scent. As sex hits the air, her nails claw his back. With his every stroke she moans, licking the sweat from his neck and whispers in his ear to 'fuck her harder.' It was a pleasure to make her grown kitty purr. The business was seeing her taste herself licking his manhood clean, her preferred dessert. Lol.

The 28 year old madam had a history of dating high rollers. Entrepreneurs and Street Kings alike. How D'Juan made her insides vibrate was something she longed for. His charisma, serious demeanor and decisiveness were rare qualities. Math was his favorite subject and he used it to his advantage; summing up large numbers within seconds. Chyna saw a king and that meant he could only be her King. Their long talks over breakfast was to introduce him to the realm of escorts, and real estate on a corporate level. Her world, and he thinks he's the one running things...

Carlosi called Dorian on the Eve of Kwanza, needing another shipment of trees with snow and ice sickles on them. 'Perfect time to travel' D'Juan thought. Aiisha was going back to Chicago anyway and willing to make that sacrifice for lawyers' fees. It would crush her heart if he would have to serve a decade locked away in any jail.

Havana's was busy during the holiday season so Tito had Aiisha making deliveries while he done the cooking.

(Phone Ringing) "Havana's Salsa Dish. Tito speaking"

"Pa, where is shorty?"

"Mijo, she's busy. Why don't you come help out?"

"I'm out of town pa, maybe someday soon." Simultaneously, D'Juan spots her from the pay phone across the street "love you pa, tell her I called."

"Hello. Mijo, you there?" D'Juan hung up, and quickly followed her until the first stoplight (horn) she looked up and saw his gold-n-diamond grill. He pulled alongside with the window down "ma-ma, I need to holla at you for a few tics."

She pulled over in a Walgreens parking lot. "Habibi where you've been? I've been coming to the house" she expressed with deep emotion. He was slightly confused considering their last conversation.

"Ma. I've been laying low. The penthouse don't feel the same."

"let me find out you fucking somebody D'Juan, I swear" she reached for his pager faster than he could react.

"What's wrong with you?"

She put her hands on her head for a couple minutes as tears began to pour. "I just miss you man, but you wit the bullshit." She cried sending

222

butterflies to his stomach. "Why can't you stop? I don't want to lose you." She buried her head in his chest.

"I miss you too ma-ma. Listen to me" he pulled her chin up and wipes away her tears "I'm working on something to secure our future. You are my only true queen, remember that."

"Come here" she demands.

"What, you want it right now?"

"Maybe, but you better get your ass over here and kiss me right now, or I swear."

They kissed as she started to come over the console until he reminded her she was on a delivery. He promised to meet her at the Bayview penthouse later that night.

"Insha'Allah" she said while shutting the door.

The beginning of a New Year is next week and D'Juan has a lot of business to get in order. He and Dorian met at uncle Hoodies to discuss some specifics. One of the major concerns was; with him being on the run who would accompany Aiisha to Chicago? Considering it was holiday season and she would be attending College there for spring semester, traveling alone was an option

"Nah she need someone with her. Preferably a seasonal vet." he suggested.

"What about Chyna?" Dorian asked.

"Chyna? You fucking crazy. She don't know jack, especially bout Shorty."

"Fam, Chyna is one of the baddest hustlers in the game. You got a boss madam on ya team kid" Dorian elaborated.

In mid conversation, Juicy bust through the door looking for dark haze and her timing couldn't have been better. After a brief interview, the collective agreed she would be best for the job. She loved to travel and enjoyed nothing more than making money to spend it. For 10 grand she was packing her luggage minutes later.

Lastly they discussed D'Juan 19th birthday bash. "Lyfe should be home in a couple days. I got something up real gigantic, you'll see." Dorian smiled and leaned back in the leather recliner chair, lounging in Haze smoke until Ameere returned their call.

(**Phone Rings**) "What iz it?" Dorian answered.

"We are ready to travel like Fed-Ex babii." Ameere confirmed the package was ready for pick up. "A'ight first thing in the a.m. peace."

"Peace."

Dorian relayed the message to D'Juan. "A'ight that's beautiful. Get the flights scheduled, I'll get shorty ready." The two shook hands and D'Juan walked out the door. "Checkmate" he hollered back from the hallway.

Dorian looked at the crystal glass chess board, leaning in for a closer look, "No shit huh. Good move kid" he thought out loud.

While flight arrangements were being made Aiisha was getting prepared to meet the love of her life. D'Juan used his key to enter the house and walked towards the kitchen. Seeing his pa wasn't home, he walked upstairs to the guest room. Aiisha's bags lay next to the door and her clothes were laid out on the bed. He decides to hide in the closet and surprise her once she enters. Moments later he heard her singing, and smiles as the sweet sound gets closer. First step in the room she shuts the door and dropped her robe to the floor. He couldn't control himself "um, um, um" He blurted out in admiration of her beauty.

"Ah habibi why you do that?" As she catches her breath, he approached with his arms out. "Pow" she slaps the smile from his face "I told you, don't ever do that."

"You right ma-ma.. I's sorry.. Come here."

Tito had yet to return home and the temperature was perfect. He grabbed her face and looked deeply into her eyes. "I need you my Queen." She reached for his belt buckle as he unbuttoned his shirt.

"Anything my king." They kissed and shared spontaneous intimacy. Making love with no fear of what may happen next. Before climaxing she reversed positions, riding him backwards while massaging his scrotum. NO question she knew what he preferred to a science.

They showered after nearly two hours of passion and embraced the moment. "It's been too long my beloved" she mention while he hugs her from behind. "Fa real, fa real."

She rubbed her face against his forearms with both eyes closed. "So, when you need me to meet Juelz?" She asked.

"Yo who said I need you to meet him?" he then kisses her neck.

"It's my duty to know, as is yours in keeping your promise." She turned to make eye contact.

"I always keep my promises my queen." He assured her with a kiss to the forehead.

The next morning Aiisha and Juicy set out to board the Amtrak heading to Seattle, Washington. "Be safe my queen and remind yourself you're a college student traveling home."

"I'm always thinking this is for my king and you gon' be good cause I got you." She winked her eye indicating, she had no worries. They hugged tightly and kissed like there was no tomorrow. "Come on lil momma. He'll remember all that ass." Juicy interrupted their moment with a slap on the lower bottom. They had a 10 hour train ride ahead, and time waits for no one...

D'Juan and Dorian went to Golden Gate Fields to relax and see the game from a different perspective. The racetrack was also a good venue to network. To rub elbows with CEOs, Politicians and the casual millionaire that could be living next door. Butch Cozie had been predicting winners for the past decade. He had it down to a science. Quiet as kept, Dorian cashed in on all the knowledge he shared. See, he had grew tired of taken great risk for little reward. Playing the horses was playing the odds. Bet big and win big, just that simple. It was no question how he earned the title of being the ' calculated one.' When the drought hit or the block was hot, he'd disappear and doubled down at the tracks.

(Phone ringing) "What iz it?" Dorian answered.

"Bra we sitting with lil folks right now. How we looking, we could keep pushing first thing in the A.M." Juicy said with enthusiasm.

"Stick to the script we gon' be a'ight" Dorian stated firmly.

"I'm just saying time is money. It's a good thought, I'll hit you when we land." "A'ight down." Dorian shook his head after the brief conversation with his sister. She was a go-getter but sometimes had a hard time following instructions. A bad and costly habit indeed...

Chapter 19

WORD WAS, LYFE'S BACK home and the South Side was buzzing. What that meant, was some profits will be cut in half or pressure would be applied to dealers and business owners alike. Dorian got a call from Lyfe around noon.

"Doe, what the bizness is?"

"All is well Cap, one strong run away nah'mean"

"I hear you loud and clear, but I been hearing a lot of good things about the kid. They tell me he the man now." Lyfe mentions with pride.

"I'll let you be the judge, we'll be over there in a minute."

"A'ight you know where I'm at. I'll be here for the next 30 days." Lyfe explained the conditions of his parole. "No matter. Just know it's good."

Lyfe was washing a 98' Green Z28 Camaro when Dorian and D'Juan pulled up "What up Capo?" They holler before embracing with handshakes and hugs. "It's good to be home. I just hope home is good to me."

"No doubt indeed" D'Juan laughed.

"Doe, you check on that for me?" Lyfe asked.

"I've been keeping him online, he's ready." Dorian assured.

"Shit we ready then" Lyfe looked at him indicating put the play in motion. Dorian nodded his head then turned to D'Juan "be easy kid. I'll holla later."

"A'ight be easy." As Dorian pulled off in his Yukon Tahoe he hit the horn three times in remembrance of Sonny Montana.

"Huh kid, take one of these rags and help me dry this cah." Lyfe then tossed over a towel.

"A'ight it's good but you know we don't wash our whips on the front lawn no more." D'Juan jokes. "That's what's wrong with y'all. Spending too much money on shit you can do yourself." Lyfe shook his head.

After just doing a nickel in Victorville, he couldn't believe how much the underworld has changed. Kids were having kids and the young man in front of him now standing over 6ft tall, 200 pounds of muscle and 16 gold teeth with over 350 diamonds. After wiping down the rear chrome wheels Lyfe grabbed the AK 47 concealed beneath the vehicle and headed toward the front door "Kid, come on that's good enough."

"A lot has changed since you been gone Capo." D'Juan explains.

"I've been hearing but that's life. Shit happens over the months then we look up and years have flown by. What's important is our growth. So what are we looking like?"

"We got a joint on 37th, moving hop and blow. On 35th is two joints, grams of hard, then you know the apartments, same business as usual. I'm working on an operation in the Globe, we just need a big score." D'Juan then shared the numbers made within the last year.

Lyfe nods his head "not bad. We may have a need for them joints in the Globe. What's up with Remo?"

"He got Silver Street on fire., they basically control that side of town far as heroin." Lyfe wasn't surprised. "You know where their success comes from?"

"They're well organized." D'Juan suggest.

"Well that's just part of it. The projects is their base so they could be organized. The Globe is our safe haven, always has been." Lyfe elaborated.

"Cap, I'm hot right now. Danielle dialed the pigs on me."

"What?" Lyfe looked in disbelief so D'Juan explained the circumstances.

"She crossed the grain. Took the bounty on one off our own, Lil Izzy. Even showed the ma'fuckaz where he laid his head."

Lyfe had heard of the beef while inside but didn't know how deep they were involved. Nonetheless, it wasn't something that should stop their operation. Lyfe was impressed of how D'Juan handled himself. After all, he was just keeping up with tradition. As in the late 80's with Sonny. Once a Globe boy was murdered a war usually followed.

"Look, we got moves to make and you on the run for some bullshit. I'm going to speak to Danielle and put that to rest. Remember, we all we got."

"No doubt indeed"

Lyfe stressed the importance for D'Juan to play his position while reiterating, his movements would be limited. D'Juan knew he was right. Izreal's death triggered an emotional and reckless response.

"What you want to eat?" Annabelle asked from behind the door. Prawns and Snapper was Lyfe's request. "Aye, Bella come here" she opened the door looking tired and stressed "What's up?"

"Did you know Danielle called the pigs and involved them in family business?" Lyfe asked.

"No I didn't but she knows the consequences. And D'Juan you not a kid neither. They would throw yo ass under the jail." She emphasized her disappointment before excusing herself to prepare their evening meal.

A basket of Butterfly Prawns, Red Snapper fillets, and a bowl of French fries rested on two portable tables. While Lyfe shared his plans for 'the great comeback.' Dorian copped over sixty pounds of dark haze just in the past six weeks. By mere coincidence, the same cats that Bishop was connected with also had ties to Lyfe. Which evidently he cared very little about. This score he hoped will bring millions back to the Familia.

"Shaka gon' meet you and Doe at the public storage on 35th. A hunnid P's is going to be stuffed in a U-Haul, probably the gas tank."

D'Juan interjected "wait these the same ma'fuckaz being watched by the FEDS?"

Lyfe's whole demeanor changed as if he was unaware of the heat. "I'll have to holla at Doe tomorrow. Either way it'll work to our advantage. They the ones hot, not us" Lyfe elaborated further, seeing that D'Juan was at unease. "Our money is worth more than their product. We're only negotiating on our terms. When Shaka unloads the U-Haul he'll keep the key until we make the drop the next morning."

"I can see that" D'Juan gesture he's in agreement. He trusted in the plan and committed to doing his job. They then enjoyed a good home cooked meal. It was the best Lyfe had in 5 years and D'Juan hadn't sat down to eat in the recent weeks.

"Bella that was really good. Thank you Madame, your service is greatly appreciated." D'Juan said with humor.

"Yea huh, where is my tip then? You ain't gotta kiss my ass..." her voice faded down the hall. Lyfe smiled as they exited the door and hit the streets...

King Arthur wasn't home six months and had a full scale operation. Heavy traffic flowed through deeper central Richmond at all times of the day. No less than thirty grand was touching his desk by the break of dawn. He was the first Street King, Lyfe chose to visit.

They pulled up to 4th street market at or around 11 p.m. "Aye, King back there?" Lyfe asked the store clerk. "Yeah he's back there. Follow Zeek." He greeted Lyfe in the best fashion. It was nothing but respect between the two.

(Door Opened)"Look at this here. What's larger than Lyfe huh?" Big King Arthur rose from his desk and embraced the two.

"Since you ask you liven pretty large from what I hear?"

"Ah now don't believe everything you hear. Business is good, but I have a feeling it's gon' get a lot better," they shared laughs in agreement.

Their conversation was all about territory and connections. The arrangement that cut Lyfe in on a pallet of Kilo's also involved Remo's vision of uniting under one banner, one banking system. Like in New York only this would be another Black Wall Street.

Rich City was home but without any stakes in it they could be banned from it at any time. Investments into City buildings and homes meant they would have a voice and chair at city council meetings. King Arthur was impressed and very much interested. They shook hands and exchanged numbers.

Next stop was the Silver Street projects. Joey and Jaquez met them in front of a safe house on 1st street.

"Soc Posse, Poppa" Joey shouted as Lyfe exited his Camaro. The young Haitians embraced their Uncle.

"Soc Posse" Lyfe smiled as he finally felt at home.

"Where Remo?"

"He and Rome flew to Hawaii last week. They got business in Tahiti." Jaquez explained.

"We got something for you though Poppa." they embraced with family love before Joey handed him a backpack. "All we ask is you holler at us for anything." Jaquez said with emphasis on **ANYTHING**.

"Damn I miss my Familia." Lyfe threw one strap over his shoulder and turned toward his Camaro. "Peace King." Their gold teeth shined as he walked away.

D'Juan recognized the two as being connected with Topaz "Hop" Deguzman's crew. He wondered if Remo was controlling the entire heroin market in Rich City.

"See this how it supposed to be. Huh" Lyfe handed the backpack to D'Juan. Inside was two kilos of heroin, two kilos of cocaine, a Mac-10 with Ingram and three 30 round magazines.

"This is how it's gon' be in due time." D'Juan rest assured.

The drive back to the South Side was like a total climate change. Although money was being made it wasn't being put back into the community.

"This city was once owned by us. Every gas station, liquor store, cleaners, laundromat, every business was ours. Now look at this" Lyfe pointed out the evident signs of power change in the urban community. D'Juan listened and couldn't help but blame the mid 80's and the epidemic of crack cocaine. Lyfe's knowledge of the city's downfall was accurate, but in reality the F.K boys were part of the problem.

The Globe was busy as usual. Lyfe didn't want to be seen that night so he parked in the lot of building 2801. They then walked to the 3200 buildings with hoods drawn over their heads. D'Juan knocked on the door of apartments where he paid rent and introduced them to Capo. Out of five joints only one would be used as a safe house. Lyfe had specific instructions concerning the other four. Then he advised D'Juan to lay low for the next four months, move like a ghost and maybe he'll be around to see the familia at its strongest yet..

Later that night Dorian considered the repercussions of this big score. Lyfe's answer to that was they're at war anyway over small change. This he reasons would set the record straight. Dorian agreed as much, "they just waiting on the call."

"So make the call. We got work to do."

Lyfe dialed Fresh Money's joint to put D'Juan on point while Dorian setup the meet. He returned 5 minutes later with good news. A hundred pounds of dark haze was wrapped and ready for cargo. The deal was set for the next night.

"We on, soon as nightfall. I'm going to slide through Fresh's joint tonight. Me and the kid gotta wrap about a few things." Dorian said before walking out the door.

"You do that. I passed the word, but he needs a face to face. Meet back here first thing." Lyfe request as he leaned back in his recliner chair.

Juicy arrived at Richmond Train station at 8:15 a.m. Dorian wasn't surprised when she handed him a bag containing only fifty grand. "Huh help me with my bags." she demanded. Giving no answers he just stared at her with a blank expression. "You really not gon' help me?" she looked him sideways.

"I got you" he popped the trunk of his Lincoln Continental and just stood with his back to the rear passenger door.

"Fa real? You ain't even cool." She pouted while tossing her luggage in the trunk.

"*I ain't cool?* You left with two bags, brought back five. Ten grand light. Nah, you got it twisted. I'm cool as I ever been." His voice was mellow but his words cut deep. Of course she had nothing to say. Little did she consider her opportunity to make a six figure salary while splurging at the outlets. It was a quite drive back to Big Hoodies joint. Before Juicy exited the Lincoln, Dorian expressed his concerns with not being able to trust her. And those who couldn't be trust had no place in his circle.

It was 2 a.m. in Chicago, Illinois. Aiisha heard the phone ring but thought she was dreaming. Her eyes opened to the sound of D'Juan's' voice coming from the answering machine.

"Aunty, peace and blessings be upon you. I was just thinking about you and my queen. Can you have her call me? Love y'all. Peace."

"Habibi!" Aiisha rushed to the phone, but he'd already hung up. She immediately called back.

(Phone Rings)"Yo, what's the drill?" D'Juan answered.

"Habibi, I missed you. How are you?" She asked with excitement. "I'm good now my queen. Your voice is like nutrition to my bones." He said with a smile. "Really? I love you sooo much, when you coming?" "Insha'Allah soon. How 've you been?"

"All praises to Allah. I love it so much here. I just rolled by Marquette earlier with Aunty. It's a big campus and I'm soo excited." she then shared events of her last couple of days.

"Sounds good, I'm feeling that. You know I've been really thinking 'bout what Losi was speaking on." He expressed fear of being just another street kid left bleeding in the gutter. "You gon' be good just trust in Allah." She encourages him to find his true purpose.

She was willing to make trips to Seattle on a regular basis in the cause of his freedom. She expressed the desire to open a hair salon and gamers' lounge for children. D'Juan loved her plans and encouraged her to follow through. However, he insisted that she not worry about the expenses, or ill-gotten gain from any criminal activity. He made arrangements to have the Lexus delivered by the dealership which she should receive within ten working days. Ending their pleasant conversation, Aiisha sang a song titled: 'Blood Isn't thicker than love' written by herself. It was the most soulful music his ears ever heard. Before closing his eyes for the night, he considered the possibility of living in Chicago under an assumed name. "Insha'Allah."

First thing in the morning D'Juan called Rome **(Phone Ringing)** "Hello" he answered, like he'd been partying all morning.

"What iz it Pa"

"Ha, Ha, the king just lounging. Me and Remo in Waikiki" He further elaborated how beautiful the Polynesians and their culture was.

"That's what's up. I gotta make that trip one day, fa real. On another note, yo it's getting heated in the city." D'Juan explained.

"Oh yeah I heard about that. You see me brodi, I'm networking and rubbing elbows with bosses. No time fa bull-shitin, ya feel me"

"I feel you bro, as long as you safe. I'll find a way out of this ma'fucka one day"

"Oh yea, I heard about that one situation. You need to be fuckin wit Chyna fa' real. She on another level."

"Word huh?"

"Bro, if you didn't know before I'm telling you. She owns damn near half this Island. Her face is on billboards everywhere. Real Estate, Clubs, you..." As Rome depicts the cities make-up, D'Juan slipped into a zone thinking of what could be "Yeah, you got you one kid" Rome reiterated.

"Fa real, huh. I gotta sit down with her. Maybe she can put me up on a few things nah'mean."

"Do that Pa, Asap ya hear me?"

"No doubt. Perfectly clear."

"A'ight, Peace king."

"Peace..." D'Juan hung up and rested his hands on his head. His heart was with Aiisha but his presence is in front of Chyna. It was no question, she had an empire to give him but the uncertainty lies in it's value.

(Phoned Ringing)"Hello" Chyna answered with a smile on her face.

"Peace Ma-ma... how are you?"

"Oh wow, I was just thinking about you."

"Oh yeah, so you miss the kid?"

"Maybe just a little. So where are you at?"

"I'm in the Globe, you in the area?" He asked while walking towards the 3100 building.

"Actually, I'm at Bella's Fish n' Chicken. You want something?"

"No doubt. Cop some butterfly prawns, fries, a large peach cobbler, and I'll tell you the rest when you get here." "Okay, whatever you saay."

"See, as long as we got that understanding. Now bring ya ass." He commanded, leaving a smile on her face.

As soon as he put the phone in his pocket, a police patrol car was moving slowly in his direction. "It's no way I'm going down today, no fucking way." He thought to himself. Rule number one, **NEVER** panic. He kept walking and not looking back until he reached the front entrance. Chyna drove slow up Carlson Blvd. as she approached the projects. He emerged from the side of a building flagging for her to stop.

(Door Opened)"Rollaz was just here," he alerted, while leaning back in the passenger's seat. "Baby you okay?" She asked.

"No doubt, I'm good." He then un holstered his Gloc 40. putting it under his leg.

"Baby what you gon' do with that?" She asked with great concern.

"If they don't pull us over, we won't have to worry about that ma. Just drive, we'll be a'ight."

Chyna avoided the main streets and took Arlington Lane from the Richmond Hills all the way to her house in Berkeley. "I don't want to lose you D'Juan, especially to some dumb shit. You've become a special part of me, let me help you." She pleaded with sincerity. He contemplated the idea, but could she really help him with the uncertainty that lies ahead or with the demons that haunt him.

"A'ight, introduce me to yo world." He looked at her with a piercing gaze.

"I got you babe." She smiled then increased her driving speed to 50 mph.

Once they reached her eight hundred thousand dollar crib, she laid it all out on the table. The funeral home and two apartment complexes were paying for themselves. A few years back, she paid the City one hundred grand for two foreclosed buildings, both of which she remodeled into five two-bedroom apartments: with Hawaiian style kitchen, bathrooms, and palm trees decorating the landscape. The property value increased immediately by five hundred percent. Her strategy was to network and invest with banks that benefited from leans on foreclosed homes. Which was the same strategy made her a multi-millionaire in Waikiki, Honolulu. Mr. Owens taught this daughter well. Chyna made herself clear, that for his heart he could have her empire. Funny thing about that, is when Annabelle was the queen of Sugar Hill that's when a young capo named Lyfe came into her life. They were married less than a year later and the rest was legendary. D'Juan had a lot to consider but while Chyna was in heat and under his command, he was going to keep the fire lit. **No question...**

Chapter 20

I T WAS 8 P.M. when Dorian called Shaka convincing him it was the best time to make the deal happen. They agreed to meet at an Exxon gas station on 23rd Street within the next two hours. Just enough time for him to employ Silas for a job. After a quick briefing, the two met Lyfe and D'Juan at the 3201 building in 'the Globe.' Fresh Money and his wife was enjoying their anniversary weekend in the Virgin Islands. The four sat at each side of a coffee table with Lyfe giving the orders, "Tonight we have to be sharp. Clear minds and eyes wide open. Silence remember, tonight you just follow 'em write down the address or location of their hangouts. Tomorrow, we'll finish it." They locked eyes and Silas nodded his head assuring, he could consider it done. After their brief meeting, they spent the next hour setting up.

Silas and Shadonje' parked in an alley behind Jones and Harris record store. Razor and Santonio were looking out of an apartment window directly across from the public storage. One held a 30 odd six with night vision scope, and the other held a military radio capable of intercepting any communications by walkie-talkie within a hundred mile radius. Lyfe and D'Juan waited inside a storage container until Dorian arrived with Socrates and Shaka. They could hear their voices as they exited the U-Haul.

"Ah, good location mon," Shaka complimented then signaled for his brother to turn the U-Haul around.

"This is why it was the best time for this to happen. You see, there's no gate man, and more importantly no eyes nah'mean." Dorian said

"Nah'mean, got'cha poppa." Said Shaka with a mischievous grin.

After receiving a page from Razor "3400" Dorian opened the container's door.

"Hey, poppa," Lyfe greeted Socrates with brotherly love.

"Lyfe mon! No fuckin way. Say mon, when you make it home?"

"A little less than a week, but it's on now. Everything we talked about." Lyfe then nodded his head.

"Yeah, we'll see. You caught wind of the situation huh?" Socrates asked.

"I heard enough, but we not gon' let a little attention stop the machine. What we doin anyway? just helping a friend unload some furniture huh."

"Ahh, right indeed my brotha." They shared laughs.

Dorian handed Shaka a lock and key, then explained its purpose. "We'll unload here tonight, lock up the container and we'll get the key from you tomorrow. Half then, and the rest next week." The one-eyed Rasta squinted as he contemplated the arrangement. On more than two occasions Lyfe sacrificed his blood and money for him during their bid in Victorville Federal prison. That surely factored into his decision. "Okay my brotha, o.k. Let's unload this truck huh."

Each pound was vacuum sealed and stuffed inside two money-green leather couches. After inspecting the product, they were satisfied and arranged to meet the next morning at Pier 19. Lyfe was fresh out, and in no hurry to go back to prison. He suggested it would probably be safer if someone other than them made the drop and pick-up.

Nonetheless, Shaka insisted on picking up the quarter million dollars himself. Dorian led them to Interstate 80 hitting the horn three times as they parted ways. As the Rastafarians discussed the potential dangers in meeting Annabelle, a white 300Z followed from four car lengths back.

D'Juan and Lyfe took a ride to the Montreal Estates in Fairfield Suisun. "Whose tilt is this?" D'Juan asked. Lyfe looked over and smiled in response. The three-car garage, luxurious estate was inspired by several designs of Frank Wright. Built from the ground up with underground bunker, security system, thirty feet ceiling, the whole nine: mobster style.

They shared ideas about buying real estate and renovating schools starting with their neighborhood. Ron's liquor store and restaurant was on the market for a reasonable price. Harry Ells Gym and Dana's Cleaners needed to be restored, and the service that those establishments provided was priceless.

"Baby how long have you been here?" a Nubian princess walked down the stairs in her nightgown and wraps her arms around Lyfe's neck, kissing him on the face.

"Millah, this is my lil' brother, D'Juan."

"Oh, hello." Kamillah then whispered into Lyfe's ear. He turned and lifted her gown as she strutted off to the kitchen. *"oooh"* She smiled, immediately covering herself. A twenty two year old college graduate from U.C, Davis with a Bachelor of Science degree. D'Juan was impressed. Not only had Lyfe copped a mini mansion while on the inside, he also had an educated mistress maintaining the joint. She returned with two Heinekens and a joint hanging from her lips. "Here, lil brother you wanna hit this?" She asked while lighting the joint.

"Nah, I need to lean back, nah'mean. Long day ma." D'Juan was clearly exhausted.

"Baby I think he'll like Jazmine." Kamillah suggested.

Lyfe thought about the kids' situation and agreed. "You got a picture of her? You gotta ask him." "You know what, I have one in the family room." she returned with graduation pictures from a few months prior. "Here D'Juan this is Jazmine,"

He grabbed the frame. "This yo sister?" He asked, drawing a smile.

"You can say that. We went to Junior high in Houston, moved to Cali, and made it all the way through college together, my bestie for sure." she explained.

"Say her name's Jasmine huh? You know what her name means in Arabic?" He asked

"In Arabic? NO, what?"

"Yasmin means beautiful. And that she is, no question. I wouldn't mind introducing her to my world." He said with confidence. She then grabbed the phone and walked up the stairs dialing a number. It wasn't long after that, he laid back and rested his eyes. Last thing he heard was, she had her own townhome and was a branch manager at Enterprise corporations. Lyfe vouched for Jazmine as being a focused and determined woman..

It was 7:21 a.m. Shaka called Dorian (Phone ringing.) "What iz it?" He answered while exhaling some dark haze.

"This me brotha, just tell me when."

"Good timing, she's en-route as we speak. You remember the location huh?"

"Yea mon, I remember."

"Be there in a half hour. Just in case, nah'mean."

"On my way brotha, if she calls, just tell her to hold tight."

"No doubt, indeed," Dorian had his confidence. Within minutes he dialed up Silas and told him to pin the tail on the Barbie. Silas assured he had the iron hot and ready.

Sitting in the parking lot of the Ramada Inn, he locked eyes on his mark. Shaka, fitted in a Johnny Blaze hoodie and cargo jeans stepped down the stairs with money on his mind. Momentarily, a tall young lady wearing provocative clothing was smoking a cigarette at the bottom of the stairwell. "Hey, lil 'momma, had a long night huh?" Looking at her up and down from her red wig to stiletto heels.

"Yeah, long and slow." She said with disappointment.

Immediately thereafter, Shaka felt a tap on his shoulder, "Excuse me sir, this yo cah?" Silas asked.

"Yeah this me whip, why? You see me talking to the lady." He responded with aggression. "Excuse me playa," Silas gave Shadonje the nod as he walked back to his 300Z.

"Rude ma'fucka . Look little birdie, I would love to talk about your long day, but I have some business to handle first." He gestured catching up with her later then on second thought, he asked her to join him. She looked at him from his Lox to timberland boots with the taste of money on her lips.

"I'll ride, but you know my time is money," she emphasized. He smiled and took her by the arm. "Money is nothing, but don't play me off like some trick willie, ya hear. I'm shotta boy, I take what I want. I can show you the good life of luxury living, not pennies and dimes, now you comin?"

Without saying a word, she rubs her arm and stomps to the passenger door letting herself into his black CLK 500 Benz. As he walked to the trunk and rearranged some bags, she pulled out a Sig Sauer 380. From her purse. **(Car door opened).** He sat behind the wheel, turned the key in the ignition and turned up the volume to some reggae music.

"Who's that?" She asked.

"Hah, this my brethren from Kingston."

She smiled, enjoying the rhythm of the beat and with his permission turned it up even louder. As he looked over his shoulder to back out of the parking spot, he never considered his fate would come from the hands of this beauty.

"BANG, BANG"

Two shots were muffled by the quacking sound system. "Ah!' she jumped, as his head leaned towards her lap. She then opened the door and strutted out of the parking lot. Silas pulled alongside her disappearing with the flow of traffic.

"Job well done momie." Silas commended while slapping her thigh. Shadonje was a little shaken up, but for ten grand she could afford the nightmares.

5:45 a.m. D'Juan awoke under a blanket with his belt unbuckled and pants unfastened. "What the fuck" he thought. His gun was still under the couch. His shoes, shirt, and coat were neatly stored in the guest closet. Guess Kamillah wanted him to feel as comfortable as possible. Upon checking his Motorola pager, he'd received the message he'd anticipated: "3400", in plain English meant the job was done. Fineto. He quickly showered and dressed. The thought of being One hundred and fifty thousand dollars richer was followed by uncertainty. He stuffed a Garcia Vega with dark haze and leaned back on the couch. Dark thoughts loomed as the cloud of smoke got thicker.

Kamillah walked down the stairs in sweat pants and sports bra "Good morning, you sleep well?" She asked with a smile. "No doubt, you?"

"I don't know, I really couldn't sleep." "I see.. My brother ain't never slept this long. That's called a **T.K.O.**" he joked. "You crazy. Nah, he in the shower he'll be down in a minute."

"Ma you good?" He asked, upon her starring at the floor.

"Oh I'm sorry." She laughed and explained: "I'm sitting here thinking about my sis. Jazzy is a really good woman, but she got bad luck with dudes. I just don't get it. She's ambitious, hella smart, and just oh-my-gawd beautiful." she explained.

"It sounds like she got a lot going on for herself. Some cats are intimidated by a good looking and successful woman." He said, excluding himself from that class.

"That might be it. I don't know, but you should meet her." She further elaborated on Jasmine's decorated track and field career. "Oh yeah, hook it up." D'Juan was definitely interested.

"Kiddo, you heard from Lil man?" Lyfe asked from the top of the staircase.

"Yeah, he said it's about that time." Kamillah's excitement was gone as she feared the worst. Asking questions into what business was so important to leave on the eve of her birthday, the answer was even more concerning. After a quick breakfast they were out the door...

It was New Year's Eve, and they had to move fast. Shaka's body was yet to be identified, but surely, Socrates and his Jamaican Posse will be coming for either their drugs or money. Lyfe called Dorian. **(Phone Rings)** "What iz it?"

"This Capo, I need you to close that account a.s.a.p."

"Al-ready done"

"100."

Within an hour of receiving a message from Silas, they blew the lock using double-odd shredders, stuffed three duffle bags, and fled on street motorbikes. It went smooth as cocoa butter. After stashing eighty pounds, they left twenty at Fresh Money's joint. Talk about an early birthday gift. Rocky finally handed over the 9mm Calico, D'Juan was itching to get his hands on. "Tuh, this what it took." He thought out-loud with a grin on his face.

Lyfe called for a meeting at Bella's after business hours. Once everyone was gathered together and in attention, he laid out the blueprints. "This was a big move. One that'll help us rebuild, and what I mean is our community. We will be the bank for the moms and pops stores on the South Side. However, we have some other business to handle first. By no means will this Jamaican Posse lay low and do a silent investigation. They are coming guns blazing', no question." Lyfe emphasized the seriousness of the threat. Reminding everyone that Socrates knew their location and faces.

"I got the young troops locked and loaded. Promise you, any dread head will be a target." Rocky was confident his army wouldn't be too trigger happy.

Silas was quiet as usual, but the more Lyfe stressed about clipping all loose ends, the more certain he was that Shadonje's days were numbered.

Dorian and D'Juan focused on the numbers. No one had Dark Haze on the market, so they could even supply the competition. Rather, they copped for leisure or to hustle, four hundred dollars an ounce was the premium. They had the right idea. Besides, nothing lasts forever.

Lastly, Dorian announced that everyone should be suited and booted by 9 p.m. Limousines would be pulling into the Globe at 9:15 p.m. and were riding out no later than 9:30. They were celebrating the New year, D'Juan's birthday, and Lyfe's return home. It's set to be an epic event...

Chapter 21

A T 9 O'CLOCK SHARP, six limousines were parked in the front lot. A mob of la familia members awaited seating assignments. Lyfe wanted the generals and lieutenants seated by the doors, and no more than nine people per vehicle. D'Juan, Dorian, Rocky, Junior, and Silk accompanied Lyfe in the black limousine. As they hit Interstate 880, a fleet of luxury whips followed. Not 45 minutes later, they were pulling into Club Echelon's parking lot. Red carpet was laid out for the stars of the special event. Suited in Brook Brothers, Giorgio Armani, and Salvatore Ferragamo, tailor-made suits. The mob rolled through in the best fashionable attires money could buy. The pretty single ladies and jazzy diva hustlers were wall-to-wall, attracting pimps, players, and hustlers. Oh my, was it the place to be.

H-Holla, the DJ for the night had the turntables on fire, only pausing for a brief announcement: "Ladies and gentlemen, let me give a shout-out to Rich City's finest. Lyfe fresh home from the FEDs and D'Juan 'the kid' starting the year off right with champagne wishes and honey-glazed chicken breasts for dinner ya dig. I see you playas." Simultaneously, champagne glasses were raised.

D'Juan had been accompanied by two attractive, sexy ladies who were educating him on how Dominicans party. "Huh, Dom Perignon, please." He slid the bartender four crispy one hundred dollar bills. "I dig your style ma-ma's, no doubt. But can I show you how we party?" He asked, while reaching for their hands. They briefly looked at each other and smiled. "Why not?"

He poured two glasses to the brim and took the bottle to the dance floor. Lyfe had two cases of Cristal and two fifths of Hennessy X.O at the tables for his entourage. He and Annabelle enjoyed a few minutes of dancing and observed D'Juan as he danced the night away with his hands as busy as his feet. Initially his accompanied guest acted a little shy, but he was able to bring out a freaky side, she probably didn't know she had in her.

"Super freak!" He thought, with his middle finger massaging her clit right on the dance floor. Covertly, she'd instigated his touch and aroused him by bending over at the waist. Offering his manhood full access to her panty less lower bottom .

After toasting to the New Year and their recent success, they chased shots of X.O. with champagne. Lyfe, Junior, Silk, Magic Mike, and Calvin T were the main attraction as cameras were flashing nonstop. Flocc City Popparazzi, a young, and upcoming photographer and film producer did the honors. Taking over five hundred pictures by the end of the night.

No question, it was just as many being taken by the FBI agents posing as Hustlers and Se-Diva-Cocksuckers! Complete focus was on the older Capos. In those days three thousand dollars suits were attractive to every-one. Ironically, it was those who envied and disliked the Mob, wanting to experience a mobster's lifestyle. Even if it was for just one night.

DJ H-Holla made another announcement around midnight: "We've got JT the Bigga Figga, San Quinn, and the Get Low records performing in five minutes." D'Juan was in lounge mode when he was approached by an Angel dressed in all white.

"Hey, lil daddy, you a pimp?" She asked,

"Nah, I would consider myself a businessman. A hustler my nature, nah mean." He explained with a smile.

"Oh, okay. I'm feeling that." She awaited his acceptance.

"What's your name lil' momma? I'm D'Juan," he reached out to shake her hand.

"I'm Mercedez, pleasure to meet you. I've had my eyes on you all night."

"Word.. So what's your interest?"

"I guess just you. You look so young to have so much power."

All he could do was smile. Whatever game she was running, she had his attention. Her poise, demeanor and walk was of pure confidence. The one piece bodysuit complimented her frame as if was her birthday suit. Pearl and platinum jewelry only added elegance to an already classy woman.

Bay Area legends, started the New year in a memorable fashion. The Get Low crew was followed by 3x Crazy, harm from the Rich, The Luniz, E-40, Magic Mike and Calvin T. All showcasing electrifying performances while supporting each other. Talking about Bay Love in a real way. King Arthur crashed the joint with his crew a little after midnight. Bringing more energy, spending more money and popping more bottles. They joined the Familia for the last group pictures, making them instant classics.

Let the record reflect, this was the night Lyfe became the top Capo of all Rich City. The DJ had a final announcement: "Please, thank our host tonight, Doe Boy, and the Artist's for the brilliant show. The ladies for keeping the gentlemen occupied, and the gangster's for showing love and respect. Welcome home Lyfe, birthday boy D'Juan the kid and ya favorite DJ, H-Holla when you see me."

Doors opened and limousines drivers were waiting. Lyfe accompanied by Annabelle, Junior and his wife, was to be ushered to the Limo first. Dorian, Rocky and Silk positioned the rest of the crew as they came out. Their only priority was protecting the Capo.

"Juan..." Lyfe yelled out, standing through the moon-roof with a Colt 45 in his left hand, signaling with his right. After arming himself with a Mac-10, D'Juan fell into formation and took the front passenger seat. Silk then signaled it was time to roll out. A caravan of fifty vehicles swerved in-and-out of lanes, basically shutting down the highway. Next stop was the Claremont Spa in the Kensington Hill's.

Dorian and Remo reserved the entire top floor for the next three days. "A hell of a way to bring in the New Year huh," Junior expressed. A spa and bar was in every suite including a masseuse on call. D'Juan called his private sexual healer to help him relax **(Phone Ring.)** No answer. Looking at his Locman watch, it was 2:48 a.m. He called a second time waking Chyna, "Hello" she whispered.

"Ma-ma, I'm at the Claremont, bring yo ass." he demanded.

"What wait, what time is it?"

"Happy New year! Baby," he said in jest.

"Babee... O.k, you right. I'll be there in ten minutes." She obviously forgot their plans; so he cared very little for her attitude.

Chyna exited the elevator in a robe, to what appeared to be an orgy. Naked women and men in their underwear running in and out each other's suites.

"What the hell." She thought. Covering herself and slowly jogging to suite number 808. D'Juan met her at the door with a gallon of orange juice and two ecstasy tabs.

"Now what's so important to get me down here half-naked in the wee hours?" she asked with one hand on her hip in akimbo.

"I was thinking, what could be more important than you being with me?" He pulled her closer by the waist. "I just miss you-ssh."

"I can't tell" she began kissing him on his neck and bare chest.

"Tonight's going to be special," He promises while putting a pill in her mouth. They shared a glass of orange juice and as he turned towards the refrigerator she jumped on his back, wrestling until they found themselves on the king-sized bed. "I'll treat you like no other than a king." She said, looking into his eyes. He felt the affection in her words. The more she talked the more he understood what she wanted: a relationship with security, power, adventure, and fantasies getting fulfilled. "Babe, I got a little sum 'thin for ya."

"Ohh, is that right?" he asked with his hands resting behind his head. She was all smiles, rolling off his chest. Then she dug into her overnight bag and pulled out a black-velvet case.

"Huh, what's this?" He asked before opening a box.

Inside was a twin set of .45 caliber Sig Sauer's, in ten karat gold with pearl handles. "This is what's really good," He said with appreciation.

"That's not it, the best is yet to come." She then opened a watch case which held an 18 karat yellow-gold Rolex with twenty-four rows of diamond clusters.

"Wow"...

"That's not even half your worth my king."

Looking into Chyna's eyes she was definitely in ecstasy. Her heart was open, and her desire wasn't a secret. Her robe dropped behind her as she rode on his erected penis.

"You Presidential baby." She whispered, before licking the inside of his ear.

"No fuckin doubt."

After a few minutes of foreplay, he enters her wet and steamy pussy again. With bodies sweating and teeth gritting, they fell asleep in ecstasy. When D'Juan opened his eyes, Chyna's 155 pounds of solid goodness rested on his chest.

For the next half hour, he reflected and on all that's happened in the past week. The 18 karat yellow gold dog tags resting on his stomach, reminded him of Izreal and the trouble that followed his death. The best thing to happen to him was laying in his arms that very moment, and he figured she had to count for something.

Chyna opened her eyes while he was still in deep thought. "Good morning, my king."

He looked at her briefly, and then returned to his thoughts.

"What's on your mind daddy?"

"Remember you were telling me about buying property from the city?"

"Yeah, what's up?" She asked with a smile.

"I was thinking, can you check into Harry Ells Gym and Recreation Center?"

"First thing Monday morning, I'll go down to the City Hall. The Mayor Chucky Newsome is my uncle. Anything to better his city he's with it."

"Make it happen for us ma-ma." he demands. By his calculation, another six month run would net a quarter mill of profits to invest.

Chyna ordered brunch and set up the dining table. D'Juan was stepping out of the shower as the meal arrived. Wrapped in a bath-towel, he sat slouched in his chair at the table.

"Damn... Ma-ma, I'm weak."

She smiled and explained that she too had a wild night. "We just need to eat daddy. Here, and drink this." She poured a tall glass of orange juice and Moet to wash down the T-bone steak and buttermilk blueberry pancakes. "I'm really glad to know you've been listening to me. I never had a man that listened. They just loved the sound of their own voice," she shared her past experiences with bitterness.

"Yeah, I listen to every word come out of them pretty lips."

"That's so, huh? Well, have you thought about the escorting business?"

"Escorting, you mean transporting?" He asked for clarity.

"No daddy, I mean putting them little bitches that jock your style to work." She further explained, gaining his interest. "I have a lot of property, homes and hotels in Hawaii. Our business would be a service that many would pay a lot of money for. The girls have to be classy with an extravagant taste for living lavishly. They'll be the ones." She laid out her vision for obtaining generational wealth.

"I can dig that, no doubt. I'm thinking more like three. The less the better. Quality over quantity nah'mean."

"Exactly. Just remember I'm always number one. I going to give you the world."

As convincing as she sounded, he revisited a conversation he had with Aiisha: "The Quran warns us about the danger of being deceived by the mere amusement of this world. Don't sell your soul my beloved." True indeed, but ecstasy can cause a man to fall in love with his selfish desires. Sex, money, and power was clouding his intellect, as if he had no true purpose.

After spending an afternoon dominating Chyna, D'Juan finally checked his pager. He returned a call to a number that's left a code: 5*600. **(Phone Ringing)** "Hello," A young lady answers, "somebody hit me from this num-"

"Is this D'Juan?" She asked, getting him to rise out of bed.

"Who dis?"

"This Mercedez. Happy Birthday!"

"Oh shit, what's really good?" "I was hoping you could answer that for me. Where are you?" She demanded directions. "You ready? I'm at Claremont Spa and Hotel, room 808."

"I know where that is. I'll call back if I get lost. Room 808, right?"

"Yes mam, and I'll be ready for you"

"Better be." She said seductively.

He hung up the phone and headed for the shower. "Daddy, we have company?" Chyna asked, stopping him in mid-stride. "Only time will tell." he answered swiftly, proceeding on his mission.

She joined him in the shower, exerting whatever energy he had left. Then she slipped in a Donna Karen dress and waited. She was anxious to see this prospect he spoke highly of.

At last, **(knock on the door)** "What's the password?" He joked.

"It's me Mercedez" He opened the door before she could finish saying her name. Her voice was all he needed to hear. She stepped in, "Who else you expecting?" She asked clothed from head to toe in Burberry. She strutted in with confidence that oozed of sex appeal and enticement. At first glance, even Chyna licked her lips.

"It's good you came, let's have a seat on the couch." He directed stepping out of the hallway. Upon which time she locked eyes with Chyna who was sitting crossed-legged reading the USA Today Newspaper.

"Hello," Chyna smiled while sitting the paper down. Mercedez looked back at D'Juan for some understanding.

"Cedez, this Chyna. We were just discussing some business opportunities in Hawaii," he explained.

"I knew you were a pimp." she said with resentment.

"Woe, wow ma. I'm far from a pimp. I'm a hustla, trying to have sum'thin. I always heard my Uncle Squally say: 'Play the game for high stakes,' so I ask you, what do you play for?" He asked, looking into her money-green eyes.

"It depends if I have to play the game to get what I want?"

"Look, what better life is there than to travel the land and be able to buy a piece of it? Shit, you seen Vegas, Hawaii, Miami, D.C.?"

"I used to live in Vegas, but what's in Hawaii?" She asked.

"It's a wide open market: adult entertainment and Real estate." She pondered on the idea for a few minutes. Meanwhile, Chyna made her way to the kitchen where she got two glasses of mimosas using just the right amount of ecstasy to spark Mercedez interest.

"Ok, I'll give you what you want. Can you give me what I want?"

"That is my intention." He received a glass form from Chyna, sipped from it and put it to Mercedez lips. "What's mine is yours." He offered her a share of his kingdom and she readily accepted.

Chyna could sense that Mercedez was uncomfortable by her presence while D'Juan was getting to know her most desired fantasy. On cue, 'Pop that coochie' by Luke blasted from the stereo. Chyna entertained them both with a strip tease, and a lot of booty clapping.

"You wanna be his number one little hefah, you gotta earn it," She whispered into Mercedez ear. Not to be outdone, she stripped down to her lace panties and bra to give D'Juan a lap dance. The Brazilian princess moved her hips, tightening her abs and inner thighs with both hands on his chest. Chyna grabbed Mercedez by her ponytail while massaging her clitoris with her free hand "Nun uh, keep that ass up," Chyna demanded. D'Juan grabbed Mercedez's head rubbing his thumb all over her powdered lips.

"If you want something, you gotta take it." He told her.

In an instant his Polo belt was unbuckled, and she was licking the head of his throbbing manhood. "Wow!" he thought as she mesmerized him with her head-game.

The ecstasy spiked mimosas served its intended purpose. D'Juan opened his eyes with Chyna laying on his chest, and Mercedez on his stomach. He re-lived the wild night scene by scene and couldn't help but smile. The thought of being a multi-millionaire by the age of twenty was grand indeed.

(Phone Rings) He woke Chyna up to answer the phone: "Hello"

"D'Juan there?"

She handed him the phone with Lyfe on the other end. "What's the drill?"

"Shit, it seems like you got it figured out" He said in jest.

"Nah, just trying to put it together, nah mean."

"No question. You the man. Try to get up wit us tonight around nine."

"A'ight, I'll be there, peace."

"One hunnid."

Chyna ordered two more bottles of champagne, a gallon of orange juice, and three fruit baskets. "Come on, miss bubble booty." She said before slapping Mercedez on her butt. "Ugh, I got a headache." Said Mercedez, burying her head under the pillows. Chyna taunted about paying the cost to be with a boss. That's as she joined D'Juan in the jet stream tub for a bubble bath...

Chapter 22

DORIAN WAS SITTING IN the apartment's parking lot when Shadonje called. She was in a panic. "Cousin, I just heard them Jamaicans were showing my picture all over east Oakland. Ten G's cousin."

"Whoa, whoa, slow down. Relax. What are you talking about?" He asked nonchalantly.

"You know the fuck I'm talking about. Y'all didn't tell me who that mother-fucker was."

She was then rudely, but understandably hung up on. Dorian called back from a telephone booth across town and advised her to lay low in Hayward with Jennifer, his children's mother. He assured her that she had nothing to worry about and put emphasis on laying low. She agreed, with the expectation of receiving another ten grand.

Dorian then immediately called Silas: "Speak on it,"

"I'm at Unc joint. Holla at me first chance."

"A'ight, down."

Unbeknownst, Silas and Santonio been trailing Shadonje and a Gray Toyota Celica all morning. From when she entered the cleaners on San Pablo Ave., made the call to Dorian, until she pulled up to a nice size home in a quiet neighborhood of Hayward.

259

"Not the place, not the time." Santonio told his brother, seeing that he was desperate.

They waited all day until around 7:30 p.m. Shadonje had changed into a pantsuit and wore a book bag over her shoulder. She was accompanied by an older woman in sweatpants and a Howard University T-Shirt. Again, as the Celica sped into traffic, they followed from three to four car lengths. They didn't stop until she reached Cal State Hayward University campus. The driver exited the vehicle, presumably talking with campus police. Silas parked at the bottom of the hill, in clear sight of their mark. Both him and Santonio, exited the vehicle while leaving it running. They patiently waited, stooping beside a family van.

Upon overhearing Shadonje and the policeman conversation, Silas moved closer towards the Celica. "Okay I'll be sure to keep an eye on her, I keep my friend with me, and she's not shy." The officer said referring to his 9mm berretta. The moment he entered his vehicle and put it in drive, **(Shots Fired)** Heavy fire entered the Toyota Celica from the passenger's side.

"**Arrrrgh!!**" a loud scream came from the car in a desperate cry for help. Santonio and Silas raced back to the idling Grand National and burnt rubber, fleeing the scene. Campus police were in their rear view mirror for all of five minutes before disappearing with vapors from the exhaust. Safely on the highway, they removed their dreadlock wigs, and with one look at each other, the job was forgotten just as quick as it happened.

Dorian and Rocky were playing chess in the back room when Santonio and Silas arrived. One couldn't help but notice the mischievous grin on Rocky's face. They all shook hands and embraced before discussing the issues at hand. Dorian did most of the talking. "I just got word the Jamaican Posse been looking for a young lady, brown skinned with red hair. They have a picture, and the word is it looked like Shadonje. Exactly to the point, she shook-up and I'm concerned about her. At the moment, she's stashed in Hayward at Jennifer's spot. Then there's this: who's her family? Where's she from? All answers leading back to home base, nah'mean!" He expressed with concern. Then his eyes beamed on Silas, as if to say: "You fucking up kid."

"Doe I got you. That Shadonje situation is not an issue, she'll be a'ight. Now these Maican's. They want war, and they'll get it." Silas said nonchalantly.

"See, I don't get you, with one snap of the finger, you're ready for an all-out war. We have to be smart. In this part of the business is when we either use our heads or lose 'em." Dorian said wisely. It was unclear how much exactly the Jamaican Posse really knew or how connected they were. However, playing defense wasn't an option.

Hakeem joined the meeting an half hour or so late as the bearers of bad news. He'd just got word from Butch Cozie that Shadonje and his niece Jennifer was gunned down in Hayward. Upon hearing the news, Dorian slammed his fist on the coffee table. "This is what I'm talking about. Our families is crossed up in this now." After a few minutes of silence, Rocky suggested they suit up that night and bring it to their front door. Hakeem offered his sincere condolences and a wiser approach.

"Socrates is the target. We hunt him, that's where the game is at."

Fuck me man" Dorian screams out-loud with fiery eyes. "You know what, you're right. I'm going to hit Lyfe and see where he is with this. I need time to think. Be on point, but don't make a move until we speak to

Lyfe." Dorian reiterated and they all agreed. "Silence, I need to holler at you for a few tics." Dorian requested a one-on-one as the meeting adjourned.

The room was emptied, and Dorian lit a backwood stuffed with Dark Haze.

"What's on ya mind?" Silas asked, taking a seat.

Dorian exhales into Silas face before starting his inquiry "I'm gon' ask you one time. You know 'bout this?" He looked into his eyes with a plea for the truth.

"Jennifer was family. I'm gonna take care of it." Silas rose from his seat like a thousand pounds of guilt was holstered on his waist.

"Nicca sit yo ass down. I ain't excuse you yet." Dorian barked.

"Fuck wrong wit you? That's my fam too and I told you I'm on it. When you need somebody hit, you call ME! Don't forget that" Silas then stormed out the room. Still, he knew Dorian was right; he was fucking up. His first mistake was trying to turn Shadonje into what she wasn't. And as a consequence, his little cousins just lost their mother to his gun. Dorian was so upset it wasn't a good time for that conversation.

8:15 p.m. Lyfe and Annabelle were sharing laughter and a bottle of Merlot when D'Juan stepped up to the dinning table. Wearing a navy-blue suede-suit with matching loafers by Brooks Brothers, he dressed the part of young Capo. "Good evening" he said calmly but with an uneasy look to him.

"Good evening, kiddo, you good?" Lyfe asked.

"I'm good as could be, what are we having?"

"We just ordered pink salmon and a crustacean platter. This is more about us enjoying each other than the food." Lyfe explained.

D'Juan indicated he understood while keeping his face planted on the menu.

"Yeah, you know if it wasn't your birthday. We'll be eating at my house." Annabelle commented, "Word up huh?" D'Juan finally smiled.

Annabelle was whispering in Lyfe's ear causing him concern. "Say kiddo, what's on your mind?" He asked. "Just a little trouble at home, nothing we can't iron out." They shared eye-contact for a few seconds communicating in silence. The waitress returned with their platter and asked if there's anything else she could get them.

"Yes. I would love to taste your chocolate mousse please." D'Juan then gave her a modest tip. They enjoyed their meal for whatever it was worth.

"Baby, me and the kid have to check on a few things." Lyfe kissed his wife on the forehead and escorted her back to their suite.

D'Juan went back to his suite and told Chyna to take Mercedez back to the crib and he'll be home later. They were already packed and waiting for his next move anyway. Judging by the nature of the phone call he received, what more needed to be said.

It was check out time. Lyfe met D'Juan at the doorway. When Chyna saw the Capo's face, she nearly stopped in her tracks as she felt the coldness of death. She long believed that he killed her oldest brother outside of little Ricky's in 86' over a gambling debt. The moment D'Juan walked into the hallway she had a vision of him walking out of her life, with the door slowly closing.

(Phone Ringing) "Speak to me," Dorian answered,

"Where are you at? Me and the kid on deck."

"Meet me in the laundry room in an half hour."

"100." Lyfe hung up while dropping D'Juan off at the back gates of the Globe. Then swung by his crib to change into street clothes. Before they walked back out the door, Annabelle told him to *be careful*. She understood all too well what time it was but hoped to remind him of the microscope he was under. Twenty minutes later, Dorian and Rocky were giving him the specifics of the hit on Shadonje and Jennifer.

"How did they know Jenny? And what did that little girl have to do with this?" Lyfe asked "Shadonje was with Silence when Shaka was hit. Jenny was just a casualty." Dorian explained. "A'ight, this kid Silas." Lyfe mumbled, grinding his teeth showing frustration

"He is a little sloppy, but no question, he's loyal." Rocky said in an attempt to ease the tension. Lyfe just stared at him with mean dark eyes before turning towards the door. "Tomorrow night, I'll check it out. Hold this down." He commanded.

"You know we good." Rocky assured.

D'Juan, Silas, and Santonio rolled out to a Jamaican Posse's hangout Shaka dropped by the night before he was executed. They pulled up to a Victorian home in the mission district **(Doors Opened)** D'Juan stepped out of the Monte Carlo SS slowly, surveying the block.

"Tone, get behind the wheel and stay there no matter what, a'ight." He asked for his word.

"I got you brodi." Silas bounced out and followed Juan to the front door. The smell of ganja was reeking from the door jam. The street was dark and the neighborhood was quiet. D'Juan knocked on the door, getting no answer, he rang the door-bell that came back muted. After a couple of minutes with no answer, they backed off the porch and turned toward the Monte Carlo. Suddenly a voice came from a bush on the side of the house.

"Hey mon, who are you looking for at dis hour? Do I know you?" A Rastafarian standing 6'4 with a fully automatic rifle approached.

"Yeah mon, we are looking for The Posse. We're here to collect on some business." D'Juan keeps his hands visible while speaking.

"Nah no business here." He looked at him with a squinted eye.

"Look, my man gave me a job and told me to come here after it's done."

With the eye of a dragon still scanning the two henchmen, the Rasta determined they were legit. "Follow me," he looked up the block to his left then turned to walk towards the back of the house. "Ya mans have a name?" He asked once in the backyard.

"Socrates," D'Juan then advised it would be best to step inside to discuss the details. They sat in the basement and got down to business. There was a bounty on Shadonje's head and Silas knew all the details to confirm the hit. The Rasta then signaled for someone he called 'Big Dread' to go get the money. "One question mon, how ya know of this joint here? Socrates don't come by here. He a hot boy." He sat up on the couch staring into D'Juan's eyes.

"We do our homework too, what do you think, we gon' take a job and not know how to get paid?" D'Juan answered with such conviction, he then rubbed his fingers together. The Rasta nodded his head then smiled as he reached to shake his hand.

"Where are you rude boys from?"

"We come and we go with the wind." He smiled.

"Okay, let me get your gouda." He met Big Dread at the steps and they were on his heels. They handed D'Juan an envelope with twenty grand in it and that was a done deal..

Santonio was on point, AK 47 on his lap, checking the rear and side views every three seconds. Although his vision was obstructed by the fog, he could feel many eyes on them. If they would have done as Lyfe instructed., it would've been suicide. Had they survived the gun battle, FBI would've surrounded them in minutes. Out of ammo, and with no room to breathe.

After being sent on an apparent suicide mission, D'Juan advised them to spend a couple days in San Fran. With Twenty grand pocket change, they hit Market Street for designers' apparel; Nike town for the latest sneakers and walked around downtown. There was definitely a lot to think about. Just to see the same street hustlers on Turk and Taylor that's been there for the past years, the same prostitutes running up and down O'Farrell, same O. G's playing chess at the Powell street Bart station, there had to be more to life.

Later that evening, Santonio hopped behind the wheel of his Monte Carlo SS and cruised with the windows down. It's was a warm night and the stars were bright, neatly decorating the glass ceiling of this beautiful world. Lo and behold, trouble was in the rearview. For two blocks they were being trailed by a black Camaro with dark tented windows.

"Bro, I seen that same car parked across from the Rasta's' joint." Santonio said while glancing in his rear-view mirror.

"It's probably them boys. Be cool, act like the not even there," D'Juan advised.

Santonio turned up Broadway and parked in front of Pink Panties strip club. They all exited the vehicles relaxed and poised. Walking to the front door, D'Juan saw through his peripheral view that the black Camaro was parked exactly four cars behind the Monte Carlo. He could see himself walking into a box without an escape route and didn't like it one bit. "Tone, this don't feel right."

"We good brodi, my boy gon keep an eye out for us. Just relax, lil bro." Santonio handed the bouncer he was referring to as his boy, a hundred dollar bill.

Tobacco smoke filled the entire room, half-naked waitresses taking orders, giving lap-dances, and the Pussy Cat Dolls were on stage. A local rap artist named Mr. Cee from R.B.L. Posse was being honored that night. The two dolls performed with his face painted on their bodies, and icing covering their private parts. One hell of a show no doubt.

D'Juan checked the bathroom and around the joint of any emergency exits. "Tone, it ain't no way outta here, and ya mans say it's getting real busy out front," D'Juan expressed his concerns.

"Relax kid. We gon' chill for the night. Spend some money wit ya stingy ass," He laughed.

"Fuck what you talkin bout? I'm trying to shake them boys." D'Juan then positioned himself by the front door. If and when they blitz, he'll slip right by them, was his logic.

As the night got older, interest brewed in the three young men looking like college athletes. Shayla Cush pulled D'Juan out of the dark corner he sat for a private V.I.P.

Approximately 3.a.m. Santonio and Silas were first to leave the titty bar. Shayla wanted more than what her current employer had to offer and bought into the kid's dream of adventure, luxury, and fantasy. "You better use this" she said, while stuffing her private number in his belt.

"We'll see" he replied with a smile.

Simultaneously their attention went to the unmarked government vehicles, parked on both sides of the street. "Tone don't go to the cah" D'Juan warned but it was a second too late. Santonio had his mind made on getting to his weapon, following a spotting of Oschino's brother.

"Blurp" Two cars hit the lights, swooping in behind his Monte Carlo. More agents poured from the strip club and parking garage. It was a wrap, and all he could do was curse himself. Three handguns, an AK 47 and a pair of hundred round drums were found in the trunk. Silas and D'Juan avoided immediate capture, only to be picked up at the pier less than an hour later.

Silas was released the next morning after twenty hours of interrogation. First was the matter of his affiliation with the Jamaican Posse. Second was the guns and ammunitions, then lastly, his affiliation with Lyfe and the familia. With his rap sheet, he knew it didn't look good for him. He'd been under investigation for the past two years and the questions they asked about Lyfe, convinced him, the jig was up. After Joseph Caramagno called the Detention Center, he was cut loose. But not without warning; the familia reign was over.

Santonio took the rap for the guns, and the federal Officers took him into custody. He was booked on illegal sells of firearms in violation of trafficking codes and promoting street terrorism. D'Juan was booked under his brother's name and taken to the West County Detention Center. He only had hours before his true identity was revealed.

"A section, prepare for chow." D'Juan jumped up in his County blues, brushed his teeth, and tried shaking off a migraine headache as he stood in line for breakfast. He returned to his cell with a cinnamon roll and prepared a shot of coffee. "Yo, O.G." he directed at his cellie.

"What's up Youngblood?"

"I need you to make a collect call, and relay a message for me. I'm trying to blow this joint like yesterday."

"First of all Youngblood, my name is Big Tex. And yeah, I can help you with that. Even do something better, watch this", He then gets on the door and flags down a tier worker.

"What's up Tex?" he asked, all the while peeking into the cell.

"I need the joint, in a hurry" he demands.

"I'm right on it. But you know you have one of them F.K boys in there with you huh" he said, whispering through the door jam. Apparently, word was buzzing about Lyfe's army and the heat he'd been under ever since being crowned as Rich City's Capo.

"All due respect folks. This my lil G, I asked you to do something and you still here. What's the meaning of that?" Tex then leans on his cane with a serious demeanor.

"My bad pimpin. Just was trying to hip you to some game. Give me ten minutes."

The tier worker returned with a T-249 mobile phone, and D'Juan made his call.

Fortunately, Chyna was home "Hello" she answered after being up all night. "Ma, I need you to get me out this joint" he said with urgency. "Babe, me and Cedez been worried about you. Where are you at?" "I'm in West County, I need you to post bail A.S.A.P. Take this information."

"Okay, hold on. Mercedez get me a pen. Okay, I'm ready."

"It's Julian Placencia, booking number: Az-1337" He gave her all the information she needed and reiterated the importance of her moving swiftly.

"Baby I got you, I'm calling Mr. Dunkley now. He'll have you out in an hour." She was confident and determined. The stars were aligning in her Universe and she vowed to let him be the Sun. "A'ight ma, it's all on you right now."

"Just never forget poppa. When you call, I come running." She immediately thereafter made the necessary arrangements.

Back in the cell, D'Juan contemplated on his next moves. Chyna would love nothing more than for him to be on the next thing smoking to Hawaii, and she wouldn't be wrong. After all, Big Vain and Young Magic were still holding it down in the Globe. Hakeem and Rashaad were making dope game music now, just a couple hundred thousand records away from becoming platinum recording artists. Lyfe, Dorian and Rocky.. They'll be a'ight, but his main man Slim, no one spoke of, or seen except Juicy. Aiisha was focused and didn't need any of the trouble that follows him. The more he searched for reasons to stay in Rich City, the more reason he had to leave. With seventy grand in cash, and another fifty in the bank, taking the money and running sounded really good.

Big Tex returned to the cell while D'Juan was staring at the ceiling. "What's on your mind Youngblood?"

"What do you know about Hawaii?"

"Hawaii, it depends on vacation, hustling', what are we talking about?"

"It's all about the hustle with me O.G." D'Juan emphasized.

"I feel you maint, but a hustler still got to know his own lane," Big Texas then gave a backstory to how he earned his fame and riches.

He had travelled to Japan, the Philippines, Amsterdam, Brazil, all in pursuit of a fifty karat blue diamond and a young Elizabeth Taylor. Visiting some relatives in Houston, Texas, he stepped off the plane with only a thousand dollars, and the silk shirt of his back. What you know, the old school Mack found himself at a Too $hort and UGK Concert. The bonafide hustlers were out that night choosing and getting chosen. Luscious had not only the walk off a se-diva hustler, she handed over ten grand choosing fee with a promising future behind her.

The California dream: Anaheim Angels, Hollywood Park, Beverly Center, Rodeo Dr., San Francisco's Mitchell and brothers, where the most prominent businessmen with elegant taste for lingerie and expensive appetites love to play. Motivated by the life of Marilyn Monroe, she too could have her name engraved on a star on Hollywood Blvd. Over the next thirty days, she made more than sixty grand in Dallas, and earned the title as Miss Texas.

The next time he was seen on the West Coast, he drove a brand new Fleetwood Cadillac with Texas license plates. Giorgio Armani suits, five hundred dollar brims, smoking hand-rolled Cuban cigars, pockets full of money along with a yellow bone in the passenger's seat to boast. D'Juan soon realized this was the same Luscious who was now working for his Uncle Kaboobi.

Four hours passed so quickly while playing dominoes and reminiscing about superstars like Sonny fo' the Money, Charlie Byrd, Easy Money and Magic Mike, it was time to go.

"Placencia Az-1337, roll up ya mattress." Came over the P.A. system.

"That's you young blood. Now remember, the name of the game is get ya money and stay sucka free." Tex advised well. D'Juan left his number to Fresh Money's joint and wasted no time getting out of them Sheriffs' faces.

Chyna and Mercedez were waiting out front in her Range Rover truck. He hopped in the back seat grinning like a crook that just evaded the law.

"I know you can't wait to get out of here." Chyna said, cruising out of the parking lot.

"We still here?" He joked. "It's really good to see y'all though. I was thinking: Y'all like diamonds of a rare quality. Canary, or some shit. I don't know, but what I do know is I'm hungry as a bear," they smiled, loving his energy.

"Don't worry Poppa, IHOP just minutes away."

"Nah, take me to the tilt, I gotta take a shower and get my mind right, nah'mean." D'Juan's eyes were heavy from not getting any decent rest in the past two days. He dozed off in the backseat.

Silas was leaving Kamillah's Globe town-apartment in the early hours of the morning with gun in hand, walking with his head down. D'Juan smiles as he watches from the stairway above. In an instant, Lyfe appears from the darkness beneath the stairs. There were footsteps then gunshots. "Fuck!" he thought while leaping down flights of stairs. He tried telling Lyfe to stop shooting, but it seems he neither saw nor heard him. As Silas crawled, attempting to grab his gun he was kicked and taunted. The faster D'Juan ran, the further Lyfe was from him. When Silas was no longer moving, Lyfe looked back over his shoulder at D'Juan. It was like looking in the mirror at his evil twin.

"Woe." D'Juan thought out loud as he opened his eyes. He couldn't make sense of the intuition but it felt like *Deja'vu.*

Chapter 23

RAZOR SPOTTED DANIELLE IN a candy-green 5.0 Mustang riding down Carlson Blvd. It appeared to be Kamal, Omar's little brother driving.

"Silence, you see this shit?" Silas zoomed in on the driver, "Follow him." He directed with his hand. Razor couldn't believe she had the audacity to be riding with the opposition. He tailed the 5.0 for a few more blocks before turning into McDonald's parking lot for a quick lunch.

"Razor, very few people know this, but she's the main witness in a case the D.A. is building against D'Juan." Silas explained.

"Wow, that's a *cold bitch*," Razor quickly reminded himself how much she knew about him and the rest of the familia, "She gotta go." He stressed. Silas thought about it while eating his fish and curry rice plate.

"Be around the hood tonight as soon as night falls, and line the trunk with plastic." They both agreed that Danielle was a liability and when a snake strikes, those whose closest get bit.

8:35 p.m. razor was at his spot on 33rd and Ohio when he got the page from Fresh's joint. He figured it had to be Silas. "Lil momma, I'll be back in an hour. Have that bagged up by the time I get back,"

"Can I..." he shut the door before she could finish her request.

273

Silas was waiting on the corner of Carlson and Pullman. Razor pulled up nearly scrapping the curb. "Fuck wrong with you" Silas questioned as he slid in the back seat.

"I was just wit Jannah, and she said she saw Danielle walking down San Pablo, you know who she is working for?" Razor asked.

"Nah, don't ever matter"

"King Arthur. He always got one of his soldiers watching his workers." Razor explained,

"Oh yeah A'ight," Silas seemed to be more concerned about the blow in his twenty dollar bill than the potential danger lying ahead.

"We can't leave any witnesses. That's still Lyfe's niece," Razor stressed.

Minutes later, he pulled up next to the Seahorse Motel on San Pablo Ave. If Danielle was working that night, he figured she'll be in a room eventually.

At approximately 10:44 p.m. Danielle was walking toward a liquor store with another worker whom Silas recognized as Tameka, one of King Arthur's top money makers. They patiently observed as they turned tricks every thirty minutes. It was no question, somebody was watching his money.

"Look at her. Wait until they walk down that street, there's no lights." Silas suggested. Suddenly they stopped in their tracks and began searching in their purses. Tameka turned on her heels, and trotted back into the store. As Razor turned on his high beams, Danielle was talking to someone in a black Grand National. At the turn of her head, a 9mm was aimed at her face.

"Bang!" she ran right into Silas arms as he jumped from the backseat.

"Ah!" she screamed and tussled before being hit across the head with stainless steel. Razor shot twice into the door of the Grand National as it pulled off.

The trunk!" Silas yelled.

It immediately flew open, and Danielle's unconscious body was tossed in.

"Heeey, help!" Tameka screamed, as they sped off.

"Bra you seen who that was?" Razor asked.

"That looked like Tydus. If it was, we definitely gotta holla at him." Silas wasn't sure what to think. So much death and betrayal has happened over the past months.

"No question, I was about to bounce out and finish him. Fuckin with that no good bitch damn near got himself clipped." Razor expressed anger as he charged Tydus with betrayal.

"If he didn't see your face, it never happened. After tonight, we torch the cah" Silas advised, hoping Razor wouldn't worry. It was well known what happens when he thought someone is a problem. Family or not, it was survival of the fittest.

Wherever they took Danielle that night, she probably wished she'd died there. She was beaten, tortured with hot curling irons and shot up with heroin for two days, who knew whatever else was done to her.

5 a.m. in Rich City, the forecast was foggy and under forty degrees. A whimpering body was found under a bench in the 4th street park. "Hey, you youngster, go to the market, tell Arthur I think this one of his girls out there, hurry up! She's barely breathing" The elder man could see she was in serious pain as he stood, and afraid to touch her.

Rico ran as fast as he could to the market, coming back with blankets and towels. Zeek accompanied him being heavily armed "O.G, we have to wrap her up until the ambulance arrive. They're on the way." Zeek rushed to Danielle aide, talking to her until she regained consciousness. Shortly thereafter, the police and ambulance arrived and rushed her to the E.R. at Doctor's Hospital. Upon checking her vitals, the nurse ordered her to be admitted into the intensive care unit.

"Baby, get up," Annabelle shook Lyfe from his sleep.

"What's up?" he wakes up gripping the Colt 45. resting beneath his pillow.

"This mother--fuckin snake had Danielle working for him and she got kidnapped, and beat half to death" she despised King Arthur and all he stood for.

Lyfe immediately rose to his feet and got dressed. "I'll handle it." He assured.

Within the next forty-five minutes Lyfe, and Silk barged through 4th street market and into King Arthur's office. Big Vain and Rocky waited outside the office's door.

"King, I need answers man. My niece is lying on her fuckin death-bed!" Lyfe pounded on the desk sending papers flying everywhere.

"I'm on it. You know I take care of mine." The 6'6, 280 pounds boss rose from behind his desk. "Oh yeah. You gone handle huh. Well, this how I take care of mine." he then drew his 44. Bulldog and knee-capped the elder man. They walked out the market with guns drawn and no regard for territory, or even human life for that matter. This was personal, and without question, Lyfe felt King Arthur was to blame.

Danielle nurses opened the window in her room letting in some fresh air. She was scarred deep, and even worse , she was damaged psychologically. Which in most cases takes a lifetime to heal. She sat on the bed and looked around the room. There were balloons wishing her to get well soon, singing teddy bears, and a bouquet of black roses. She then picked up her diary and began writing.

The Doctors told her it'll be a long road to recovery, but she'll only make it by taking one day at a time. She'd lived life by the minute up to that point. Being powerless made her reflect on how short life really is. Also how beautiful it is just to wake up. After a few hours of jotting down her life story, her head began to spin.

"Ughhh!" She ran to the bathroom, throwing up blood. Wiping her mouth and holding her stomach, she stumbled pass the bouquet of roses. Easing into bed, she moaned in pain. In search of strength, she opened the greeting card and it read.

"How does it feel to be alive?"
P.S 'LOL'

The Capo series continues with Diamonds and Pearl Handles...

Made in the USA
Columbia, SC
02 December 2022

72334108R00159